CHARLESTON NOIR

A NICK JANZEK CHARLESTON MYSTERY
(BOOK 3)

TOM TURNER

JOIN TOM'S AUTHOR NEWSLETTER

Get the latest news on Tom's upcoming novels when you sign up for his free author newsletter at tomturnerbooks.com/news.

ONE

SHE WAS BREAKING HER IRONCLAD LAW: NEVER LET A MAN set foot into her penthouse apartment on King Street. But, in this case, it didn't really matter since her visitor wouldn't be leaving under his own steam.

Which was to say, vertically.

She remembered his cockiness from fourteen years before.

The way he sat on a horse—all loose and smirky and self-assured, like he was goddamn Roy Rogers or something. And the way he looked her over that first time, his stare stripping away her tank top and cut-off jeans. And those two other cretins with him.... like he was the sheriff, and they were the posse.

He was drunk now—really drunk—his washed-out blue eyes cruising the room after just having tried to paw her. She had shoved him away but knew he'd try again. He seemed to focus every once in a while but, she could tell, was mostly seeing blurs.

"What's that thing?" he asked, pointing to an expensive tortoise-shell box on her mantel.

"A tea caddy," she said, stifling a yawn.

"Doesn't look like any of the caddies up at Yeaman's," he said with a smirk.

It was a lame joke. Yeaman's Hall was a prestigious golf club north of Charleston where all the local blue bloods and rich Yankees played.

Fourteen years ago—when she was sixteen—he'd seemed like the coolest guy she'd ever run across. He didn't say much back then. He let that rich-kid swagger and arrogance do the talking, and she'd been impressed.

"What are those blue and white things?" He pointed to an expensive Delft Garniture set.

"Dutch porcelain figurines," she said.

"Look like pieces from an old chess set," he said.

She glanced over at them. *Yeah, if you're drunk, stupid, and totally unsophisticated, they do.*

She'd had enough of his blather as she watched him take another pull of his Maker's Mark. Now was as good a time as any.

She stood up and straightened her skirt, because she could see he was getting itchy to start pawing her again.

"Where you goin'?"

"To powder my nose," she said, not looking back.

He smiled, thinking that was code for getting prepped to do the deed.

She walked across the room, opened the mahogany door, and closed it behind her.

HE LOOKED around the room at a few framed pictures of her with people he didn't recognize. Then his eyes lit on one of her riding a horse. She looked to be in her teens. That was how old she'd been when they first met. He was surprised she didn't seem to have any bad feelings about what had happened back then. Come to think of it...how could she *not?*

He looked at his watch and wondered what she was doing beside powdering her nose.

A moment later, the bathroom door opened and a man in blue jeans and a Lacoste shirt hurried out.

He had a pool cue in one hand and something long, sharp, and shiny in the other.

TWO

NICK JANZEK WAS ON HIS WAY TO THE CHARLESTON police station on Lockwood at seven in the morning when he got the call from the dispatcher. She told him in short, choppy, but detailed sentences that a woman who had been walking her dog in White Point Garden in the Battery had called in a possible homicide. The woman had been unusually specific, the dispatcher said. She'd first noticed the vic on a bench reading a book. Something about him made her keep an eye on him, she explained. A minute or two later, as she watched him out of the corner of her eye, he suddenly pitched forward, holding his book in a "vice grip," and his forehead "bounced" on the macadam pathway. The caller ran up to the body and saw a gash on the man's forehead but not one drop of blood.

Janzek, doing seventy down Murray Boulevard, pulled up to White Point Garden and skidded to a stop next to a black and white Charger. He saw a uniform talking to a woman with a dog and walked over to join them. The cop's name was Robert Prioleau.

As he got closer, he saw a man's body on the pavement behind the two.

"Hey, Robert," Janzek said, looking down at the body.

"Nick," Prioleau said, nodding. "This is Ms. Hobbes. She came in here to walk her dog about a half hour ago and found the deceased."

Janzek looked up from the body to the woman.

"Hello, Ms. Hobbes, I'm Detective Janzek," he said, pulling out his murder book and pen from his inside jacket pocket. "Can you tell me exactly what happened from the moment you first got here? Just one second, please—" he turned to Prioleau "—tape off the scene, will you, Robert? Keep everyone out of here." Then he turned back to the woman. "I'm sorry, you came here to walk your dog and—"

"I saw this man sitting on the bench here and didn't think much of it," she said. "Then as I was walking past him I said, 'good morning' and he didn't look up or say anything back. So, I kept going and walked past him again later and the man hadn't moved. I mean, literally not moved an inch. I got the feeling he hadn't turned a page in his book either. Something about him was strange, not just that he didn't look up or say anything."

"But his eyes were open?" Janzek asked.

"Yes."

"Just that he hadn't moved?" Janzek said.

"Yes, he was dead still," she said, then realizing what she had just said, nodded. "Dead is right."

"So, then what happened, Ms. Hobbes?" Janzek asked.

"So then, my dog, Haimish, went up to the man and, you know, kind of sniffed him. I pulled the leash back and at the same time I did, the man fell forward," Hobbes said. "His head hit first, really hard. It ended up facing to the side and I saw this big cut, but there was no blood at all."

"So that's when you called us?"

5

"No, first, I went to see if I could help him," Hobbes said. "I thought maybe he had fallen asleep on the bench, though his eyes were still wide open. But at that point I could just tell..."

"That he was dead?"

"Yes, not breathing at all," she said. "And when I touched him, he was cold... and stiff."

"Like he had been dead for a while?"

She nodded.

"So then you called?"

She nodded again.

Janzek looked down at the dead man. His eyes were still open and Janzek saw dried blood-spatter on his pants below the crotch. He heard the blare of sirens. One was coming from the north, the other from the east.

He put on a pair of latex gloves, squatted next to the man, and patted him for a wallet. Feeling a bulge in a back pocket of the man's pants, he reached into the pocket and pulled it out. He found a South Carolina license in the plastic window. It said James M. Swiggett and gave his address. He returned the wallet to the man's pants and looked up at Ms. Hobbes.

"When you first got here, before the man fell over, were there other people in the park?"

"No, I didn't see anyone until a few minutes after I got here. It was just starting to get light."

"And can you describe those people?"

Hobbes pushed a strand of hair out of her eyes.

"One was a woman jogger. In her twenties, I'd say. Running fast, didn't even slow down," Hobbes said. "Then an older woman pushing a baby carriage. Like maybe she was a nanny or something."

"And that was all?"

Hobbes nodded. "Until Officer Prioleau got here."

Janzek glanced around. The curious had started to gather.

There were six people outside the yellow tape that Prioleau had strung.

"Well, thank you very much, Ms. Hobbes. Can you give me your phone number and an email address in case I have more questions, please?"

"Sure," Hobbes said. "What do you think could have happened to him?"

"At this stage, I really have no idea," Janzek said. "But I appreciate all your help."

She gave him her cell number and email and, as Janzek was taking them down, he heard steps behind him and turned.

It was his partner, Delvin Rhett.

Rhett was a bespectacled, trim, black man in his late twenties who sported a Fu Manchu. Janzek suspected it was to make up for his otherwise scholarly look. A cop had once called him Urkel, meaning the nerdy kid Steve Urkel from an old TV sitcom. Janzek figured the Fu Manchu and Rhett's occasional sprinkling of ghetto-speak into conversations were his partner's attempt at countering the Urkel charge. He wore khaki pants, a white button-down shirt, a tie that was not perfectly centered, and a loose-fitting brown corduroy jacket. Superfly, he was not.

"Hey, Delvin," Janzek said, nodding to him, "this is Ms. Hobbes, the witness who called it in."

Rhett nodded. "Hello, Ms. Hobbes," he said, then got down in a crouch next to the victim. His eyes went right to the spots of blood on the victim's pants.

Ms. Hobbes nodded and smiled at Delvin, then moved away with her dog and ducked under the yellow tape.

Rhett looked up at Janzek. "Strange place to see blood."

Janzek nodded, got down next to him, and pointed at the victim's forehead. "Yeah, but not a drop from that cut."

Rhett nodded. "Never seen a guy so pale before," he said. "Like Casper."

7

"Who?"

"The friendly ghost."

Rhett had an offbeat sense of humor and Janzek was still trying to warm up to it. They had been together a little over a year.

"Guy's name is James Swiggett. Looks like he bled out somehow before he took the header on the pavement."

"So someone brought him here, you figure?" Rhett asked. "Already dead?"

"That's my guess," Janzek said as Rhett pulled out his cell phone and started snapping pictures.

As he watched, Janzek noticed a goose-egg-sized bump on the top of the man's head.

"Get a few of this, too," Janzek said to Rhett, pointing to the bump. "Looks like a tree fell on the poor bastard."

"Yeah, or a Louisville Slugger."

"I wanna show you something else." Janzek's old football knee popped as he stood. He took a few steps down the path, Rhett following, then pointed at a tire-track imprint next to the macadam path.

Rhett's eye followed the tire track. "Goes right up to the bench."

"Yeah," Janzek said, crouching down to inspect it. "But the tires are too close together to be a car or a truck."

"And who would drive a car or a truck into the park anyway?" Rhett said. "A uniform spots it and he's all over the guy."

"I'm guessing a golf cart," Janzek said.

Golf carts were a common means of transportation in downtown Charleston.

"Yup. That'd fit," said Rhett.

"I'm gonna go check the surrounding area," Janzek said, "see what else I come up with."

Rhett nodded and started taking snapshots of the tire tracks.

JANZEK DIDN'T FIND anything else related to the dead man in the park, but at the far end he came across a large monument he'd never noticed before. It commemorated the hanging, on the site, of twenty-two pirates back in 1718. Their captain was Stede Bonnet. One of the things Janzek liked about Charleston was that it had a lot of history, much of it infamous. The monument noted that there had been twenty-nine pirates, but only the twenty-two had been hanged. Janzek wondered what happened to the other seven.

He glanced over at the dead body a football field away. The tradition of violent death in the beautifully landscaped park was still going strong.

THREE

Billy Hobart had been through the house on lower Meeting Street with the realtor twice before. This time they'd be meeting Miranda Bennett there.

The Miranda Bennett.

From one of the oldest families in Charleston.

Billy and the realtor were up on the second floor when Miranda walked in the open front door.

"Yoo-hoo, Billy, the checkbook has arrived." Miranda warbled in her signature, free-spirited voice.

Billy walked down the steps from the second floor, the realtor trailing along behind him.

"Hey, honey," Billy said, walking down the steps and wrapping Miranda in a big hug. "Get that checkbook out and start writing. There's gonna be lots of zeroes in this offer. I'm thinking a million four. They don't take it, well then, screw 'em."

He looked over at the realtor.

"Oh, Mark, this is my friend Miranda Bennett," Billy said.

"Hello, Mrs. Bennett, pleased to meet you," said Mark, the

chinless realtor from a nondescript office in West Ashley, clearly impressed to meet the grand dame of Church Street. She had the nicest house "on the bricks," as opposed to the slightly less-desirable houses a little farther north on the paved section of Church Street.

Miranda shot chinless Mark a curt nod, her standard acknowledgement for the sub-classes, which included real-estate agents, waiters, hairdressers, and people who worked for the Department of Motor Vehicles.

"What are we going to sell it for, once you've worked your magic?" she asked Billy.

Billy glanced at chinless Mark. "Two million five, maybe. I don't know, what do you think, Mark?" Billy asked, testing the agent. "Assuming new HVAC"—heating, ventilation and air conditioning—"a refurbished kitchen and baths, plus a fountain to make that backyard fabulous?"

The agent was licking his chops at the prospect of getting a $2.5-million listing once Billy fixed it up and put it back on the market. "At least that much," he said.

Billy frowned and shook his head. "Nah, on second thought, best case is two million two." He turned back to Miranda and lowered his voice so the agent couldn't hear. "The good news is I figure we'll only need to put three-hundred-thousand into it."

Miranda—sixty, savvy, rich, and thirty pounds overweight—hooked her arm onto Billy's.

"You know I'm lousy with numbers, honey," she said, "so how much does that mean we make?"

"Net around four hundred thousand," he said. The reality was closer to six hundred thousand, but four hundred was certainly enough to get Miranda to stroke a nice, fat check.

Their deal was that Miranda would put up all the money and get a guaranteed fifteen percent return. That would mean

that she'd get around $90,000 and he'd get the rest—
$510,000. Not bad, particularly since he didn't have to put up
a dime.

Miranda liked the money, but what was more important to
her was the fact that she got the companionship and attention
of a good-looking thirty-year-old man. Billy, at five ten, had a
slight build, but was rakishly handsome—high cheekbones, brilliant blue eyes, and thick, wavy blond hair. Miranda still wasn't
totally clear about his sexuality.

"So how much should I make the check out for?" Miranda
asked Billy.

Billy looked at the realtor.

"How much do you think?" Billy asked chinless Mark.
Another test.

"I don't know, I'd say twenty thousand would be a meaningful deposit," Mark said.

"I'd say *too* meaningful." Billy turned to Miranda, "Make it
ten thousand, honey."

Mark started to say something but stopped.

"Who to?" Miranda asked.

"Carolina One Trust Account," Mark said.

Miranda signed the check with a flourish and looked up.
"So, Billy, will you use Tipton for the sale on this?"

Billy nodded, and Mark looked as if he'd just been pick-
pocketed. "Absolutely. Girl's the best realtor in town." He
turned back to Mark. "Since we're all cash buyers and it's
gonna be an easy deal for you, we're gonna need you to take a
four percent commission."

Mark reacted like Billy had not only snatched his wallet,
but grabbed all his loose change, too.

"Oh, I can't do that," Mark said, "my broker would never go
along with it."

Billy started walking toward the door. "Come on, Miranda.

I guess we'll have to go buy that one up on Tradd Street instead."

Mark moved swiftly to block the door. "Wait, wait," he said. "Let me see what I can do."

———

TIPTON HILL HAD BEEN the highest producer at Carriage Properties for the past three years. She was in her late twenties, unmarried and possessed of near model-like good looks. Few people wondered if this beauty helped her stellar sales-record. She was showing the Bingham house to Donald Knott, who ran a big fund up in New York. It was Knott's third time seeing the house, and Tipton was eighty percent sure she'd be writing up an offer. They were in the Bingham house's living room, which featured fine English furniture and more books than Tipton had ever seen in any Charleston house.

She slid a Thomas Pynchon novel out from a bookshelf. Yep, just as she expected, it was stiff...starchy, almost. Clearly, no one had gotten past the jacket copy.

Then something caught her eye that she hadn't spotted before, up on a shelf above her head. It was a penwork box, probably from the late 1700s, in a unique pagoda shape. A classic, she could tell at first glance, and she wondered if the owner knew what he had. It elicited a visceral response in her—her heart rate ticking up, nerves in her fingers jangling—and she felt an ardent yearning for it, approaching lust almost. A few times in the past she'd actually started sweating while picturing certain exceptional pieces owned by others placed in a prominent spot in her living room.

"How long's it been on the market?" Knott asked, snapping Tipton out of her reverie.

He had asked her that same question the first time he saw

the house. He was a self- important and humorless man with an off-kilter handlebar mustache.

"Four and a half months," she said, knowing he loved numbers. "No offers so far. It works out to $655 per square foot. Last sale was in 2014 for 2.1 million. They redid the kitchen and the master bath at a cost of around ninety thousand at that time."

Knott did his best not to look impressed. "And what do the comps say?"

She put her hand on the back of a chintz loveseat. "They range from about $620 to 660 a square foot," she said, watching him blink a few times, processing.

"So this is on the high side of that range," he said, slipping a book out of a bookshelf. It was a Robert Caro biography of LBJ and looked brand new. Knott put his hand on his chin, doing a poor Thinker impression. "Let's make 'em an offer of 2.75," he said. "That works out to six hundred a foot."

Six hundred ten, actually, thought Tipton. Instead of correcting Knott, she did the quick math on the commission of a $2.75 million sale. It came out a $165,000, eighty percent of which she'd get for herself.

That money would go a long way to buying the furniture in the new house she was building, and she'd do anything neces- sary to make sure the deal went through.

FOUR

Janzek was hanging up his phone when Delvin Rhett walked into his office with two pieces of paper in his hand.

"You hear?" Delvin asked before Janzek had time to mention the phone call he'd just ended.

Janzek looked at him. "Hear what?"

"Poor bastard got Bobbitted."

Janzek leaned back in his chair. "What the hell does that mean?"

"Jesus, man, you haven't read this?" Rhett held up three sheets of paper. "Check your email. Lorena Bobbitt was that pookie who cut off her hubby's John Henry Johnson."

Some of Rhett's patter Janzek could decipher, but not all. "Jesus. That's what happened to Swiggett?"

Rhett nodded.

It made a sick kind of sense, given all the blood they'd seen on the vic's pants.

Janzek reached for the pages. "Let me see that."

"You got it in your email," Rhett said. "Guy was four quarts low, too."

Janzek turned to his computer and clicked on his email. The first message he saw was from the Medical Examiner.

Rhett sat as Janzek started reading. It was one of the more gruesome write-ups Janzek had ever read. It confirmed that the vic was James McClain Swiggett. Janzek could only hope for Swiggett's sake that he was unconscious when the killer surgically removed his manhood—or, in the parlance of Delvin Rhett, his John Henry Johnson.

Janzek skimmed through the rest of the report, which was chock full of blood and gore. The killer had apparently bludgeoned Swiggett, the ME speculated, then slashed his femoral artery, leading—as Janzek had previously surmised—to Swiggett bleeding out. *Exsanguinated*, as the ME termed it. The big question, of course, was where had it all happened? Figure that out and it would be case closed.

When he finished with the report, Janzek looked up at Rhett, who was on his iPhone checking messages.

"Hey, I need some time to read this whole thing again," Janzek said. "How 'bout you come back in fifteen minutes and we'll talk it over."

Rhett nodded. "Killer's one sick mofo," he said, getting up. "Aight, check you later."

Janzek read through the report carefully this time. Then he did some internet research. The first thing he learned was that if someone lost one-third to half of his blood, he was going to die. The obvious conclusion that Janzek came to was that this had been no spur-of-the-moment murder. Whoever killed Swiggett had a well-thought-out plan, a key part of which was to execute it in a place where no trace of blood would ever be found. A place where multiple quarts of blood would drain away. A bathtub was the first place that came to mind.

Janzek thought back to the infamous John Wayne Bobbitt incident. At the time, he had been working a particularly grisly murder/suicide up in Boston. Flash forward to a little over a year ago, when Janzek put Boston in the rearview mirror and signed on with the Charleston PD. A series of devastating incidents had taken place up there to make him want a change of scenery—the worst being the murder of his wife. Twenty-five years before that, his father, who had been a "close personal associate" of the murderous mobster, Whitey Bulger, had been killed executioner-style in an alley behind a bar in Waltham. Whitey himself was a leading suspect. But then he disappeared. There were just too many ghosts in Boston for Janzek, so he packed up a U-Haul truck, hitched his car behind it, and headed south.

At six feet and a solid 175 pounds, Janzek had emerald-green eyes and dark hair he wore on the long side. A three-inch scar from below his eye ran down the left side of his face and stopped just above a sturdy cleft chin that had taken a few shots over his forty years of hard living.

His mind wandered back to Bobbitt again. Aside from all the jokes on Letterman and Leno, he recalled thinking that Bobbitt must have been incredibly abusive and aggressively unfaithful to warrant that kind of punishment.

He didn't hear Rhett walk in.

"Pretty fuckin' sick, huh?"

Janzek looked up, startled. "Jesus, man," he said, "they got this thing called knocking."

"Sorry. Readin' all that shit freaked you out, huh?" Rhett smiled. "What's the matter, you never had a dickless vic before?"

"Okay, Delvin, can it, will you? Let's talk about what we got and what we're gonna do next."

While the M.E. and techs had been preparing their gruesome report, Delvin and Janzek had dug up plenty on the vic over the last twenty-four hours.

James McClain Swiggett, thirty-four, was a lawyer who specialized in tax law. He had gone to Porter-Gaud, the private school in nearby West Ashley, then to the University of Virginia, and after that, UVA's law school. He seemed like a rich kid and, from what Janzek was able to piece together, had conducted a pretty serious party-hearty lifestyle along with a few run-ins with the law. He'd had a DUI seven years back and had been the defendant in a paternity suit four years before that. All this while married and bringing up three sons.

In the breast pocket of Swiggett's blue blazer, a crime-scene tech found a couple of tabs of something called rohypnol and another called Nymphomax, whose ingredients, Janzek learned, were designed to get women in the mood. *Bill Cosby specials*, Rhett called them.

Janzek's working theory was that Swiggett had a date with someone he was not married to and planned to ply her with more than just a few cocktails. Rhett theorized that maybe in the middle of Swiggett's tryst, a husband or a boyfriend had caught the pair in the act, then spared the woman and killed Swiggett. Only problem with the theory was that he didn't feel the signs pointed to Swiggett having been killed on the spur of the moment.

No, this killing seemed elaborately premeditated.

Delvin sat, his expression turning serious. "Whatcha thinking?"

Janzek nodded at his desk phone. "I just got a call from a bartender at the Carolina Yacht Club on East Bay. He read about the murder and told me Swiggett had a drink there with some other guy at around seven the night it happened."

"Did he know who the other guy was?"

"No, he didn't," Janzek said. " I asked him to describe him and he wasn't much help. Blond guy, around thirty, on the short side. Then I asked him who else was in the bar at the same time. Thinking maybe someone else could ID him."

"Any luck?"

"Yeah, he gave me a list of five people there. I'm gonna start calling them, then go pay a visit to Swiggett's widow. Meanwhile, why don't we split up the people in Swiggett's law firm?" Janzek handed Rhett a printout of the partners and associates he had found listed on the office's website. "I'll take A through M, you take the rest."

Rhett nodded as he read through the list.

Janzek looked out his window and saw a new hotel being built off in the distance. Charleston had been booming in the year he had been there while the rest of the country seemed to be limping along.

Janzek swung back to Rhett. "I also got a list of names and numbers of all residents within a half mile of the park," Janzek said. "That's about three hundred phone calls. We can split those up, too. You take two hundred, I'll take a hundred."

Rhett groaned. "Oh, gee, Nick. Thanks. That's real fair."

"Hey, you're a much better talker than me."

Rhett shook his head in weak protest.

Janzek shrugged. "Nobody ever said this was a glamorous gig, my friend."

FIVE

AFTER MAKING FIVE UNSUCCESSFUL CALLS TO BAR-GOERS who might have seen Swiggett's blond drink-mate on the night of his murder, Janzek paid a visit to the vic's widow on James Island. Camille Swiggett lived in a modest two-story brick house in Riverland Terrace, one of the more desirable areas of the Charleston suburb.

Janzek was surprised at the plainness of Swiggett's house based on two things: One, how the dead man had been dressed when discovered in White Point Garden. He'd been wearing a Brooks Brothers blue blazer, a yellow Hermes tie, and expensive-looking English shoes. Two, the fact that he was a lawyer. But then Janzek remembered something that his boss, Chief of Police Ernie Brindle, had told him when he first got to Charleston. Something about how lawyers, for the most part, were a dime a dozen in Charleston, but the only ones who made real money were the ambulance chasers. The others just got by.

Swiggett's house was nice enough but certainly not fancy, and it had a wooden accessibility ramp leading up to a side entrance. Camille Swiggett opened the front door and let him in wordlessly. Janzek caught a glimpse of an old man hooked up to a respirator through a half-opened door off of the living room. Camille was blonde, pretty, slightly overweight, with dead eyes, slumped shoulders, and a whispery, forlorn voice. Her beaten-down first-impression formed a surprising mismatch with how forthcoming she was about her husband. It almost seemed as if she wanted to be the one to put her husband's secrets out there and on the record before someone else dug them up. Without mincing words, she began by telling Janzek that her husband was a serial philanderer. Within the first three minutes of their conversation, she told him that Swiggett had cheated on her the night before their wedding, fourteen years before.

He wished all his interviewees were so forthcoming.

Camille speculated that her husband's proclivity to stray far and wide had something to do with his death. Janzek even thought he heard a note of 'he got what he deserved' in her tone. He asked her about the events of the night Swiggett was killed. She said they'd had an early dinner at six o'clock in front of the TV, then Swiggett had taken a shower and said he was going to go meet a friend for a drink at the Yacht Club on East Bay Street. She'd suspected the friend might be a woman, but she hadn't bothered questioning him further.

Janzek asked her if she had any idea who the woman might have been. She had four candidates and allowed that there were likely others she didn't know about. He wrote all the names down, figuring he and Rhett would split them up and interview them.

Following her candid admissions, he proceeded to ask all the standard questions: Did Swiggett have any enemies who might want to do harm to him? She answered that with a question: Two of the women he'd been sleeping with had husbands, so wouldn't they be possible suspects? She didn't know either of the women, but again volunteered that you never knew what a cuckolded husband might do...right? Unless, of course, the cuckold was *her* husband. Jamie wouldn't have given a damn who Camille slept with. To which she added, "Well, late husband, I guess that would be."

He asked if there had been any incidents in the past, any threats on her husband's life, anything that she might have overheard or that he had told her about. She thought for a second, then answered no, not that she could think of.

He got brazen and asked if they'd had any money problems. Glancing around the house, he'd noticed how everything looked a little threadbare. Like maybe too much of their money went toward Jamie's wardrobe instead of a new carpet or replacements for the see-through curtains. Before Camille could answer, he asked if Swiggett owed anyone money or had any debts of any consequence.

That opened up the floodgates. Camille broke into a long, stream-of-consciousness ramble, starting with how she could barely afford to shop at Whole Foods anymore. How between taking care of her father-in-law, who had no insurance but huge medical bills, and Jamie insisting that their kids, Brett and Olivia, go to the expensive private schools—Porter-Gaud and Ashley Hall, respectively—they'd come perilously close to a hand-to-mouth existence.

"What had gone so wrong?" she bemoaned. After all, Jamie had grown up rich. His parents had had three houses. On Sullivan's Island, across the bridge from Charleston, Boca Grande, Florida, not to mention the big hunting place down south. But then it all fell apart. She said Jamie kept telling her not to worry, no need to put the kids in public schools, he was going to take care of everything. But she *did* worry. A lot, and, fact was, their financial situation had kept getting worse.

Just last week, he had stumbled home at eleven p.m.

—"from one of his sordid little affairs," Camille said—and told her that this time he really meant it. *This* time, their financial problems were going to be over. He had never gotten around to telling her how this little miracle was going to happen. For her part, Camille had responded sarcastically: "Good, so does this mean I can buy dog food now?"

That was the first and only time Camille resorted to humor in the hour and fifteen minutes Janzek spent at her house... but maybe she hadn't been joking at all.

SIX

BILLY HOBART DIALED MIRANDA BENNETT AS HE PACED around his apartment on King Street, looking down at the boats on the Ashley River. Billy's contractor was about two months from finishing another house he was flipping on Atlantic Street, and Billy, who had a nose for promoting his renovated houses, had just had a brainstorm.

Miranda's voicemail finally picked up and he left a message. As he waited for Miranda to call back, he went to the window that looked out over the tops of the live oak trees of White Point Garden. On the other side of the Garden were three spectacular houses on South Battery that loomed up above the trees. They had to be five or six stories tall. Beyond them, he saw an enormous white structure. Incredibly, it was *moving*. That's when he realized it was a colossal Carnival cruise ship slowly steaming into its slip at 32 Washington Street. It would soon be disgorging the great unwashed—gawkers and selfie-snappers from New Jersey, Pennsylvania or wherever it was they came from—and dumping them onto the pristine, hallowed streets of Charleston. Later that day, the ship would raise its twenty-ton anchor and depart, its passengers nattily outfitted in their newly purchased, *Someone in Carolina Loves Me* T-shirts and sated on Market Street hot dogs and ice cream cones.

That *someone* in Carolina who loved them sure as hell was not Billy Hobart.

Miranda called him right back and said that she had been on the phone with "that stultifying bore, Weedie Cheslow."

Billy, still watching the monster ship dock, told her about his brainstorm. "Wouldn't it be fantastic if we had a big party at the house on Atlantic—like a giant open house—so people could come and see how fabulous it turned out? Maybe even sell it to someone who attends. Just think...we wouldn't even have to pay a broker's commission."

"But what about Tipton?" Miranda asked.

"Don't worry about Tipton," Billy said. "We give her plenty of business."

Miranda said she thought it was a marvelous idea and wondered why they hadn't done it before. Then she volunteered the use of her impressive Rolodex of who's-who in Charleston, which was, of course, Billy's whole point in suggesting the idea in the first place.

Suddenly, though, as if a light bulb had popped on over his head, he had an even better idea.

"Wait a minute... what if, instead of a big, fancy open house with all the movers and shakers of Charleston—along with the rich, nouveau Yankees who desperately want in on Charleston society—we make it a big, fancy benefit? It could be for the Preservation Society or... what's that illustrious do-gooder environmental group called?"

"Oh," Miranda said, "you mean the Conservation Coastal League?"

"Yeah, yeah, exactly, that's it," Billy said, his mind racing now. "What we could do is have a bunch of silent auction items that people or companies donate. Lay them out on big tables. You know, with a little piece of paper in front of the item where people write their bids. Then someone else comes along and writes down a higher bid below it? Well, you of all people know the drill."

"Of course, I do," said Miranda. "I've been to a million of 'em."

"The trick," he said, "is to get really good stuff."

"Yes, exactly," Miranda agreed. "I've been to ones where the silent auction stuff is all garbage. So, we could go to a place like *Goat. Sheep. Cow* and get them to donate a case of really good French wine."

"Absolutely," he said. "And get a nice, little tax donation and a bunch of free press."

"Or get somebody to donate a trip to somewhere really exotic and fabulous," Miranda said, really getting into it now. "Like St. Barth's or Anguilla or Harbor Island."

"Exactly," Billy said, though he didn't have a clue where the last two were. "Maybe a round of golf up at Yeaman's. Throw in a couple of lessons with the golf pro."

"I don't know," Miranda said. "That doesn't have much *panache* to it. We need to have the absolute best of everything. *Ne plus ultra*," she added enthusiastically.

"Definitely," agreed Billy, not sure what the phrase meant, but pretty sure it was French. He was still watching the Brobdingnagian cruise ship, which had come to a dead stop now, towering over the mighty houses south of Broad.

"Oh, it's *such* a marvelous idea, Billy, why in the world didn't we think of it before?" said Miranda. "Throw a party, raise money for a good cause, and get a little publicity for our house. Win-win, for everybody."

"And you know what the key is, right?" Billy asked.

"What?"

"Booze," he said. "Lots and lots of top-shelf booze. That's what makes silent auctions so successful. Give 'em a few stiff ones, shed their inhibitions, makes everyone a little more competitive."

Miranda laughed. "Starting with a waiter serving flutes of champagne at the front door."

"Brilliant," he agreed, and then sprung the coup de grace on her. "What about having 101 Atlantic as the sole item in the *live* auction?"

Miranda went silent for a second, then said, "Oh my God, Billy. *You really are a genius!*"

A live auction typically featured an auctioneer, preferably clad in a dinner jacket, whose sole function was to incite spirited, inebriated bidders to grossly overpay for top-of-the-line items. Sometimes auctioneers were local celebrities, like a newscaster from the local TV station who could talk fast and rev up a crowd. But Billy and Miranda agreed that they would aim higher. Much higher.

"All right, then. I'll get to work on the silent-auction donors tomorrow," Billy said.

"Divine," Miranda said. "Oh, this is going to be *such* fun."

SEVEN

You went to a victim's funeral as routinely as you interviewed their bereaved spouse. Nothing much ever came of it, Janzek thought, spooling back through the years. Well, once...sort of.

James McClain Swiggett's funeral took place on a drizzly Thursday morning at Magnolia cemetery on Cunningham Avenue. It was not the turnout that Janzek would have expected. Twenty or twenty-five people was all. Janzek kept an eye out for a sobbing girlfriend or two but didn't see anyone fitting the bill.

Camille Swiggett and their two kids were there, of course. Next to Camille stood the man on the respirator, who had to be Swiggett's father. The elder Swiggett had gaunt cheeks and the vacuous, faraway look of a man who was not all there. He was skinny as a scarecrow and Janzek guessed that he had probably once stood an inch or two taller.

A cluster of men—a half-dozen or so—in black and gray suits sat off to one side. Lawyers from Swiggett's firm, Janzek knew, from having seen their pictures on the office's website.

They looked like a pretty grim lot, much as one might look after spending their life trying to figure out how to wiggle around tax laws and get one over on the IRS.

There was another little cluster of people—two husbands and their wives, plus a fifth man—who had all arrived together in an Audi station wagon. Janzek watched them share a quiet joke or two, looking much more relaxed than the lawyers, who were showing a fraternal display of respect for their fallen comrade.

The sole single guy in the Audi group got up fifteen minutes after arriving. He looked to be around Swiggett's age, had longish curly dark hair that swirled around his ears and a red birth mark covering part of his cheek that, at a quick glance, looked like a miniature state of Texas. He took a few steps forward, then turned to face the others. He looked from face to face, long enough so the silence got a little uncomfortable, then finally he spoke.

"I realize that except for you, Mr. Swiggett," the man began, "I've probably known your son the longest of anyone here."

Mr. Swiggett did not react. Camille smiled wanly.

"I was thinking back to my first memory of Jamie, which was when we smoked cigarettes behind my folks' barn out in Awendaw." A few gratuitous titters. "My second memory was of you, Mr. Swiggett, with Jimmy bent over your knee after you caught us with a bottle of your best bourbon."

A few more titters, but nada from the old man. To Janzek, it seemed that he half-reacted to hearing his name but nothing else.

"I won't bore you with any longwinded stories. I just want to say that Jamie was the leader of the pack back then. A guy I looked up to and respected. He had an aura about him. And even when times got tough for Jamie, he still had it." He looked down at the casket and patted it gently. "I'm gonna miss runnin' with you, buddy. You're the man...and always will be."

Camille smiled like it was expected of her as the man returned to his seat.

A long, awkward pause followed as nobody said anything. Finally, a man in green corduroys, which were out-of-place for the hot summer day, stepped forward. He didn't turn and face the other mourners, but looked straight ahead, his back to them.

Given the man's dry, serious eulogy, you would have thought James Bryant Swiggett was Saint Peter. He spoke of Swiggett's commitment to his church, to his kids, to his profession, and to his friends but—fittingly—he made no mention of Swiggett's wife. The man ended it solemnly: "So I just want to say, so long, Jamie. Charleston's going to miss you, old friend. Fare-thee-well, brother."

Janzek didn't know people still said "fare-thee-well." He glanced at Camille Swiggett for her reaction, which was nonexistent. It made Janzek wonder what his late wife, Diana, would be thinking if this were his funeral. Possibilities bounced around in his mind as the intermittent drizzle matted down his hair, the rain and the somber occasion darkening his mood and sparking a pang of regret. All the "if onlys..." If only he hadn't let his job become his lord and master back in Boston. If only he'd put Diana first and remained as attentive and loving as he had been those first few years. If only he had been as free-spirited and, well, fun, as he had been when they met.

If only she was still alive, and they were still together.

He heard footsteps and looked up to see a woman who had just arrived.

She was in her late forties, early fifties, Janzek guessed. Blonde, attractive, shorter than average, and wearing what looked like expensive, conservatively cut clothes. Grey pants with a knife-like crease, a cream-colored, silk shirt with a wide collar, and big diamond studs in her ears, the kind that looked at home on a pro football player who had just landed a fat signing bonus. The earrings made for a bold contrast, the conservative alongside the flashy. She had oversized, black Jackie O sunglasses perched on her head and Janzek noticed how everyone immediately started sneaking glances at her. Although when the funeral was over, nobody approached her or said anything to her. Almost as if they were scared of her. Or intimidated. Or maybe none of them were on her social level. Janzek couldn't get a clear read.

He stayed in back off to one side and watched everyone walk back to their cars. Janzek knew that walk. Slow. Deliberate. No one went too quickly, or it might be perceived that they were in a hurry to get back to their office or out on the golf course.

The blonde woman who had arrived late was the first to leave. She also walked significantly faster than the others. But before leaving, her eyes darted to Swiggett's father's face. She stopped and stared at him for an uncomfortable moment. Swiggett's father finally looked up at her, but his eyes remained blank, not registering the slightest recognition. Janzek watched to see whether she made eye contact with anyone else, but she didn't even acknowledge the presence of any other person.

From a distance, though, Janzek thought he saw tears in her eyes.

She approached a long Mercedes limo, where a man in a black suit and white shirt and tie hopped out and opened the door for her.

A second later, she was gone in a whisper of white exhaust smoke.

EIGHT

Fifteen years ago....

JENNY WAS BORN IN A LITTLE TOWN IN SOUTHERN Georgia called Thomasville. Her father worked as a foreman on a plantation named *Bellevoir,* which was owned by a rich man from Charleston. Her family had a house on the plantation that they didn't own. It came with her father's job and only had two bedrooms.

The man from Charleston and his wife frequently hosted houseguests who came to shoot and ride at *Bellevoir.* During those sessions, Jenny's father worked long hours coordinating the shoots to make them come off as effortlessly relaxed adventures, when in reality, only a perfect symphony of timing and precise attention to detail made it all work.

One day in the fall, Jenny, eleven at the time, came home from school sick with the flu. As she walked into her house, she heard noises unlike anything she had ever heard before.

As she went by her parents' bedroom she saw, through the door which was open a crack, her mother lying naked on her bed, tightly gripping the bedposts, her legs wrapped around a man standing and thrusting at her. The man, who was not Jenny's father, was sweating and grunting and wore nothing but perfectly polished black leather hunting boots which came up to his knees. She noticed a little scratch on the top of one of the boots. She almost cried out before realizing her mother was not in danger. Instead, she tiptoed quietly to her bedroom, shut the door, closed her eyes as tightly as she could, and put her hands over her ears.

Two days later it was the weekend and Jenny was feeling better. Her father, who had taught her to ride and shoot, sometimes recruited her to help him serve drinks when the fancy people from Charleston took a break from the hunt. Together Jenny and her father would locate the hunting party traveling in an old-fashioned horse-drawn carriage loaded with beer, wine, liquor, soft drinks, and mixers in a big, ice-filled vat in the rear of the buggy. Jenny, in a demure smock, would help her father serve the hunters.

She was always dazzled by the beauty of the women in their hunting attire. They looked as if they'd stepped out of the cover of *Town & Country* magazine. The men—young and old —wore crisp Tattersall pattern shirts, ties, and tweed, pleated hunting jackets with suede shoulder pads and huge pockets to carry game.

Her father, by contrast, in mud-splattered blue jeans and a canvas jacket with a rip in the right sleeve, looked like what he was—a man who said, 'yes, sir,' 'no, ma'am,' and served other people. And though Jenny dearly loved her father, she sometimes wished he was a different man, a man like the one who owned *Bellevoir,* with all his self-assurance and swagger.

That Saturday as she served the men and women drinks, she encountered two things she would never forget. The first was the son of the man who owned *Bellevoir.* She observed and studied him. No more than fifteen or sixteen, he looked like a little prince with penetrating blue eye and a haughty air. He sat rigidly erect on his horse and eyed Jenny with an expression she couldn't decipher.

She asked him if he wanted something to drink.

"Yeah, a beer," he said without hesitation.

His father, on a regal chestnut quarter horse next to him, shook his head and rolled his eyes. "For God's sake," his father said, then to Jenny, "He'll have a Coke."

The man looked back at his son, caught his eye, and smiled. He seemed amused at his son's effrontery, a chip off the old block, maybe. Then the father nudged his horse and rode forward.

Jenny noticed his black hunting boots, which were polished to a lustrous glaze and had a little scratch at the top of one.

NINE

JANZEK HUNG UP THE PHONE AND WALKED OVER TO Delvin Rhett's office.

"I have a question for you," he said at Rhett's doorway.

Rhett looked up. "Fire away."

"Who is Sheila Lessing?"

Rhett smiled, like, *You got a couple hours?*

"Jesus, Nick," he said. "Are you totally clueless? Just stumble off a cruise ship or something? Sheila Lessing is like the patron saint of South Carolina. Not to mention a billionaire, president of the College of Charleston, and, if she wants, the next senator of the Palmetto State."

Rhett was stretched out in his Aeron chair knock-off, feet up on his desk, as he peered up at Janzek in khaki pants, a blue shirt and his favorite red and silver Old Navy tie.

"Okay, then the question is, what was she doing at Jamie Swiggett's funeral?" Janzek asked.

"Sure it was her?"

"Yeah, definitely. Looking all regal and mysterious. I ran the license on her Mercedes limo."

35

Rhett nodded. "I've seen it. Long as a football field."

"A little ostentatious for a college president, wouldn't you say?"

"Yeah, well, she's not your typical college president. Whatever that might be."

Janzek sat down and looked out the window. He didn't say anything for a few moments. Then Rhett rapped his knuckles on his desk. "What exactly's goin' through that brain of yours, Nick?"

Rhett took a bite of a half-eaten Kit Kat bar that Janzek had seen festering on his desk for at least a month.

"So that's her official job, running the college?"

"Yup."

"How'd she get to be a billionaire?"

"She was a big deal up in New York. Wall Street, I think. Then, just to make sure, she married a billionaire."

Janzek was staring at a bug making its way slowly across the floor. He nodded, eyeing the bug. "I got news for you, brother: You got termites in here."

"Yeah, I know. I called a guy at Buzz Off."

Janzek chuckled. "That's really the name of the place?"

Rhett nodded.

"So I'm guessing Swiggett was either Sheila Lessing's lawyer or her—"

"—shorty?"

"What the hell's that mean?" Janzek asked.

"That would be slang for a boyfriend in the African-American community," Rhett said.

Janzek shrugged. "Sorry, I'm just an unhip white guy."

"No shit... I think it mighta been Snoop who came up with *shorty*."

"Just so you know, I have the greatest respect for Mr. Dogg." Janzek looked away. "I've been thinking about some-

36

thing Camille Swiggett told me. How she and Swiggett were having financial problems and how, just before he bought it, he told Camille all those problems were about to go away."

"So... you thinkin' maybe his friend Miss Sheila was gonna bail him out or something?" Rhett asked. "Is that where you're going?"

"I don't know," Janzek said, standing up. "Could be." He went over and stepped on the bug that had almost made it to the far wall. "You friend from Buzz Off's got one less termite to terminate."

"You're a cruel man, Nick," Rhett said. "Oh, hey, speakin' of Sheila Lessing, wanna know how she ended up being a widow?"

Janzek's head swung around. "You have my full, undivided attention."

TEN

Tipton always went to the big hullabaloo for the Preservation Society. For a variety of reasons. It was an annual event and everybody who was anybody made an appearance.

For one thing, she always got a lot of attention from men. Married men and single men alike. She liked that, even though nothing ever went very far. For another, she almost always managed to wangle a real-estate listing at big galas. Last year she had actually landed two, a big house on Legare and a townhouse with a spectacular view of the water on East Bay. She had also gotten cozy with a couple who were interested in buying a place. Maybe not right at the moment, the husband kept saying; but if something 'really special' came along, the wife added. And sure enough, four months later, something really special on Tradd Street did come along. The couple paid a shade over three million for it. Tipton's commission was $182,000.

The other reason she liked the Preservation Society gala was that they didn't hesitate to break the bank to get special guests for the annual blowout. Usually it was a big-time author, politician, public figure, or someone in the news. This year it was Heather Clawson, the longtime special correspondent at NPR, who had written all those ponderous six-hundred-page tomes about pompous statesmen, and knew exactly where the bodies were buried in D.C. Clawson's reputation was for keeping it high-minded but Tipton had heard she could also dish with the best of them. Charleston society queen bees included. That was saying something. And that was all Tipton had to tell her friend, Kitty Savage, to get her to go to the gala. Kitty was a soft touch for any kind of gossip, be it local, state, or national. Since Tipton didn't feel comfortable going alone, taking along good-time Kitty worked out perfectly.

There was another reason why Tipton wanted to go—actually, the main reason—but she kept that one close to her vest.

THE PRESERVATION SOCIETY put on an amazing show—as well they should, at five hundred dollars a pop. The usual drill was that a leading member of Charleston Society would lend their house for a cocktail party that would kick off the whole thing. Estelle Raintree, head of Preservation, wasn't about to settle for any old Charleston house south of Broad. No, the house she selected had to combine history, elegance and, most importantly, exclusivity. That meant she was only in the market for a house whose owners had been extraordinarily discriminating, meaning that they had only allowed the upper, upper, upper echelon of Charleston society through their home's hallowed doors. The idea, of course, was to get those who were on the outside looking in—i.e., the dreaded, nauseatingly rich Yankees—curious enough to want to see what all the fuss was about. To allow the excluded...to be included, but for a hefty price, natch.

This year it was Lucien and Dede Wiedemann's house.

Tipton talked Kitty Savage into taking a bike taxi to the house on Water Street, despite Kitty's protest that the humid air was going to seriously mess with her hair. They got to the house at six twenty and Kitty told the young pedaler to keep the meter running while she re-teased her bleached-blond tresses in the seat behind him. Five minutes later, the two walked into the five-story, ten-thousand-square-foot house.

Tipton's first impression was, 'What's all the noise about?' The ceiling was high, the moldings and details were authentic and impressive, but the furnishings were, for the most part, quite pedestrian. But the more Tipton looked, the more she realized that—like a *Where's Waldo* face—there were quite a few museum-quality pieces sprinkled among the kitsch. She and Kitty introduced themselves to Lucian Wiedemann and his wife, then quickly made their way to a bar. On the way there, Tipton turned a few heads as Kitty nattered on about some buff guy from her spin class.

Tipton got a pinot grigio and Kitty a cabernet sauvignon and they walked back into the living room. She noticed a penwork box on a mantelpiece bracketed by much more ordinary pieces on either side.

"The two most beautiful women in the room," came the voice from behind Tipton.

Oh, God, she thought, *Bertie Wemphill*. The biggest bore in the room... though she had already spotted several contenders for the title.

Bertie planted himself in their space, making himself impossible to ignore.

"Hi, Bertie," Tipton said, eschewing his lame nickname.

"Hey, Wempie," Kitty said, opting to go with it.

"How goes the disposition of domiciles?" Wemphill asked Tipton.

That was the way he asked questions. Thinking his hifa-lutin' verbiage somehow added luster to his ho-hum questions.

"Pretty good," Tipton said, "how goes the shepherding of strangers around our fair city?"

Two could play his lame-ass game.

Wemphill, the son of a prosperous doctor, was a tour guide whose specialty was the "Olde" Charleston jail. He knew its history cold and not much else.

Kitty looked over Wemphill's shoulder in an undisguised room-scan. Evidently, she spotted an eligible bachelor. "Well, nice talking to you, Wempie," she said—even though she hadn't —and moved on to greener pastures.

Tipton, not quite so insensitive, spent another three minutes with Wemphill, finally making her getaway under the pretext of needing another hit of pinot.

She refilled her glass and walked up to the third floor. On a mission.

Along the way, she had a few more fluffy conversations with people she knew, then hightailed it when she saw the second most boring person in the house, Johnny Baldwin, beel-ining toward her.

She beat it up to the fourth floor and left Baldwin in her dust, figuring the higher the floor, the fewer the people. Walking up four flights in heels or dress shoes was only for the hardy—generally limited to the under-fifty crowd. She spotted a small famille rose tureen on a bookshelf in a corner. On the right of the tureen were eight copies of Lucien Wiedemann's memoir, *A Man of Four Letters*.

She had heard of the book but was never curious enough even to find out what the title referred to. She figured he prob-ably had boxes and boxes of his books stashed in a corner of the attic. In another room, which had three distinguished period fireplaces and mantels, she spotted two hand-painted papier-mâché snuff boxes. She looked around and saw a couple ten feet away, laughing uproariously, then watched the man actually slap his knee. Could anything really be *that* funny? she wondered.

She thought how easily she could just sweep the valuable snuff boxes into her purse.

But she was after bigger booty.

Then it dawned on her.

The Wiedemanns would almost certainly have put their prize treasure away. Just to be safe.

Probably in a big Mosler wall safe somewhere, along with Dede Wiedemann's fabled Marie Antoinette necklace.

Tipton decided to cut her losses and walk back down to the more populous second and third floors, where she could cultivate prospective house buyers and sellers. She was rarely the initiator of real-estate conversations—people tended to come to her. It would start out something like, 'Tipton, the kids are all gone, we don't need all the bedrooms we have,' or, 'We need more room; got anything on the bricks on Church Street?'

But the little voice in Tipton's head told her, *You've come this far, might as well go up just one more flight and check out the top floor.*

So, she hiked up the stairs, thinking it was probably a wasted climb.

She walked into a half-furnished, somewhat dreary room. The Wiedemanns must have figured that no one would ever get this high, so why waste their decorating budget on anything up here.

She audibly gasped when she spotted it. It was sitting proudly on a shelf next to what looked like a fake Queen Anne highboy.

There was no mistaking it. It was a Faberge egg.

ELEVEN

"You gotta be kidding me," Janzek said.

He was sitting in Rhett's office, his feet up on Rhett's desk.

Rhett shook his head. "No, man, supposedly there was a similar case up in New York," he said. "But, like, a million years ago. Some big society woman shot her husband the same way."

Janzek knew all about the case, though he didn't want to tell Rhett how he knew. He didn't think it would be good if word got around that he had read a nonfiction account of the incident, even though odds were a hundred to one that nobody at Charleston PD had ever heard of the book.

"I remember I read about it once on Google," Janzek lied. "Like you said, this society woman on Long Island shot her husband with a shotgun, I think it was back in the 1950s. She claimed she thought he was a burglar. I guess there had been a few robberies in the area and—long story short—she got away with it."

"You think she did it on purpose?" Rhett asked.

"I don't know. Maybe she had a young stud on the side or something. I forget the details."

What he did remember was that, a few years later, the woman killed herself after getting snubbed by society people.

"The difference was, as I remember it, " Rhett said, "Sheila's husband was coming home from a business trip in the middle of the night."

"So the story goes, anyway," Janzek said.

Rhett nodded. "Yeah, word on the street was maybe he was coming home from seeing the farmer's daughter."

"And she claimed she thought he was a burglar?"

"Yeah, same thing as that Long Island woman. But in this case, a con had just busted out of McDougall Correctional twenty miles away and had hit a few houses in the area."

"Was there a trial or anything?"

"No," Rhett said. "Mainly 'cause the con got caught a couple days later burglarizing a house a mile from hers. Everyone gave her the benefit of the doubt, figured she had legit reason for the hair-trigger."

"After it happened, I bet the local cops stepped up their efforts to catch the con," Janzek said.

Rhett nodded. "I see where you're going. I don't know the answer to that."

"Obviously it didn't hurt her reputation or anything."

"Nah, never slowed down old Sheila," Rhett said. "I think it was that no way in hell anybody figured her for a murderer."

Janzek thought for a second. "I'm not sure what this has to do with our case, but what was your take on it?"

"I don't know, man," Rhett said. "I always wondered, wouldn't the husband have said something? Like, "Hey, honey, I'm home.' You know, just to let her know it was him."

Janzek tapped Rhett's desk a few times. "Not if she shoots first and asks questions later."

TWELVE

Tipton, who'd only had a pinot grigio and a half at the Wiedemanns' home, was drunk. Drunk on exhilaration and jazzed up with lust for her new possession, now in a pocket of her silver lamé Judith Lieber handbag.

She and Kitty Savage had just walked down the steps of the Wiedemann house and spotted the driver of the bike taxi waiting for them across the street. He was texting, of course, as all kids his age seemed to do every minute of the day.

It was seven forty-five now and the gala's dinner would be served at the Library Society in another forty-five minutes. The Preservation Society had to rent the elegant main room of the Library Society building, which galled Estelle Raintree to no end since she felt her organization—*Pres Soc*, as she called it—was way more prestigious than *Lib Soc*, though maybe disadvantaged when it came to real estate.

Tipton and Kitty got drinks at the Library Society bar—it was Kitty's fourth—and Tipton suggested that Kitty pace herself, advice which Kitty had never heeded before and probably wouldn't start listening to now.

After dinner, scheduled for eight thirty, Heather Clawson would take the mic, presumably to tumultuous applause, even though she was way more liberal than most in the room. (Although Tipton knew that Charleston had more closet liberals than one might think.)

A speaker usually spoke for about half an hour at the event, followed by five or ten minutes of Q & A. Then the mildly to heavily inebriated guests would strut their stuff to the mellifluous strains of Charleston's Peter Duchin knock-off, the Darryl Hobcaw Five.

———

TIPTON HAD the third most boring man in Charleston on her right. Stephen Shand was an orthopedic surgeon who, if you gave him a chance, would regale you with all the gory details of every operation he'd ever performed. Every laminectomy, arthroscopy, and discectomy. Somewhere along the way, the man had come to believe that people actually gave a damn about his scalpel mastery.

Thank God for a man from New York, seated to Tipton's left. His name was Zach Taylor, and he was a breath of fresh air. He never told her what he did for a living and she didn't ask, but he had a facile—and it turned out deep—grasp of everything from movies to literature to which restaurants in Charleston were ridiculously overpriced.

She would have spent all her time talking to him if she didn't feel sorry for Poppy De Sirico, on the other side of Steve Shand, who kept shooting Tipton imploring looks that said, 'Get me the hell out of this horrible conversation.'

"I don't want to monopolize you," Tipton finally said to Zach Taylor. "But I'm afraid it's time to switch partners."

Taylor nodded, smiled, and turned to his left.

Shand, it turned out, was not only boring, but also hammered.

He drunkenly launched into a blow-by-blow of a double hip replacement he had nimbly performed on some hobbled geezer who had been the football team captain at Clemson a hundred years ago.

Tipton had totally forgotten about another characteristic of Shand's that repelled her equally. The guy was a 'toucher,' or, more accurately, a 'pawer' or, even more accurately, a 'mauler.' He kept putting his hands on her arm as he described his deft strokes in the OR. She kept pulling her arm away, but there wasn't anywhere to put it that was out of his lecherous reach.

So, finally, she had had an anxiety attack. A pretty bad one, in fact.

Hyperventilation mixed with panic. Genuine, too, she wasn't faking it. She tried to hide her short, fast breathing. Fortunately, Shand had greatly diminished powers of observation, which was to say, none at all. The symptoms quickly enveloped her: lightheadedness, dizziness, and a palpable tingling and numbness in her lips. She wanted to run, get as far away from Shand as possible.

She excused herself, walked across the wide expanse of the marble floor and hid out in the stall of the women's bathroom for five long minutes. Then, feeling better, she went back to the table, hoping that Shand would by now have again snagged the ear of poor Poppy De Sirico. But, as it turned out, Shand was lying in wait and picked up exactly where he had left off: the spellbinding climax of how he had neatly implanted the new hips of the ex-pigskin hero from Clemson.

No sooner had she sat down than Shand's hand was back on her shoulder, then he slid it back down to the same place on her arm. Immediately, she felt a spasm in her leg, the result of

47

her breathing so fast that she didn't have enough oxygen in her system.

She had seen several doctors about it. The inescapable conclusion was that it was caused by men touching her. Even lightly. Even without sexual motivation. The worst cases resulted in her having sharp chest pains and palpitations, and often she had difficulty sleeping for days afterward.

She had an overpowering urge to drive her steak knife deep into Shand's chest and mute the obnoxious bore for good. But instead she decided it was time to make a run for it. After all, she had the precious egg in her Judith Lieber bag, the same bag she had shoplifted from the Nieman-Marcus flagship store in Hudson Yards.

She turned to Shand and reeking with sarcasm said: "Oh, Steve, I had an absolutely marvelous time listening to you for the last two hours, hearing all about that man's pair of sturdy new hips, but now I must go."

Then, she glanced over at Poppy De Sirico. Her pleading eyes said it all: *please, please, don't leave me with this blathering, egotistical jackass.*

THIRTEEN

Janzek walked into Red Truck Books and went straight to the historical fiction section. He pulled out a book on an upper shelf by Bernard Cornwell titled *1356*. He remembered someone telling him it was one of Cornwell's better ones, though Janzek was partial to his Richard Sharpe series.

Janzek knew that the historical fiction section was directly across from Geneva Crane's office, which meant that chances were good that, sooner or later, she'd look up and see him.

Geneva, owner of Red Truck Books, possessed an old blue blood name, a spectacular figure and had been—for three steamy, passion-filled months—Janzek's lover.

They had broken up two months before and communication had tapered off, but they still kept in touch from time to time. What had happened was Geneva had wanted to push the relationship to the next level. She wasn't hinting around for a ring or anything, she just wanted to see more of him. Which, when you think about it, was not an unreasonable request.

Nevertheless, it had spooked Janzek, resulting in one of those heated, wine-fueled fights during which the charge of him being a "commitment-phobe" had been leveled. Of course, that made him even more spooked.

Afterward, Geneva—in her inimitable straightforward manner—had given him her take: She suspected that seventy-five percent of his reluctance had to do with him not having gotten over the tragic murder of his wife a year and a half before and the other twenty-five percent was because he was a workaholic cop.

Janzek might have adjusted the percentages slightly, but Geneva wasn't far off.

So, their relationship had evolved into 'platonic' status, which worked fine for him, but Geneva was far from thrilled about it.

Out of the corner of his eye, Janzek saw Geneva look up, smile, then walk over to him.

"So, Nick, what do you need from me this time?"

Janzek looked up, pretending to be surprised.

"Oh, hi, Geneva," he said, kissing her on the cheek. "What did you say?"

She laughed. "Come on, now, you forget. I know you cold."

He patted her arm and smiled. "Busted," he said. "Okay, I could really use a little of your insider knowledge about a woman in Charleston."

"And what's my reward?"

"Ah...take your pick. Breakfast, lunch, or dinner?"

"Sex."

Janzek glanced around and noted a customer perusing books in the nearby biography section.

"Jesus, Geneva," he whispered. "You know that's a terrible idea."

She sighed. "Yeah, I guess you're right. Lunch, then."

"So, Virginia's tomorrow?"

"Sounds good. All right, so go ahead... pump me." She caught herself and laughed. "Figure of speech."

He laughed. "So tell me what you know about Sheila Lessing."

"She's too old for you."

"Seriously."

"Well, what do you want to know?" Geneva asked. "I mean, she's a multi-billionaire, but you know that. She beat the boys on Wall Street at their own game, then married a fellow billionaire, just to be sure she wouldn't starve; then, sadly, shot him. After that became the best president the College of Charleston has ever had—"

"Wait, back up. Do you think that was an accident? Shooting her husband?"

Geneva took a deep breath. "Yes, I definitely do."

"Why do you say that?"

"'Cause she loved the guy."

"But there was a story going around that he might have been...messing around on her?"

"That's bullshit. He was one of the rare, good guys."

Janzek slipped the Cornwell novel back into the shelf. "Ever read *The Two Mrs. Grenvilles*?"

"That Dominick Dunne hatchet job?" Geneva said. Then it clicked. "Oh, so you're suggesting that's where Sheila got the idea? That woman on Long Island killing her husband? Pretty highbrow detective work, Nick."

Janzek smiled and nodded, coloring a bit. "Let me ask you something else. Why would she want to become president of the College of Charleston? Strikes me as kind of a demotion. I mean, being this big... she-wolf of Wall Street, running a place that's—well, a good college, but it sure ain't up there with Harvard or Yale."

"*She-wolf?*"

"Sorry, how about *titan?*"

"Better," Geneva said. "I think you just put your finger on it."

He narrowed his eyes. "What do you mean?"

"Her goal is to make the college into Harvard or Yale."

He rubbed his chin. "That's a tall order."

"It may be. But you don't know Sheila. She thinks big. She has all her life. You know about Colonial Lake?"

"What about it?"

"It always bothered her. This lake in a great location in the middle of Charleston with a bunch of mostly nondescript houses around it. She looked at it and envisioned what it could be—Central Park, or that beautiful park down in Savannah...I forget the name."

"What's this got to do—"

Geneva held up a hand. "Hang on, let me finish. So, what she did was personally commit to spend five million dollars of her own money to revamp Colonial Lake. Make it into a mini-Central Park—" Geneva held up her hand again to stop him. "Okay, so now I'm getting around to your question, 'Why would she want to become president of the college?' And this is straight from the horse's mouth. See, Sheila and I had a few cocktails at a dinner party back before I met you—a year or so ago—and she told me she intended to turn the college into an Ivy League contender. Up there with University of Virginia. Told me how Charleston as a town has more going for it than Cambridge and a hell of a lot more than New Haven. So, she was going to make the college a lot tougher to get into. You know, like only take kids with 1500s on their college boards, for starters."

"You're kidding. She actually thinks she can do that? Be that selective?"

"Absolutely. It already has changed. Just wait another ten

years. See, my theory is she wants that to be her legacy. She doesn't really give a damn about being the richest woman in South Carolina or having a business school named after her. She wants her legacy to be Lessing College."

Janzek's eyes grew bigger and greener. "She's going to change the name?"

Geneva nodded. "She supposedly told someone that. Not me. She'd probably deny it if you asked her. Hey, look at Harvard and Yale and Brown, they're all named after someone that gave 'em a bunch of money, right?"

Janzek scratched his head. *Interesting, but what does any of this have to do with my murder case?*

"What do you know about her personal life?"

Geneva put her hand on her chin. "What are you really asking, Nick?"

There was no way to put one over on Geneva Crane.

"Ever heard her name mentioned in the same breath with James Swiggett?"

"No," she said, after thinking for a moment, "I mean, maybe he was her lawyer or something. Attractive to some women, I guess. But no, I don't see Sheila messing around with married guys. I would have heard something."

Janzek stepped up to Geneva and gave her a kiss on the cheek. "Thank you," he said. "As usual, the best-informed woman in Charleston. You earned a four-course lunch."

"Just don't let me drink," she said with a sigh. "Or I might try to jump you."

FOURTEEN

BELLEVOIR HAD A SWIMMING POOL BEHIND THE MANOR with a pool house on the far side that included a huge game room with billiards, a foosball table, and two arcade video games. It also included two bedrooms and two baths off of the game room.

It was a rainy day and the plantation owner's son and his two friends were playing pool when Jenny walked in. It was her sixteenth birthday, and she was wearing something her mother had bought her that she really wanted: a black bra from the Nordstrom in Tallahassee.

She had a crush on the plantation owner's son, who was three years older than she. He had a kind of a smug arrogance, but, boy, was he handsome. Smoldering eyes that always followed her when she was near him. She thought maybe he found her sexy. A little, anyway.

Boldly, she walked into the game room and approached the boys. "Any of you guys want something to drink?"

As if they couldn't get just about anything they wanted from the oversized stainless-steel refrigerator in the galley kitchen just a few feet away. But this was her job, getting drinks for guests at *Bellevoir*.

The owner's son chalked his cue stick, then blew the end of it as if he had seen some guy do it in a movie once. "Sure, whaddaya offering, girlfriend?"

She liked him calling her that.

"Oh, you know, the usual," she said, "Coke, root beer, Dr. Pepper."

The owner's son caught one of his friend's eyes and smirked.

"I'll have a Coke," he said, "with three fingers of Mount Gay rum in it."

His friends laughed.

She had no idea what three fingers meant.

One of his friends took a shot at the eleven ball, then turned to Jenny.

"And I'll have a root beer," he said. "Hold the root."

The plantation owner's son laughed and high-fived his friend.

"Make that two Mount Gay and Cokes," said the third boy.

"I'll have to go to the main house and get a bottle," said Jenny, eager to please.

"We're not going anywhere," the owner's son said, lining up a shot. Then he turned to her. "Hey, check and see if my parents went into town, will you?" He tapped the butt end of the pool stick on the shiny hardwood floor.

"I'm pretty sure they were planning to."

"Beautiful," he said, "then make that two bottles of rum."

Jenny shot him a thumbs-up and smiled.

JENNY WAS LEANING over the pool table, stick in hand,

showing a lot of thigh and a peek at her new black bra from Nordstrom. She wasn't trying to look provocative—that wasn't her style—but the boys couldn't miss it.

The owner's son looked over at one of them, smirked, and took a long pull on his third Mount Gay and Coke.

Jenny took a shot, but her cue stick slid off the side of the cue ball, which limped into a side pocket.

The three boys laughed.

"Okay, you need help." The owner's son stepped up behind her.

"Minnesota Fats to the rescue," said one of the other boys.

"Who's Minnesota Fats?" she asked the son.

"A pool hustler," he said, pulling the cue ball out of the side pocket.

He placed it where it had been before.

"Okay, try it again," he said, touching her from behind now.

Suddenly, she felt uncomfortable, like maybe she shouldn't be there. The boys were already drunk and acting different than before.

"Go on," he said, "I'm going to help you."

She leaned onto the table and stretched out, holding the butt of the stick with her right hand, and resting it between the thumb and forefinger of her left hand like she had seen them do.

He leaned into her and put his hands on hers.

"So what you want to do is make sure it's a long, slow, firm motion," he said dragging out the last four words.

One of the boys laughed and she felt even more uncomfortable now.

"Okay, I got the idea," she said, hoping he'd back away. "I can do it."

She tried to free her hands, but he squeezed his palms around hers, pushing into her from behind even harder.

"Okay, stop, please," she said, trying to sound forceful.

This time he took his hands off of hers, then reached up inside her top and cupped her breasts inside her new black bra.

For the first time in her short life, Jenny felt completely and totally helpless.

FIFTEEN

For a billionaire, Sheila Lessing wasn't hard to get on the phone.

Geneva had given Janzek the name of the town in Dorchester County where Sheila lived alone in an old, ancestral farmhouse, when she wasn't in Charleston. The town was called Pasco. Her other house was on Tradd Street. "More like a castle," was how Geneva described it. She told Janzek that Sheila usually went to the country house on weekends. Since it was a Saturday, he tried information for the Pasco house and found that it was actually listed. He dialed the number and got her housekeeper on the first ring. He told her that he was a detective with the Charleston Police Department and had a few important questions for Ms. Lessing, and the housekeeper went and got her. Easy as that.

Sheila Lessing was friendly but businesslike. Although she said she preferred to answer his questions right then and there on the phone, he insisted on seeing her in person, explaining it was about the murder of James Swiggett. She finally relented and ten minutes later he was on the road to Pasco, an hour and a half away.

As Janzek drove up to the house, he wasn't sure he had the right address. The farmhouse was quite unassuming but surrounded by what seemed like hundreds of acres of perfectly groomed land. A two-story colonial, it had simple Doric columns and a porch with four wicker chairs on it. At most, the house looked to be four or five thousand square feet. Janzek's impression was that was on the small side—for most billion-aires' second homes, anyway. But then he realized, what did he know?

Inside was a different story. Spectacular art and antiques greeted Janzek wherever he looked, starting with the front foyer.

Sheila Lessing answered the door herself, wearing white pants, a beige cashmere sweater and a self-assured smile. Late-forties was Janzek's guess. She looked like she'd maybe been a brainy cheerleader once upon a time who figured out early on that doing Bikram yoga and eating right would keep her looking ten years younger.

"Hello, detective, welcome to Redfern Farm," she said, giving him a surprisingly firm handshake and locking eyes.

"Thank you, Ms. Lessing, I appreciate you taking the time to see me."

"Call me Sheila," she said, turning toward a cozy living room and gesturing. "Have a seat anywhere you like."

Janzek chose a soft, blue club chair.

A few moments later an older black man entered the room.

"Cedril," Sheila said, "this is Detective Janzek from Charleston—" then to Janzek—"Would you like something to drink?"

Janzek nodded to Cedril. "Just a glass of water would be great. Thanks."

"Yes, sir," Cedril said. "Tea, ma'am?"

She nodded. "Thanks."

Janzek pointed at a hundred-year-old American Impressionist painting on the wall above where Sheila was sitting. "That's a beautiful painting. It reminds me of the New England coastline."

She blinked. "Thank you, it's a Frederick Judd Waugh—probably Rockport, Maine—you have a good eye," she said, running her tongue over her upper lip.

"Well, ma'am, I'll get right to the point."

"Before you do," she said with a smile. "I'd appreciate it if you wouldn't call me *ma'am*."

"Oh, sorry," he said, surprised. He thought that was a polite southern thing.

She explained. "To me, it's how people address a doddering, old woman. And by the way, it's perfectly okay to have a little warm-up chit chat before you grill me, or whatever it is you're going to do."

Janzek nodded, smiled, and looked back at the painting above her. "Okay, then," he said, pointing at the painting. "Is that a Rothko, by any chance?"

"I am very impressed, detective."

"Don't be," Janzek said. "I took an art class in college 'cause it was a gut."

"You mean, shoehorned in between Homicide 101 and Advanced Forensics."

He laughed. "Exactly. But turns out, I'm actually kind of a collector myself."

"Really?"

"Yeah, I've got a Joe McGuirk, a Ralph Eppsley and a Morton Riegleman in my living room... the last one was from Mort's early Hyannis period. Got a package deal on all three at a tag sale in Boston."

She laughed and put her hand up to her chin. "I'm sorry, I can't say I'm familiar with Jim, Ralph, and Mort."

"Joe, actually," Janzek said, "Old masters... the Cape Cod School."

"I'll have to check 'em out."

He smiled and sat up straight. "What can you tell me about James Swiggett, Ms. Lessing?"

She brushed back a low-hanging strand of blonde hair. "The old abrupt-change-of-subject gambit," she said. "Nice technique, detective."

Janzek smiled and eyed a stack of coffee-table books. One was titled 'Mustique' in big white letters; the one below said, 'Harbor Island.' He thought they were fancy places somewhere but didn't have a clue where.

"If you don't mind, I'd appreciate you telling me about your relationship with Mr. Swiggett, please?"

"Sure. My relationship with Mr. Swiggett was cordial and businesslike."

Janzek leaned forward. "'Cause you know how you hear stuff in Charleston—"

"Oh yes I do know, detective. What exactly did you hear?"

"Well, I just know that Mr. Swiggett was a nice-looking man, popular with the ladies."

"Look, detective, whatever you heard about my relationship with Jamie Swiggett in any kind of a romantic context is pure bullshit."

Hunch confirmed: you didn't get to be a billionaire by pussyfooting around.

"I was just about to say, I never believe rumors. Unless, of course, I hear the same one so many times that—"

"I'm guessing Geneva Crane is one of your sources?"

It was a perfectly timed *gotcha*. She had clearly made some calls and checked him out.

"I know Ms. Crane but wouldn't exactly characterize her as a 'source.'"

"Okay, so she never told you anything about me?"

"Can we go back to Swiggett, please?"

She sighed. "Of course, I'm very sorry about what happened to Jamie. Despite what people may have said, he was a good lawyer and... a friend."

Janzek fixed her with his *Miss Dooley eye*. Miss Dooley had been his high-school algebra teacher, and she'd had the unique ability to scare the hell out of him with her eerie stare. Turned out she had a lazy eye.

Sheila simply stared back at him with unblinking, penetrating eyes.

"When did you last see Mr. Swiggett?"

"Two weeks ago. Well, that's not quite accurate. I saw him in the casket at his funeral, where I saw you, too."

Touché. Another one for Sheila.

"Two weeks ago... was that when you and he had a late dinner at Hall's Steakhouse?"

"Yes. That's exactly when it was."

"Was that the same time you and he had an early breakfast at the Peninsula Grille the next morning?"

"There's an implication there which I strongly resent," Sheila said tersely.

He ran a hand over the crease of his pants. "Like I said, Jamie Swiggett was an attractive man."

Sheila shook her head. "Oh, please. Do you hear yourself? Jamie was handsome, so what? You're an attractive man, too. And somehow, I'm able to restrain myself from throwing myself at you. What you're implying is really insulting. Jamie was handsome, ergo I must've been sleeping with him? I mean, are you *kidding*?"

"I didn't mean—"

"So, because I was seen having a late-night dinner at Hall's with Jamie, means we then went somewhere and had sex? Is that what you're suggesting?"

"No, I—"

"And then the next morning, after we spent the night together, we went and had eggs Benedict at the Peninsula Grill. Is that how your logic works?"

"I just—"

"You just made the connection... late night drinks, breakfast in the morning, a lot of screwing in between."

Janzek put his hands together and rested his chin on them. "You, ah, don't by chance happen to have a law degree, do you, Ms. Lessing?"

She shifted her weight and stared at him. "No, an MBA."

"Could have fooled me," Janzek said. "I apologize for implying—"

She put up her hands. "Apology accepted," she said, getting up. "But we're done here."

Whoa, he still had half a dozen more questions. But what could he say? The Q&A was clearly over and he hadn't even knocked off half the glass of water in front of him. He pushed up from the club chair, stood, and shook her hand.

"Well, thank you, Ms. Lessing."

"You're welcome," she said, heading toward the front door. "I just want to make one final point."

"What's that?"

She turned and looked him in the eyes. "The fact that Jamie Swiggett was married," she said. "Call me old-fashioned, but I *do not* mess around with married men."

SIXTEEN

ONE OF JANZEK'S BASIC RULES WAS, IF HE WAS STUCK AND going nowhere on a case, he dug into the department's files and checked out cold cases. He was three days into Swiggett and had absolutely nothing of value at this point. Statistically —as everyone who's ever watched a cop show knows—if it's older than forty-eight hours and you haven't solved it, the odds are, you never will. The true math, he had read somewhere, was that the chance of solving a homicide is cut in half if you don't get a critical lead in the first forty-eight hours.

For six straight hours, Janzek rifled through cold cases in the file room until he finally found one that had a few similarities to the Swiggett murder. It turned out that only sixteen months before, a body had been found washed up on the shore not far from the Coast Guard station at the end of Tradd Street. That was roughly ten blocks from where Swiggett's body had been found in White Point Garden. The first thing that caught Janzek's attention was that the victim, Whitredge Landrum, was thirty-three years old at the time of death.

Sixteen months later, Jamie Swiggett died at age thirty-four, roughly the same age.

The second thing that he noticed was that while Swiggett had been found with no penis, Whitredge Landrum had been discovered with no hands. That gave Janzek a perhaps-irrational hope that the two cases were indeed related. Jack Martin, the ME on the case and not one of Janzek's favorite men in law enforcement, had theorized in his report at the time that because Whitredge's body had been in the water so long, sea creatures had nibbled away at the hands until there was nothing left. That sounded plausible enough on its own, but a later report directly contradicted it, concluding that the hands had actually been cut or sawed off. Forensics revealed a clean, straight cut on the left hand that reinforced the second theory.

Janzek shuddered. Either explanation created disturbing images. Was it really possible that someone had actually sawed the guy's hands off? Wasn't that more of a Mexican-drug-cartel thing?

Whitredge Landrum had lived in nearby Mt. Pleasant, next door to where Jamie Swiggett grew up on Sullivan's Island.

His murder, if that's what it was, took place four months before Janzek moved from Boston to Charleston; the investigating detective on the case, he saw, was Les Holmes.

Janzek went straight to Holmes's office after reading the file. Holmes was leafing through the *City News* and eating an apple.

"Come on in, Nick," Holmes said, looking over the paper. "What can I do for you?"

"Tell me about Whitredge Landrum, if you recall the case."

Holmes took a bite of his apple, looked away and chewed. Then his eyes returned to Janzek. "That was a strange one," he said. "Everyone had a different theory. One was that it was a suicide. He lived in Old Village in Mount Pleasant right on the water, so—I forget who it was—someone figured he just waded into the water and took a swim to nowhere. He had a history of depression and shit. But then the ME's report said it looked like he had been strangled, so I talked to Jack Martin, and he was theorizing it was auto-asphyxiation. You know...that Landrum might've been a gasper...."

"You're kidding."

"Nope." Holmes took another bite and chewed for a few moments. "Fact is, no one knows. Body was in the water so damned long. Nobody agrees on how long it was in there either, but somewhere between three days and a week."

"Guy was thirty-three, right?"

"Yeah," Holmes said. "That sounds right. Bought it on his birthday, as I remember."

"But how do you know exactly when he died?"

"Well, 'cause I used the date he was reported missing."

"Gotcha," Janzek said with a nod. "And you never had any credible suspects?"

"No, not a one. I mean, trust me, we dug and dug. Guy didn't have anything sketchy going on in his life. Just that depression thing."

Janzek wrote down a few things, then stood up. "Well, thanks, man, I appreciate it."

"No problem," Holmes said and went back to his apple.

———

JANZEK CALLED Camille Swiggett and asked her if she knew the name Whitredge Landrum.

"Know the name?" she said. "Jamie was godfather to one of Whit's boys." She went on to explain that Swiggett and Landrum had been classmates and best friends at Porter-Gaud.

Janzek clenched his fist and pumped it in silent triumph.

Maybe he was finally getting somewhere.

He asked her for the names of the two men who had given the eulogies at her husband's funeral. She said the first one was named Peabo Gardner and the second was Alex Smith.

Janzek first called Smith, the one who'd been wearing the green corduroy pants at the funeral. Smith answered and Janzek asked him if he could come over to his house and ask him some questions. Smith said sure, but he needed to change. Janzek said that wasn't necessary, but Smith said he was still in his pajamas.

Janzek checked his wall clock. It was two in the afternoon; Smith was clearly not a member of Charleston's workforce.

SMITH LIVED in a big house on Limehouse Street, in the fashionable part of town south of Broad. Despite the toney neighborhood, the house looked neglected and smelled of cats. They sat in a family room off of the kitchen, where Smith told Janzek that Swiggett and Whitredge had been charter members of the so-called "bad boy" crowd at their private high school. Way out in front of the pack when it came to pot, booze, and sex.

Sounded like Swiggett was the leader and Landrum, along with Peabo Gardner, were first lieutenants.

Janzek asked him if Landrum had gone to Davidson, too, the college in North Carolina Swiggett had attended. No, Smith said, he went to Wofford.

"Where's that?" Janzek asked.

"Oh, up in Spartanburg," Smith said. "I'm pretty sure Jamie and Landrum kept in touch over the years, in case that helps you."

Janzek asked a few more questions, then the conversation wound down. He thanked Smith and went back to the station.

He was only in his office a few minutes when Rhett walked in and sat down across from him. "Got something for you."

"First, I gotta tell you what I just found out."

"Let's hear it, man."

"Jamie Swiggett and a guy named Whitredge Landrum—who were close friends in high school—both end up dead sixteen months apart. Kicker is, just like Swiggett, Landrum was missing certain essential body parts."

He laid out everything he had learned.

"Wow, man, that's money," Rhett said. "Looks like we're finally getting somewhere. And from a cold case." He smiled and shook his head appreciatively. "Now listen to what I got."

It turned out Rhett's scoop was even bigger than Janzek's.

SEVENTEEN

RHETT'S BIG NEWS WAS THAT HE'D TALKED TO AN eyewitness who claimed to have seen two men ride into White Point Garden on a golf cart the same night Jamie Swiggett's body had been found.

The eyewitness subsequently saw Swiggett's picture in the paper and told Rhett that he was certain the man in the passenger seat of the golf cart was the victim. The only problem was that the eyewitness, by his own admission, had been inebriated—"kinda shitfaced" was how he sheepishly described his condition. He described "weaving" his way home on foot after spending a few hours in a couple of nearby bars.

"So, what time was it when he *weaved* his way home?" Janzek asked.

"That's the problem, he didn't really know."

"Ball park?"

"I asked. Same answer."

"He didn't really know?"

Rhett nodded.

"So you found this guy on one of your phone calls?"

"Uh-huh. About the fiftieth one. Alan Victor's his name. When I first showed him the picture of Swiggett, he kind of hemmed and hawed a little. You know, couldn't look me in the eye. So, I said, 'Come on, Mr. Victor, I know you know something,' and gradually dragged it out of him. But it took a while. Turned out he was scared, like he was wondering if he could get arrested for drunk-walking or something." Janzek chuckled and tapped on his desk a few times. "If that was the case, half this town would be in the slammer. So, he finally admitted he saw Swiggett and this other guy?"

"Yeah," Rhett said. "Came out after a while he was with another man when he saw those two."

Something clicked and Janzek nodded. "So that's what it was."

"Whaddya mean?"

"Victor didn't want to tell you he was going home with another guy."

Rhett's eyes widened and he snapped his fingers. "God*damn,* you're right. That's exactly what it was. It didn't even occur to me."

"He say anything else?"

"Just that the two guys on the golf cart were coming from the west, going east. On Battery. He saw them just for a second. No headlights on the golf cart or anything."

"So what did he say the other guy looked like? The guy driving?"

"Not much help there and, trust me, I asked and asked. Finally, he says, 'Like David Bowie.'"

"What?"

"Said kinda blond, skinny, and pretty."

"Well, what's wrong with that? That's a damned good description."

Rhett shrugged. "I don't know, struck me as kind of strange."

"Yeah, well, that's the way this whole case is shaping up."

"Maybe his 'Thin White Duke' period?"

"Bowie, you mean?"

Rhett nodded.

"I'm impressed you know about that."

Rhett shook his head and glowered at him. "You know, Janzek, sometimes you really piss me off. What do you think, all I know is Kanye and Beyonce? Is that how your cracker-ass brain works?"

Janzek put up his hands. "Whoa, whoa, big fella," he said, and a smile lit up his face. "What can I tell ya? I guess I'm just another racist profiler. But, for the record, I'm a big fan of Little Wayne."

Rhett started laughing. "Motherfucker. And, just for the record, it's Lil Wayne."

"So what else did you get from this guy Victor?"

"That's about it," Rhett said. "I figured you'd want to talk to him."

"Yeah, I do," Janzek said. "How 'bout we let him give a description to the sketch guy, too?"

Rhett shook his head. "If you want, but all his sketches always look like the same guy to me."

Rick Dodge was a square-jawed, former marine with a spiky crewcut and clearly lacked a sheepskin from any art school.

"Nobody ever called him Van Gogh," Janzek said. "But it doesn't hurt to see what he comes up with."

"Yeah, I guess," Rhett said, "but sometimes I think we'd be better off with an Identi- Kit."

An Identi-Kit was a computer program which, with a few clicks of a mouse, could illustrate hairstyles, jawlines, noses, and other features to form a composite image of a suspect based on a witness's description.

"Maybe," Janzek said, "but let's see what Dodge comes up with."

"All we gotta tell him is sketch the Thin White Duke."

Janzek laughed. "I can hear him now... the thin white *who?*"

EIGHTEEN

RHETT CALLED IT.

Rick Dodge's sketch of the man driving the golf cart with Jamie Swiggett in the passenger seat looked like half the men in Charleston under the age of forty.

"Light-colored hair, eyes like a shark, and Angelina Jolie lips," Rhett said, looking at the sketch Janzek was holding, "I'm not seeing a whole lotta Bowie."

"Yeah, I agree," Janzek said, standing up and grabbing his coat from the back of his door. "I got another idea. A real artist."

———

HE HAD REACHED Torborg Randall on her cell phone. She was taking a few minutes off from her job, sketching St. Michael's church on Meeting Street. That was the beauty of her work: she could take time off, pull out her sketch pad, and simply paint.

"Hey, I got a paying gig for you," Janzek said into his iPhone.

"Tell me about it," she said. "Are we talking official police business here?"

"Absolutely. Where are you anyway?"

"St. Michaels. On Meeting."

"That a church?"

She snorted a laugh. "No, Nick, it's a pizza parlor. I know you haven't been here that long, but come on, dude."

"Don't be a wiseass or you won't get this big, career-changing gig."

Janzek had met Torborg a month before, back when Charleston had gone murder-free for eight weeks and he had a little spare time. For a change, he wasn't putting in the four-teen-hour days that he had been since his arrival the year before.

He'd met her at the Oyster Point Gallery on Broad Street. Going to galleries was his mental-health break but was not information he shared with Delvin Rhett or any of his other fellow cops. In fact, he typically visited galleries in a modified disguise. Otherwise, there was a chance he'd be spotted going in or coming out of one and the last thing he needed was to get branded as a cop who liked art. *What about ballet, Nick? You like opera, too bro?* He'd never hear the end of it.

Torborg was tall, slender, and blonde, and would have stood out anywhere, but especially in a gallery where the only people in there were a short, nondescript couple in their 60s. She was looking at a landscape painting of a barn as it caught the early morning light, surrounded by stately trees in the back-ground. She hadn't seen him come in and had her head cocked to one side, her stance wide. She wore charcoal-gray sweatpants and a faded white T-shirt from the College of Charleston that had plenty of mileage on it. She had a hell of a profile, Janzek thought, as he came up beside her—high cheekbones, large brown eyes, and full lips. A nice tan, too. He figured she must spend a lot of time in the sun.

"Where do you s'pose that is?" he asked her.

She glanced over at him and smiled.

"Doesn't seem local," he said. "I mean, not with all those big elm trees."

She looked back at the painting. "I don't know," she said. "Hard to tell."

"I'm guessing up north. New Hampshire, maybe."

"Why do you think that?"

He pointed at the little white card below the painting. "New Hampshire Barn," it said, followed by the artist's name.

She laughed. "You cheated."

He smiled. "My name's Nick."

"Hi, Nick," she put out her hand. Long, slender fingers, no rings. "I'm Torborg."

They shook.

"You come here a lot?"

"Quite a bit," she said. "The owner's a friend."

They moved together to the next painting. It didn't grab either of them. They moved on to the next.

"Notice how every gallery has the inevitable South Carolina low-country landscape," he said.

It was a marsh scene—tall brown grass, tranquil water, a long dock.

"Yeah, but that's a pretty good one," she said.

"I agree." He moved to his right as Torborg, ahead of him, skipped over three smaller portraits.

"Not your cup of tea?" He pointed to the paintings they had passed.

"They're all right," she said, pointing to another in front of them. "This is one by the owner of the gallery."

It was a picture of three houses on East Bay Street.

75

"Did I hear my name?" A short woman in her forties with a wide smile and a black headband came up to them, holding a mug of coffee in one hand.

Torborg put an arm around her shoulder and kissed her on the cheek.

"Careful, honey," said the woman, "steaming java."

"I was just about to start singing your praises," Torborg said, pointing at the woman's painting. "Sasha, this is Nick. We just met."

"Hi, Nick," Sasha said. "Welcome to Oyster Point."

"Thanks, nice to meet you," Nick said, gesturing to her painting. "I like it."

"Thanks," Sasha said, "but it doesn't hold a candle to any of hers."

Nick turned to Torborg.

"You're a painter?"

Her face turned a little red under the tan.

"Best painter I got," Sasha whispered. "But don't tell any of my other ones I said that."

Janzek looked around, then at Torborg.

"Well, where are yours?"

Sasha pointed. "You just went past them."

Nick looked at the three portrait paintings, then at Torborg.

"Ah, the ones that you said were 'all right.'"

Torborg flushed again as Janzek moved over to view her work more closely. Torborg and Sasha followed him, Torborg reluctantly.

Two of the portraits were of men, one of a woman. They were precise and three-dimensional with realistic, lifelike coloring.

"They're a lot more than all right," Janzek said. "They're really good."

"Yeah, right, what else *could* you say."

Janzek laughed. "Hey, I mean it, I'm not really the flattery type. Your figures are amazing. I mean, the expressions and features are dead-on."

"She's not too shabby at watercolors either," Sasha said.

"No kidding," Nick said.

"Okay, okay, that's enough," Torborg said. "Not like the Met is breaking down my door.'"

Janzek laughed as the bell on the door to the gallery tinkled and three people walked in.

"Oh, excuse me," Sasha said, then, under her breath, "I see checkbooks."

Torborg laughed and grabbed Nick's arm.

"Come on, let's keep going."

"You really are talented." He shrugged. "Just sayin'".

They walked out of the Oyster Point together ten minutes later. Torborg shielded her eyes to block the sun and looked up at Nick.

"What do you do, Nick?"

He looked down at her. "I'm a cop."

Her eyes got bigger. "Wow. Now that's something I never would have guessed. I was going with architect. Lawyer was my second choice."

"Please don't tell me I look like a lawyer," he said. "What about you? You paint full-time?"

"Nah, I drive a rickshaw." She pointed at a bicycle with a cab behind it.

"Get out of here!"

She shook her head and smiled. "I get to work my own hours, stay in shape, and the tips are pretty good, too. Not exactly a corporate chick."

Janzek leaned back on his heels. "You know, come to think of it," he said, "I think I've seen you around."

She pulled a headband out of her pocket, put it on over her

hair, and looked up at him again. "Well, Nick," she said, "it's nice to have met you. Time for me to get pedaling. Pay the rent and all that."

Janzek pulled out his notepad and a pen and glanced over at a little sign on the bike taxi. He took down the phone number. "Just in case my trusty Charger ever lets me down, I know who to call."

She fished a pair of sunglasses from a pocket of her sweatpants. "You could always call anyway."

"I got a better idea, why not save a call," he said. "What are you doing this Thursday?"

It turned out she had no plans. They went to a place called the Pour House out on Maybank Highway on James Island, where a cover band was playing Grateful Dead songs. Torborg knew a lot of the words and sang along to a few of them. Janzek was not really a sing-along kind of guy and kept quiet.

Afterward, he drove her home to her place up on Chapel Street. She invited him up to have a drink. He never said no to invitations like that from women who looked like her. Her apartment was a good-sized one-bedroom on the second floor with paintings covering just about every square inch of wall space.

He had one drink, kissed her on the cheek, and left.

He never liked to push his luck on the first date.

NINETEEN

TORBORG WAS A PORTRAIT-PAINTER BUT THE HUMAN FACE and form were only part of her repertoire. She also painted precise architectural details—photorealistic, almost—of houses, fences, and walls. Partly to pay the bills but mostly for her own pleasure. And she had no lack of spectacular architectural subjects in Charleston.

She was finishing her rendering of the ancient, wrought-iron fence surrounding St. Michael's church when Janzek pulled up, double-parked, got out of his car, and walked over to her.

"Hi," he said, shading his eyes to look at what she was painting.

"Hi," she said.

"I like it," he said, pointing. "That shadow is very cool."

"Thanks," she said. "So what's this job you got for me? I'm dying of curiosity."

He reached into his pocket and took out the computer-generated sketch of the man at the wheel of the golf cart.

"This is what is called 'a person of interest,'" Janzek said, handing the sketch to Torborg.

"I know what that means," she said, eyeing the sketch. "Hey, what *Law and Order* fan doesn't?"

"The problem is, this guy could be anybody."

She looked up. "I know what you mean. Generic man, age forty to fifty-five."

"Which is exactly the problem," Janzek nodded, "an eyewitness described him as around thirty."

She cocked her head. "So you want me to—"

"Go with me, get a description from the man who saw this guy, and see if you can't come up with something better."

"No offense, but that would be impossible *not* to do."

"I know," Janzek said, glancing over at her bike. "Can you leave your wheels here?"

"Sure, how long are we going to be gone for?"

"An hour, two at most," Janzek said.

Torborg put her brush in a glass jar that had formerly been a Hellman's mayonnaise jar and looked up at Janzek. "So, what's a gig like this pay, anyway? Are we talkin' minimum wage?"

"Come on. I did some heavy arm-twisting and got CPD to break the bank," Nick said. "Fifty an hour, plus I'm throwing in dinner at a restaurant of your choice."

"Better not do that," Torborg said, "that'll break *your* bank."

Janzek laughed. "Come on, let's go," he tilted his head at the Crown Vic, "we gotta get to this guy before he starts hitting the sauce."

Torborg looked at her watch. "But it's only quarter to one."

"Yeah, but I got a feeling he starts early. Likes vodka on his Wheaties."

"One of those, huh?" she said. "Not so uncommon in this town."

TWENTY

VICTOR LIVED IN A THIRD-FLOOR APARTMENT ON SOUTH Battery. It was a good address, a so-so building, and a crummy apartment. It had a totally bizarre layout, where you had to walk through a bathroom to get to the living room and where the kitchen was so small that the dishwasher was in the tiny dining room. The furniture was a combination of Habitat, Haut Home Liquidators, and IKEA closeouts.

Janzek and Torborg had spent an hour and forty-five minutes in Victor's den that smelled of cigarettes and spilled cocktails. When they got there, Victor asked them if they'd join him in a Bloody Mary. Janzek said thanks but he was on the job and Torborg said ditto, but she'd take him up on a Virgin Mary.

Once Victor had his drink in hand, Janzek asked him to describe the man he had seen driving the golf cart on the morning of Jamie Swiggett's death. He made sure to ask Victor for the exact time as well.

Victor smiled nervously, then confessed that he wasn't sure exactly what time it was when he saw the man. Just that it was dark. When Janzek pointed out that could have been anywhere between eight-thirty at night and six in the morning, Victor just nodded.

Janzek shot Torborg a frustrated look and told Victor that he'd be asking him some more questions while Torborg painted.

Victor agreed, but Janzek noticed a thin sheen of sweat forming on Victor's forehead, along with a few beads on his upper lip.

Torborg began painting in short, precise strokes, taking in Victor's description as the witness began with the suspect's eyes, then filled in the rest of the face. Torborg worked quickly and paused only to listen to Victor.

While she worked, Janzek asked if Victor had ever seen the man before. Victor said he thought so but wasn't sure where. Janzek said it was really important and Victor said he thought maybe he had seen him at an opening of the Matisse exhibit at the Gibbes Museum. But, he allowed, it might also have been at Trader Joe's.

Janzek wrote 'Matisse opening—Gibbes' in his murder book. He hoped to get a list of people who had attended the opening, if the museum had such a thing, then show them Torborg's finished painting.

As Torborg neared completion, Janzek asked Victor to call him if he ever saw the man again.

Victor's eyes brightened at that. "So, I'll be like your...C.I.?"

"Exactly," Janzek said.

Torborg looked up at them. "C.I.?"

"Thought you watched *Law and Order*," Janzek said. "Confidential Informer. Alan's gonna help me crack the case."

Victor beamed.

Torborg went back to her painting, putting a finishing touch on the lips of the suspect.

Janzek was amazed at how detailed and precise it was. The

woman had a future in law enforcement if she wanted it. *Rick Dodge... look out!*

––––––––––––

JANZEK AND TORBORG were at Lana that night, a restaurant at the corner of Rutledge and Cannon Streets. Three of the four corners at the intersection were restaurants, all of which ranked among Janzek's favorites. Hominy Grill was his go-to weekend breakfast spot, though sometimes you had to wait in line for a half-hour or more because it was so popular. On the northeast corner was Fuel, where he watched football games and drank a local IPA beer called Dale's. Lana—across the street from Fuel—was in his rotation as a favorite place to take a date for dinner. One time he had spent a whole Sunday at the intersection: Hominy for a late breakfast, Fuel for a double-header of football games, then Lana's for dinner.

He was showing Torborg something on his iPhone.

"See," he said, "according to the Daily Beast—and I'm not exactly sure what the Daily Beast is—Charleston is the fourth-drunkest city in the country."

Torborg was squinting to read the article. "Wow, what an honor."

"Yeah, I know. Right behind my hometown, Beantown, then Norfolk, Virginia, and, of course, Milwaukee—Beer City, USA."

Torborg took a pull of her red wine. "And just how do these Daily Beasts determine such things? I mean, how do you become a contender for the drunkest city in America?"

"No clue," he said. "Some highly scientific algorithm, I'm sure. And I'm guessing Boston is number one because of all the colleges there."

"Sounds like a plausible theory." She set her wine glass down. "So about that guy, Alan Victor...."

He put down his menu. "Yeah, what about him?"

"Well, the phrase 'odd duck' comes to mind," she said. "I mean, I felt sorry for him. One foot out of the closet *and* a major drinking jones.... Is he the only person who saw your suspect?"

"A guy was with Victor that night. Me and Delvin had a long conversation with him. He was no help at all. Said he was so drunk he said he couldn't see ten feet in front of him."

"You believe him?"

Janzek nodded. "Yeah, I did. Said he'd been bouncing from one bar to the next since he got off work... I love your sketch, by the way."

"Thank you, Nick."

Janzek had finished his veal and was on his last bite of risotto and they were still talking about Alan Victor.

"Did he strike you as being... all there?" Janzek asked. "Alan?"

Torborg picked at her swordfish. "He struck me as a guy whose brain has been slowly nibbled away by alcohol."

"How poetic," Janzek said. "That sounds a lot like *not all there*."

"Umm...yeah, pretty close." She popped a bite of swordfish into her mouth.

"But then he brought that thing up about being a C.I. I don't think he's totally out of it. It's almost like he...comes and goes a little."

Torborg's head was cocked, observing him. "You know, Nick, I've been noticing, you're a bit of a stereotype."

Janzek scrunched his eyes. "What's that s'posed to mean?"

"I don't mean it as an insult," she said, taking a sip of her wine. "It's just you're like a dog with a bone. I can see why you're such a good detective."

"That's not an insult?" Janzek said. "I think what you're saying is, I'm obsessed."

"Who said anything about being obsessed? You're just...."

"Consumed?"

"Well, maybe a little. But in a good way."

He chuckled. "Yeah, I've heard it before. But last person who said it didn't mean it as a compliment at all."

Torborg shrugged. "But who...who wants a man who's not really into what he does? Who's not...engaged?"

"Maybe there's a fine line between obsessed and engaged," he said. "Come clean, though: You think it's closer to obsessed, don't you?"

"Don't put words in my mouth."

"Married to the job," Janzek said. "All those other clichés."

"You sound a bit defensive. I don't know you well enough to reach that conclusion."

"But if the shoe fits...?"

She smiled. "See what I mean? Dog with a bone."

TWENTY-ONE

BILLY HOBART AND MIRANDA BENNETT, ALONG WITH THE head of the Coastal Conservation League, greeted arriving guests in the voluminous foyer of the newly refurbished house at 101 Atlantic Street.

They had sent more than two hundred invitations, and at least that many had accepted. It had quickly become such a hot ticket that people called Billy and Miranda directly, practically begging to be invited. Which meant printing even more invitations and sending them out. Part of the draw was that the names of Miranda's most socially prominent friends on the committee had been emblazoned in raised type and a regal font on the linen white Crane invitation. But what really got the buzz going was the inclusion of the Baron Richardson Easterling-Northgate and the stage actress Cornelia Whiting, though nobody seemed to know or care that a baron was the lowest rank in British peerage and Whiting hadn't been offered a good role in years. Of course, Miranda had also gone out of her way to hype the party, telling friends she bumped into at the local Harris Teeter and her bridge club, "Oh, you absolutely *must* come to my party on the 19th. *Tout le monde* will be there."

Billy preferred to call it an "event" instead of a "party." Granted, "event" had a slightly tacky, or at least affected, ring to it, but he felt it gave the whole shindig a sense of a greater purpose. It was, after all, for the Coastal Conservation League, which was high society's philanthropy *du jour*. He vaguely remembered hearing something about their recent campaign to save the white-faced whistling ducks, though he wasn't entirely sure from what. He'd also seen them decry nasty developers running amok and despoiling the Cainhoy Plantation, which Billy thought might be on nearby Wadmalaw Island. But he wasn't sure. Nor did he care.

Billy had decided to give all the proceeds of the silent auction to the League, but only a half a percent of the big enchilada: the live auction of the house at 101 Atlantic. He knew he needn't consult Miranda about such details; she couldn't be bothered. Billy calculated that the silent auction would net the League somewhere between three and five thousand dollars, once the expenses—booze, hors d'oeuvres, plus a new, white linen suit for himself—were subtracted. Assuming an additional half percent of, say, three million dollars, made another seven to eight thousand for the foundation. Okay, it wasn't exactly a home run, but the duck-savers would surely be appreciative.

Getting donated items had been no sweat. When prospective donors heard that Miranda Bennett was involved, they lined up to donate stuff. Brooks Brothers—not a regular in philanthropy circles—donated a royal-blue, double-breasted blazer that retailed for eight hundred dollars. (Their manager got the word that the "event" was going to attract a high-end crowd and thought it wise to provide a presence for his store.) Billy called Meghan Tuggle, a woman he knew who was the manager at Williams-Sonoma, and told her that her invitation was in the mail, and—oh, by the way—do you folks want to donate something for a really good cause? Meghan thought for a second and said, 'Sure.' She started out offering a plain-jane $99 blender, but Billy—negotiator he was—had talked her up to a Vitamix Professional Blender—$749 retail—which now sat on one of the tables, ready for bidders to step up and pen their bids.

A lot of other King Street retailers had also made donations —Billy Reid had kicked in a pair of stylishly funky men's shoes (any size); Calypso St. Barth's had donated something described as a Jomeri Hand Embellished Max Dress, which retailed for $725; C Wonder, which was not long for the world and would soon go belly-up, donated a Diego Narciso cocktail dress; and Blue Mercury kicked in a large selection of Kiehl cosmetics, including three tiny .17 ounce bottles of Facial Fuel Eye De-Puffers, which were sure to be in great demand with this crowd.

Throw in the Morrison family's donation of their beach house in Kiawah for President's Day weekend, two season tickets for Bill Murray's baseball team, the River Dogs, dinner for two at Lucca—liquor and wine not included—a Garmin S3 GPS golf watch, and a smattering of other crap.... All in all, they had a much better array of booty than most other benefits.

After greeting the last of the guests, Billy gave Miranda a peck on her well-rouged cheek and whispered, "Let the drinking begin!" But by then, most people were already on their second cocktail, and Billy had prepped the bartenders to go heavy on the pour.

"I wonder what happened to Tipton," Miranda said, looking around the room. "She was invited."

Billy shrugged. "You never know about Tipton."

A woman named Sandra Wilson was already three sheets

to the wind, Billy could see, her tell being that she was giving men 'hello kisses' on the lips instead of the cheeks.

Geneva Crane came up to Miranda, who was getting her first drink at the bar.

"I love this house," Geneva said, "I remember coming here to play with Betsy when I was a kid." Then, whispering, "Place was a real dump back then."

Betsy was Betsy Westendorf, whose parents had needed cash quick and sold the house to Billy for a below-market price of under two million.

Miranda laughed heartily, raised her glass, lowered her voice, and clinked Geneva's. "Nobody puts lipstick on a pig better than Billy."

"Yeah, well, it doesn't hurt to have *your* taste in the equation," the bookseller said.

"Damn right," Miranda said with a flourish of her fleshy arms.

THE SILENT AUCTION WAS OVER, and, after a quick scan, Billy realized that the total take was going to be over ten thousand dollars, which boded well for what they were going to get for the house. A photographer from the Charleston *Mercury* was making the rounds—taking pictures of the rich and inebriated—and Billy knew he and Miranda would make the front page, which couldn't be bad for future business.

He scanned the room for house-buying prospects and found several. Rad Cottingswell had pulled him aside earlier and asked him what he'd have to pay for the house. Apparently, Cottingswell and his wife Constance had just sold their Fort Sumter building penthouse and were in the market for something that had a great back yard. Billy had assured him that

Atlantic was the house for him and added that he had no clue how high it would go, but Cottingswell had better be prepared to spend upward of three million. Cottingham feigned shock, but Billy still thought he'd be in the mix, raising his paddle until the end...or close to it.

Then there was a guy from "off"—the local patois for some-one, usually a Yankee, who was not from Charleston. The man had been introduced to Billy by Sully Noonan, a white-shoe lawyer with McMaster & Kaye. The guy—typical aggressive New Yorker—didn't beat around the bush and asked Billy straight-up what the bottom line was.

"What do you mean?" Billy asked, playing dumb.

The guy looked at him like Billy had a tree growing out of his nose. "Whaddya think I meant? How much to get the house, right here, right now?"

Sully, the man said, had already drawn up a contract and he was ready to sign it. No need to screw around with any auction bullshit.

Billy put on a shocked look and told the New Yorker that they couldn't just sell it and ignore the live auction. "That's the whole event," Billy said. "That's what people are paying to see: how much we can raise for the Coastal Conservative League."

The man looked at him and chuckled. "I think you mean the Coastal Conservation League."

Billy laughed it off and joked that maybe he should go a little easy on the Jack Daniels.

Then—at the last minute—a society real-estate agent by the name of Tommy Richard (pronounced REE-shard) came up to Billy and said that he represented a man who wanted to buy the house, sight-unseen.

Billy balked for a second, then recovered. "Okay...so you mean you're going to bid for him, right?"

Richard shook his head and explained that the man was a

big art collector and wanted to bid over the phone, the way he always did when he bought a painting or sculpture.

Billy had to think about the logistics of that for a second. Quickly, he realized what a home run the idea was. The telephone-bidder wrinkle would bestow the aura of a Christie's or Sotheby's sale upon his little auction. There'd be high drama, electricity in the air, a bid coming in from London or Paris or Abu Dhabi, or wherever the hell the telephone bidder happened to be. He pictured heads nodding artfully, paddles raised subtly, as whispered bids came through iPhones and Samsung Galaxies. Billy told the agent he would welcome the phantom phone bidder as long as Richard could personally vouch for him. Richard looked offended and told him the man had bought an eleven-million-dollar painting just last week. "Who knows?" Richard said with a wink. "He might even hang that painting on the wall over there."

Billy smiled and clapped him on the shoulder. "Then he's more than welcome to participate."

Billy was particularly pleased he had signed up George Leeds as auctioneer. Because—speaking of Christie's—Leeds had once worked there and now had an art-appraisal business on Gillon Street that quietly did 3 million a year, advising big-name buyers and sellers what to buy and how to avoid fakes. Oprah was reputed to be one of his clients.

Sheila Lessing was another one.

TWENTY-TWO

Janzek was on his way to the home of Peabo Gardner, the second eulogist from Jamie Swiggett's funeral. When Janzek called him, Gardner had said, "Sure, come on over any time." From that, Janzek got the sense that Gardner, like Alex Smith, either didn't work or had a job that wasn't especially taxing.

Gardner was a thirty-four-year-old architect who apparently hadn't built up much of a following. At least judging by the rathole of an apartment/office he occupied.

It was a one-bedroom walk-up on Perry St., that, in one section of the living room, looked more like a shrine than a living space. Gardner, it turned out, had been a big-time football player. He'd been a star halfback at Porter-Gaud, then gone on to play for the Cavaliers at the University of Virginia. One wall was nothing but framed newspaper articles of Gardner's football exploits. On a long, crescent-shaped table against another wall stood an army of trophies, at least thirty of them, all crammed together.

Janzek was reading the headlines of the articles while Gardner looked on proudly.

"How was your record at Virginia?" Janzek asked.

"It sucked. We had a bad coach back then. They got rid of him after I left. We had a lot of injuries, too. Torn ACLs, blown-out knees, stuff like that."

"Looks like you still ran for a lot of yards," Janzek said, reading a headline, and pointing. "Was this your senior year?"

"Yeah, I had the seventh-best total in the country," Gardner said. "Not good enough for the pros, though. Actually, I got a tryout with the Bengals, but I was four-tenths of a second too slow for them. Claimed I fumbled too much, too. Which was bullshit. It was really because I was white."

Janzek turned to him. "But twelve years back, weren't there still quite a few white guys running the ball?"

"Name one."

Janzek thought. "Shaun Alexander, wasn't he white?"

Gardner shook his head.

Janzek nodded, still thinking, but couldn't come up with another name.

Okay, enough of the small talk.

"Mr. Gardner—"

"Peabo."

Maybe his dumb first name was the real reason why the pros didn't take him. After all, the sport had a proud tradition of players with names like the Refrigerator, Megatron and the Bus.

"Mind if I ask you a few questions about Jamie Swiggett?"

Gardner gestured at a dilapidated-looking couch. "Sure, have a seat."

Janzek sat and looked up at Gardner. "So I gather you stayed in touch with Mr. Swiggett after you two graduated from Porter-Gaud?"

93

Gardner ran a hand through his thinning brown hair. "Yeah, I did," he said. "We got together at least once a month. You know, played a round of golf, had a couple of beers, whatever."

'Did he ever mention anyone who... I don't know, might have threatened him or who he had a problem with?"

"No, never. I mean, Jamie was a pretty easy-going guy," Gardner said. "He didn't have like a dark side or anything. I'd have known about it. You know how you read about some guys who have a secret life? Not Swig."

"Yeah, I know what you mean," Janzek said. "So he wasn't like that?"

"No, not at all. Guy was a tax attorney. Doesn't that say it all?"

Janzek looked down at a stain on the couch's arm.

"I will say, he definitely changed a lot." Gardner said. "Toned down, over the years."

Janzek looked up. "How so?"

"Well, I mean, from the guy he was back in high school. He was pretty wild back then."

"Like how?" Janzek asked. "What did he do?"

Gardner laughed. "Oh, you know, mostly harmless shit."

"Like what?"

Gardner shrugged. "Well, like one time, we were all in the locker room after a football game and Jamie grabs this kid who's about to take a shower and drags him out into the corridor, then locks the door on him. Kids are going past, walking to classes and there's Benjy Kantrell, our equipment manager, buck-ass-naked, trying to cover up his scrawny little body."

Janzek looked at Gardner blankly. "Quite the prankster, huh?"

"Yeah, you know, it all was pretty harmless."

"What else?"

Gardner thrummed his fingers on the side of his chair, as if deciding which not-so-harmless anecdote to tell next. "There was this other thing that happened," Gardner said, "that wasn't so cool."

"What was that?"

"I guess I can tell you," Gardner said. "Jamie scored a bunch of tabs of Blue Heaven from this black dude—"

"Blue Heaven, what's that?"

"It's like acid. I never tried it...really powerful supposedly," Gardner said. "Anyway there was this dance, and Jamie told this kid, Benjy again, that he had some Ecstasy. Benjy, who was dyin' to be one of the guys, practically begged for it. So, Jamie sold him the Blue Heaven."

"And what happened?"

"He had a real bad trip; his parents took him to the emergency room at Roper."

Janzek shook his head. "Seems to me your friend Jamie actually had kind of a dark side to him. I mean, I'm not hearing a lot of... good, clean fun in something like that."

"Yeah, on second thought, maybe you're right."

"What was with him anyway? I mean, how come he singled out this guy Benjy?"

Gardner shrugged and glanced away, his gaze landing on a spot on the wall.

"I think Jamie maybe had a Jewish problem." Gardner's voice dropped an octave.

"So Benjy Kantrell was Jewish?"

"Yeah, just this harmless little nerd," Gardner said, "I remember Jamie going off on Jews a couple of times when he was drunk. One time it was a guy in his firm."

"Why'd he do that?"

"No reason I know of," Gardner said. "Some guys are just like that."

"Anti-Semitic, you mean?"

Gardner shrugged and lowered his voice. "Yeah, I guess you could call it that."

"This Benjy Kantrell?" Janzek said. "You know what ever happened to him? Where he ended up?"

"Sure do," Gardner said. "About two blocks from here. Over on King St. He's got a software company—like a hundred employees, I heard. Old Benj did pretty well for himself."

"So you got any theories about who might have wanted to kill Jamie? I mean, it sounds like you knew him as well as anybody."

Gardner shook his head. "No, I really don't have a clue."

"Same question about Whitredge Landrum," Janzek said. "He was part of your crowd too, right?"

Gardner nodded. "Pretty scary when you think about it. Yeah, we were like the Three Musketeers back in the day. I sort of lost track of Whit, though."

Janzek rubbed his forehead. "The fact that Landrum's hands were cut off and Swiggett's penis was too. What did you think when you heard that?"

Gardner exhaled loudly. "I thought it was pretty sick," he said, almost in a whisper. "I mean—"

"Maybe the deaths are unrelated," Janzek said, "but maybe... they weren't."

Gardner nodded slowly; the grisly images seemed to have lodged firmly in his head.

"Did anything ever happen—I don't know—way back when you guys were kids together? Maybe something Swiggett and Landrum did?"

Gardner shook his head and, again, glanced away. "Hey, not like I was with them every minute," he said. "But nothing I can think of. I mean, it's not like any of us were angels, but...."

"Did Jamie ever mention Sheila Lessing?"

Gardner looked up, clearly relieved to change the subject. "Yeah, he did, once or twice. Just that she was a client of his. But I think he'd known her for a long time."

"From where?"

"I don't know, like they were old family friends maybe. Something like that."

"Did he ever say, or imply, that there was anything more between them?"

Gardner's head snapped back. "You mean—"

Janzek nodded. "I mean sexual."

"No, not at all."

"What about...other women?"

Gardner leaned back in his chair. "Well, now that's a different story. I guess you could say that was Jamie's weakness, but I don't really know anything about any of the women."

Janzek studied the man's eyes and decided he had gotten all he would get out of Peabo Gardner.

"Well, thanks—" Janzek started to put his hands on the couch to push himself up, but he used his legs instead. "Thank you for your help. If you think of anything else, I'd appreciate you giving me a call." He reached for his wallet and slid out a card. "Here you go, here's how you can reach me."

He left wondering whether Gardner had a few more Benjy Kantrell stories to tell.

TWENTY-THREE

IT WAS A LITTLE AFTER EIGHT. STANDING IN FRONT OF THE floor-to-ceiling window in the massive living room of 101 Atlantic Street, Billy and Miranda faced more than two hundred people crowded around them and spilling into the adjacent dining room and den. Miranda had just addressed the guests, graciously welcoming and thanking them for their help with the noble cause that they were all supporting. As Miranda spoke, Billy repeated the name—Coastal Conservation League... Coastal Conservation League—ten times in his head so he wouldn't screw it up again.

Miranda was wrapping up her remarks, thanking the silent-auction participants for their bids and urging those interested in this "marvelous house that has bones almost as old as mine" to not hold back, since a chunk of the winning bid went to this "incredibly worthwhile cause."

Once again, Billy calculated what he and Miranda might make on the deal. At three million, she'd get a little less than $100,000 and he'd get slightly over half a million. Not bad for a four-month renovation. Not bad at all.

Concluding her remarks, Miranda turned the mike over to George Leeds, the gentleman auctioneer.

"Okay, ladies and gentlemen," Leeds said, taking the mike and getting right down to business, "I welcome you all to this great benefit for the Coastal Conservation League. Though most of you know already, let me explain exactly how the bidding works. Those of you who have expressed interest in this magnificent home have gotten paddles"—he raised one that had a number on it. Below the number, it read in bold lettering: *Bid it up for the CCL!*

"So just raise your paddle to acknowledge that you will pay the dollar amount which I just called out. There is a reserve price on the home, meaning it has to sell at or above a certain minimum for the sale to be official. Anyway, it's that simple, so then let's get on with it, and let the best man—or *woman*—win."

Billy liked that touch. It was a call to action for competitive people, male and female alike. He looked around and could see a lot of *extremely* competitive people—the vast majority men—who had their game faces on. Jaws muscles bulging, eyes unblinking and focused, much as they might have looked forty years ago in the locker room before "THE Game" against Yale.

Only difference was they had a few cocktails under their belts. Some, more than a few.

"Two million seven fifty," bellowed a man with a meaty red face in a blue, serge suit.

George Leeds laughed. "Now, Arthur, that's not the way it works," he castigated the bidder.

"Cash money," the man said even more loudly. Arthur Mitchell was a self-made man who had succeeded by being brash and aggressive.

"Okay, I'm going to start the bidding with Arthur's bid. Two million, seven-fifty. Thank you, Arthur." Leeds pointed at the man. "Do I hear two eight? Do I hear two million eight hundred thousand?"

The broker, Tommy Richard, cell phone to his ear, raised his paddle.

"I have two eight from a phone bidder," Leeds said.

That caused a rustle of hushed voices. There was palpable tension in the air, the kind that was created when big-money offers were slung around a room. Billy looked over at Miranda and winked. She puckered her lips and blew a kiss back at him.

"Two eight, two eight, I have two eight. Do I hear two eight fifty?" Leeds looked at Arthur Mitchell.

Arthur waved his hand dismissively at Leeds. He had shot his wad on his first bid and was done, a mere flash in the pan.

The Yankee from "off," standing next to his lawyer, Sully Noonan, raised his paddle discreetly and caught Leeds's attention.

"I have two eight fifty from the man in the red tie," Leeds said. "Two nine, do I hear two nine?"

Tommy Richard glared at the man from "off"—the dreaded carpetbagger—and hissed into his phone. His eyes got big. "Three million!" he said, jumping the bid to the next level.

There was a spontaneous burst of applause from a knot of officials from the Coastal Conservation League.

Billy assumed the man at the other end of the phone was a seasoned negotiator trying to scare away the man from "off" with his price jump.

Billy caught Rad Cottingswell's eye. He thought Cottingswell would join the mix, if for no other reason than to show everyone he had a couple million to throw around. But Rad simply shook his head at Billy, not nearly in the same league as the man from "off" or the man on the telephone.

"Three million dollars. I have three million dollars," Leeds said, staring hard at the man from "off." "Do I hear three one?"

The man from "off" flashed his paddle.

"Yes, thank you," Leeds said enthusiastically, turning to Tommy Richard on the phone, "I have three million one, do I hear, three two? Who'll give me three million two?"

Richard waited.

And waited.

Then his eyes brightened, and he thrust up his paddle.

"I have three million two, three million two, do I hear three million three?"

The man from "off" shook his head and lowered his paddle to his knee.

Leeds knew how to milk it. "Come on, gentlemen. Do I hear three two fifty, three million two hundred fifty?"

The man from "off" shook his head again.

Leeds turned to Tommy Richard and smiled.

"Well, people, Tommy's our high bidder at three two," he said, "I have three million two hundred thousand dollars, going once, going twice—"

"Three million five," came the lilting Southern accent.

It was a woman. The crowd swung around and gasped collectively.

Sarah Rentschler was something of a local legend. Daughter of a low-key, scholarly gentleman lawyer, she had outraged more than a few local Gamecock loyalists (her father and grandfather having attended the University of South Carolina) by going to the University of North Carolina and earning Phi Beta Kappa. Then she went up to New York where, twelve years later, she became head of Private Wealth Management at JP Morgan. Her salary was on the public record: four million a year. She could certainly afford 101 Atlantic.

Billy wanted to race over and tongue-kiss her.

Tommy Richard looked to be in shock. Like someone had

walloped him in the gut with a two-by-four. He said something into his phone half-heartedly, then moments later his shoulders slumped forward. He looked up at George Leeds and shook his head forlornly.

Leeds looked out over the crowd.

"Three million five, three million five hundred thousand dollars, going once... going twice... going three times. Sold to Ms. Sarah Rentschler, the pride of Charleston. I thank you, Sarah, the Coastal Conservation League thanks you"—he shot a look over at Billy—"and, probably most of all, Billy Hobart thanks you."

TWENTY-FOUR

BENJY KANTRELL WAS WEARING A BLUE POLO SHIRT, creased blue jeans, and beige white bucks. Best Janzek could tell, Kantrell's company was the largest provider of some kind of service-industry software. Judging by the expensive-looking, quasi-funky reception area and lavish conference room where they were meeting, Kantrell had done quite well for himself.

Janzek had told Kantrell on the phone that he wanted to talk to him in connection with Jamie Swiggett's murder. Kantrell didn't sound too broken-up about what had happened to his former classmate and told Janzek that meeting him would be a waste of time, but Janzek insisted and Kantrell acquiesced.

"Who brought my name up?" Kantrell asked Janzek across the conference table

"Peabo Gardner."

Kantrell nodded, like Gardner was yet another bad memory.

"The football hero," he said simply.

"From what he told me, sounds like Jamie Swiggett made your life pretty difficult?"

"You mean the fact that the guy was a total anti-Semitic bully asshole?"

Janzek nodded.

"So what do you want from me, detective?" Kantrell said. "Or maybe you think I killed the guy?"

Janzek leaned back and crossed his arms. "In the course of an investigation, Mr. Kantrell, I question many people—sometimes a hundred or more. Some people have nice things to say about the victim, others not so nice. Sometimes I get useful information when I talk to someone, sometimes not. Tell me about Swiggett, please, Mr. Kantrell."

"I just did. The guy was a raging anti-Semite, a bully, and a so-so tax attorney, I hear." Kantrell did a long exhale, then his voice dropped to just above a whisper. "And maybe even the secret to my success."

Janzek uncrossed his arms and leaned forward. "Can you explain what you mean by that?"

"Sure. The guy was the best teacher I ever had. Taught me that there were a lot of assholes out there, who want to fuck you over for no good reason," Kantrell said matter-of-factly.

Janzek leaned back. He could tell Kantrell was just warming up.

"But as Nietzsche said—or maybe it was Frank Sinatra—revenge is sweet."

"If you'd explain that, please?"

"Two years ago, I made a million- dollar pledge to Roper Hospital," Kantrell said. "Then I found out that my old friend, Jamie, was on the board. So, I told them that I was withdrawing the offer. The head of the board called me up and asked me why. I told him and—lo and behold—next thing I knew Swiggett had resigned from the board. I guess a man is replaceable, but a million bucks is not."

Janzek could understand Kantrell's vengeful attitude.

"So, okay, when you heard he had been killed, what did you think? You strike me as a man who might have a theory... about what happened to him?"

"I have no idea what happened to him. Don't really give a shit," Kantrell said. "It's not like I followed his life. Last thing I remember about the guy was senior year, him bragging about gang banging some girl or something."

Janzek reached for his water bottle, took a quick sip, and leaned close to Kantrell. "Okay, I need you to tell me everything you know about that incident you just mentioned."

"All I know is he seemed pretty proud of it," Kantrell said. "He and his dickhead buddies."

"Who, specifically?"

Kantrell thought for a second. "I'm pretty sure that guy Landrum was involved."

"And did it take place around here?"

"No. Swiggett's old man had a place somewhere down south, as I remember."

"So, it happened there?"

"Yeah, I'm pretty sure."

"But you don't know any specific details?"

Kantrell shook his head. "Sorry, can't help you there."

"What about, do you know if Peabo Gardner was involved?"

"I have no idea," Said Kantrell. "If he was, I'm sure he'll tell you the girl was asking for it. You know, the way assholes like that always do."

TWENTY-FIVE

JANZEK THOUGHT ABOUT GOING DIRECTLY TO PEABO Gardner's house but chose instead to call him from his office. He got Gardner's message machine and asked him to call him.

Just as he clicked off, he got a call.

It was Torborg. A jazzed-up Torborg.

"I just saw the guy," she blurted.

"What guy?"

"Who do you think?" she said. "The guy in my sketch."

Janzek was halfway to his door. He grabbed his jacket on the fly.

"Where'd you see him?" he asked, as he got to the elevator.

"Down on lower Meeting. I followed him... from a safe distance," she said, "He just walked into the Fort Sumter House."

"Where's that?"

"1 King Street. Right next to the White Point Garden, where the body was found. That's where I am now. Right in front."

"I'll be there in five."

HE WAS DRIVING SO FAST he almost ran a horse and carriage off the road at Broad and King. Four minutes after the call, he pulled up to the front entrance of 1 King Street and saw Torborg across the street, trying to look casual. He parked and walked up to her.

"Hi," she said, cocking her head, and shading her eyes.

"Hi," he said. "Thanks for following the guy. You sure it's him?"

"Definitely," she said. "And he was dressed pretty close to how Alan Victor said he was that night."

"I guess you get to be my C.I. instead of Alan."

"Gee, thanks. What an honor."

Janzek looked over at the front door of Number One King Street and calculated that it was only a few hundred yards between it and the park bench where Jamie Swiggett's body was found.

"Okay, I'll take it from here," he said. "Hey, thanks again."

"You're welcome. Is this going to be dangerous?"

"You mean, am I going to get into a shootout?"

"Yeah."

He looked around and not seeing anybody, leaned forward, and kissed her on the cheek.

"I doubt it," he said and walked toward the front door.

There was a brass buzzer marked 'building manager' at the bottom of the building's directory. Janzek pressed it.

A bald, older man shuffled up to the door a minute later.

Janzek showed him ID and said he needed to speak to a tenant in the building. Janzek described the tenant and the building manager knew him right away—his name was Billy Hobart. Then he eyed Janzek and asked the predictable question: "Is there some kind of a problem, Detective?"

Janzek responded with the equally predictable, "No. I just need to ask him a question or two."

The manager nodded and walked over to two elevators, Janzek following. He pushed the button and one of the elevators opened. The manager walked in and Janzek followed. They went up and the elevator stopped. They walked down the carpeted hallway and the manager pointed to the apartment where Billy Hobart lived. Janzek thanked him and, as the manager walked back to the elevator, he knocked on the door of apartment 704.

1 King Street had been a hotel before it went condo back in the nineties and it had its share of Charleston history. One story was that John F. Kennedy, when he was in Charleston in his Navy days back in the late 1930s, dated a woman from the building who people claimed was a German spy: Danish journalist Inga Arvad, who had twice interviewed Hitler and been his guest at the 1936 Olympics. Rumor was that J. Edgar Hoover had Kennedy and Inga followed, going so far as to plant a bug in her apartment which, reputedly, captured a lot of shrieking and moaning coming from the Dane's bedroom.

As Janzek waited at the door, he heard it open and a man appeared.

He was a dead ringer for the man in Torborg's sketch and indeed had more than a little 'Thin White Duke' to him. He reminded Janzek of someone else, too. Someone else famous, but he couldn't come up with the name. The only surprise was that Janzek had figured he'd be taller. He stood around five nine or ten, had a slight build, and—no question about it—matinee-idol looks.

"Mr. Hobart, my name is Detective Janzek, I just want to ask you a few questions about an investigation I'm working on."

Hobart nodded and smiled. "Sure, detective, come on in."

Janzek walked in and followed Hobart down a hallway. The apartment had floor-to-ceiling windows on two sides, one looking out over the Cooper River to James Island and the other onto White Point Garden.

"Happy to help in any way I can," Billy added, leading Janzek into his living room.

"Thanks. Beautiful view you have here."

Hobart pointed out the window. "If you've got good eyesight, you can see the building's namesake out there. Fort Sumter itself."

It was a speck in the distance.

"Oh, yeah, I see it," Janzek said, then shifted his glance to one of the windows that faced White Point Garden. He could see the bench where Jamie Swiggett's body had been found.

"Sure beats my view," Janzek said. "The parking lot at Harris Teeter."

Hobart laughed. "Have a seat, detective." He pointed to a plush love seat.

Janzek sat down in it. It was chintz, as clean and elegant as the one in Peabo Gardner's apartment had been dirty and threadbare.

Hobart sat on a couch across from him as Janzek slid his murder book out from the breast pocket of his jacket.

"Sorry, I didn't ask," Billy said, "but can I get you something to drink?"

Janzek noticed how long and slim Hobart's fingers were. He shook his head. "No, thanks. I'm good. I'm investigating the murder of Jamie Swiggett, which occurred on—"

"I'm aware of when it occurred, detective. I was with him that night."

Janzek felt a rush of adrenaline. "Where was that? Where you and he were together?"

"The Yacht Club," Billy said. "We had drinks. He came and parked in back of the building here, then we took my golf cart and drove over there."

Janzek nodded. "Oh, so you're the man who was with him at the Yacht Club. I've been trying to track you down. What time did you go there?"

"A little after seven, I'd say."

"You were friends?"

"Not exactly, he was my lawyer. To tell you the truth, I was trying to get around having to meet him at his office and get charged two hundred bucks an hour."

"So you wanted to ask him something business-related?"

"Yeah, a tax thing. We had drinks and were just shooting the breeze; then I snuck in my tax question. Probably get billed for it anyway."

"Probably not this time."

Billy nodded. "Yeah, I guess you're right. Did... ah, whoever killed him really cut off—"

"Yeah, they really did." Janzek said. "So you had drinks at the Yacht Club and then what?"

"Then a little past eight we left. Drove him back here to the parking lot."

"And he drove off?"

"Yes."

"And did he say where he was going?"

"No, but I'm sure it wasn't home to the little woman."

Janzek glanced out the window. Fort Sumter looked really small. Then his gaze returned to meet Hobart's azure-blue eyes. "How did you know he wasn't going home?"

"Well, I didn't for sure. Except he went to the men's room

at the Yacht Club, he came back smelling like he'd just splashed a whole bottle of bay rum on his face."

"So you think he was getting ready for a... date?"

"Sure smelled like it. Hey, Charleston's a small town, detective. You know how it is. Everybody knows everyone else's business. Jamie was a player, as I'm sure you know by now."

"Did you have any first-hand knowledge of that? Or was it just hearsay?"

"First-hand. I saw him at Oak once with a woman. He wasn't even hiding it. Didn't bother introducing her as his client or something."

"How long ago was this?"

"Oh, maybe six months back."

"I might want to talk to her."

Hobart shut his eyes for a second and tapped the arm of the couch. "Her last name was Wentworth, I'm pretty sure. Holly or Helen maybe. I don't remember for sure."

Janzek wrote down the name and looked up at Hobart.

"And, just for the record, where did you go after he left?"

Hobart's blazing blue eyes seemed to turn a shade darker. "Right here. I went on a *Succession* binge. Watched three and a half episodes, then crashed."

"So Swiggett never mentioned who he was going to see?"

"Nah, he wouldn't just volunteer that."

Janzek nodded.

"But wait a minute," Billy said, raising his hand. "I remember, there were rumors."

"About?"

"About Sheila Lessing. I'm sure you know who she is. Bet her name has come up before."

"What about her?"

"I don't know. Just from what I heard, they seemed to have a little more than an attorney-client relationship."

"Like what kind?"

Billy's eyes started blinking. He threw up his hands. "Actually, I have no idea. You'd better ask her. I'd just be repeating gossip."

"Mr. Hobart, an eyewitness said he saw you and Mr. Swiggett driving your golf cart into White Point Garden from this direction—going east, that is—" Janzek winged the time —"at approximately two in the morning."

Billy's face suddenly betrayed a few wrinkles. "Is that what this is all about," he said, his stare turning fierce. "You think I had something to do with what happened to Jamie?"

"I'm just asking questions. Did you drive Swiggett into White Point Garden at two o'clock in the morning?"

"No, of course not. I told you. I was sound asleep. Just who the hell is this so-called witness, anyway?"

"A man who was walking down King Street at the time."

"Who the hell walks down King Street at two o'clock in the morning?" Hobart asked. "Unless they're dead drunk or something."

Janzek paused a split-second too long.

"So that's it. He *was*."

"He claims he saw you then," Janzek said pulling out a copy of the sketch. "This is what he said the man looked like."

Billy shot the sketch a quick, dismissive look.

"For Chrissake, it's not about whether it was me with Swiggett, but what time it was. Your witness clearly had no idea when it was. He was off by—" Billy did the match "—seven goddamn hours."

"Did you know Whitredge Landrum?"

"Who?"

"Whitredge Landrum," Janzek said. "His body was found a year ago, washed up in front of the Coast Guard station."

"Oh, yeah, I remember reading about that. No, I had no idea who he was."

Janzek drilled into Billy's stony blue eyes, then stood. "Thank you, Mr, Hobart. I appreciate your time," he said, casting a hard glance down at the park bench in White Point Garden.

TWENTY-SIX

Fifteen years before....

JENNY, TEARS STREAMING DOWN HER FACE AND BODY
convulsing, went to her mother and told her how she had been
brutally raped by the three boys. Her father, fifty miles away
buying a new hunting dog, was unreachable by phone, so Jenny
and her mother went to the Thomasville, Georgia, police chief
and told him exactly what had happened.

Jenny could tell from the chief's shifty-eyed reaction that
this was the last thing he wanted to hear about. Nevertheless,
he went and dug out an old Grundig tape recorder and
recorded Jenny's explanation of her version of what happened
that afternoon in the pool house at *Bellevoir*.

The sheriff took her statement and went and arrested the
three boys. Five months later, there was a trial, in which all
three were charged with rape and sodomy. The local prosecutor was no match for the high-priced defense attorney from
Atlanta, whose strategy was far from novel. He portrayed Jenny
as a sixteen-year-old Lolita and implied that she was no

stranger to sex, all but telling the jury that she'd been asking for it.

Jenny, whose experience with the opposite sex was limited to kissing a ham-handed boy next door once, appeared skittish and jittery on the stand. The jurors seemed to think that meant she had something to hide, like she was holding back a dark secret. Even a teacher who vouched for her exemplary character and her "wonderful wholesomeness" was discredited when the slick defense attorney implied that the teacher had an unnatural—read: closet-lesbian—interest in the beguiling teenager.

The three boys were well-coached, well-scrubbed, and angelic looking. The jury took less than an hour to announce a not-guilty verdict.

Then, in rapid succession, Jenny's father lost his job, her mother and father separated, and Jenny and her mother moved away in a hurry. Her father had seethed and raged when his wife and daughter went to the Thomasville police chief without discussing the consequences or alternatives with him. It had been an irreparable tear in an already flimsy marriage.

Jenny and her mother got in their car and drove, stopping in Fort Lauderdale, Florida, where her mother ended up getting a clerical job at an insurance agency. For the next two years, Jenny attended Stranahan High School in Fort Lauderdale, where she kept to herself, read hundreds of books, and worked part time at a fast-food restaurant in a marginal neighborhood.

Between what she and her mother saved, she had only enough money for a local community college. After paying for books, Jenny had literally nothing left to her name. She needed more than what she made at the fast-food restaurant to get by.

Every job advertised in the Fort Lauderdale paper either paid minimum wage or was full-time. In desperation, she picked up a so-called, 'alternative' newspaper. Articles about obscure, unheralded causes and ads for weight-losing miracle drugs and strip joints made up most of the content. In the back, she saw ads for SWM seeking SWF and a BiBM in the market for just about anything. She wondered how anybody knew what all the abbreviations stood for, naively searching for a glossary below.

On the adjacent page were classified ads. One caught her attention. It said simply, "COMPANIONS. $$$$$. (954) 484-2222." She was pretty sure a companion, as it was used in the ad, meant more than the dictionary definition.

Sure enough, it turned out to be an escort service.

"We arrange dates where you accompany gentlemen," the female voice with the strange Slavic accent explained. Jenny was wary when she heard the word, "gentlemen."

The plantation owner in Thomasville and his son had often been referred to as gentlemen, too.

She almost hung up, but then the woman asked. "Can you describe yourself? You can make a *lot* of money, you know."

That got her attention.

"I'm eighteen, first year at community coll—"

"What do you look like?" The woman clearly didn't have all day.

Jenny described herself, then the woman told her the job paid sixty to eighty dollars an hour and asked when they could meet.

Jenny said she'd think about it.

Two days later, she called the woman back and they met at a restaurant. The woman picked up the tab, told her she would make at least a hundred dollars an hour, and a week later Jenny had her first date. It lasted two hours and she made two hundred dollars. She went and bought her mother a new pair of shoes from TJ Maxx, a turquoise leather purse for herself, and took a long, cleansing bath.

After a while, Jenny invented a trick to make her dates more bearable. She created a fictitious man her "dates" morphed into. He was tall, chiseled, had piercing green eyes, and reminded her of the actor Liam Neeson. She trained herself to look at her Johns but see only Neeson.

In the winter of her freshman year at college, she had a date with a man who took her back to his house. He lived at 900 South Ocean Drive in Palm Beach, twenty miles away. His house was a Mediterranean villa with sixteen-foot ceilings and designed by a famous decorator. It had a tunnel from the basement of the house that went under South Ocean Drive and came out on the beach and had a cabana and a shower. That first night, they had sex on a fluffy white towel on the beach, but after that they met at the Chesterfield Hotel.

She began to see the man, who was married, on a regular basis and he was generous with her. It soon became clear that the man was infatuated with Jenny. One time, she happened to mention that she got straight As and wanted to go to a better college than Fort Lauderdale Community College. The man, whose primary residence was in Merion, on the Main Line outside of Philadelphia, had an idea. He was on the Board of Directors at his alma mater, the University of Pennsylvania, and thought he might be able to help get her admitted there as a transfer for her sophomore year.

She said she had never heard of the college and asked him how much it cost. He explained that it was an Ivy League school and one of the best colleges in the country and told her not to worry about how much it cost. He would pay for it as well as an apartment off-campus for her. In return, he would have the key to her apartment. The man, who owned the biggest chain of real-estate offices in the Philadelphia metropolitan area, also had her hired part-time at his main office and personally helped teach her the business.

And that was how Jenny Riles, a poor man's daughter from Thomasville, Georgia, got a first-rate education, and graduated magna cum laude from an Ivy League university.

But the day after graduation, the small apartment building she had been living in burned to the ground and her horrifically burned body was found on the shower floor.

TWENTY-SEVEN

Janzek could tell that Alan Victor had had a few already.

When Janzek called him, on the heels of his meeting with Billy Hobart, Victor had said to come on over, he wasn't going anywhere. So Janzek had returned to Victor's dingy, booze-infested lair.

"Alan, I need to ask you a question, and you need to be very sure of your answer," Janzek said. "Okay?"

Victor nodded sheepishly.

Janzek felt like a teacher reading the riot act to a misbehaving pupil.

Alan Victor took a pull from a can of ginger ale that Janzek was pretty sure was spiked with either vodka or gin. Janzek figured it was a stand-in for the Bloody Mary he had knocked back last time he was there. On the kitchen countertop were half-opened bottles of both Gilbey's gin and Popov vodka.

"Exactly what time did you see those two men on the golf cart? Again, I need you to be absolutely sure of your answer."

Victor sighed. "I wish I'd never said anything about seeing them," he said, then took a long, noisy sip from his ginger ale.

"It's okay," Janzek said. "Just think hard. What time was it?"

"I'm gonna say...." Victor rubbed his forehead hard. "I'm gonna say... somewhere between, um, ten and two."

"I need you to be more specific than that."

"Okay, midnight, then."

"Christ, Alan," Janzek said, raising his hands, "you really have no idea, do you?"

Victor shook his head ruefully.

In his eighteen years of being first a cop, then a detective, Janzek had learned that there are solid witnesses, somewhat reliable ones, and complete disasters. Cases could be closed on the testimony of the first one, and maybe the second, but witnesses like Alan Victor were case-killers, pure and simple.

TWENTY-EIGHT

IT WAS EIGHT P.M. AT THE STATION HOUSE AND JANZEK WAS on his computer. He had just called Peabo Gardner again after not having heard back from him in the last four hours.

He rarely felt as dead-in-the-water on a case as he did now. Actually, it had been this bad a few times before. And, Janzek reminded himself, the majority of those he had cleared.

One of his sources of frustration was that he couldn't find anything on Billy Hobart, anywhere. He had logged onto all the usual databases. First, DAVID, which stored records on people —misdemeanors, from traffic violations to shoplifting, on up to serious felonies. Then he logged into SLED—South Carolina Law Enforcement Division's database and found nothing there either.

Finally, he had tried Facebook, desperate now to find *anything* about the man, and he'd struck out again. Hobart had a Facebook page and lots of friends but no information of any real use.

At that point, Janzek suddenly realized that he had never tried James Swiggett on Facebook. He typed him in, figuring the chances were that his page had been taken down. But there Jamie was, smiling broadly and looking like a million bucks. He had about ten times as many friends as the meager turnout at his funeral.

Sheila Lessing was one of Swiggett's friends, and there was a weird photo of Peabo Gardner cradling a shotgun, black cigar butt dangling from his mouth with a Confederate flag in the background. Janzek decided to see if Gardner had a Facebook page. He did. According to it, Gardner lived in Charleston, was a former All-American halfback for UVA and listened to Pink Martino, Warren Zevon, and Maria Callas operas. Janzek read further and saw a post from an old University of Virginia football friend, then saw a new one from his sister congratulating him on his thirty-fourth birthday.

Janzek jumped to his feet, slammed his computer shut, sprinted to his car, hit the remote button to unlock the Crown Vic, jumped in, and gunned it. He flicked the switches for his blue light and siren as he roared up Lockwood. He took the corner onto Rutledge and skidded, coming within a few feet of a bicyclist who seemed to think he owned the road.

Janzek blasted past the bike, steering with his left hand, and scrolling down his cell phone, looking for Peabo Gardner's number with his right, things ordinary citizens would get arrested for.

He came up to a red light, eased through it at twenty, then stomped on the accelerator. He found Gardner's number, dialed it, and hit the green button on his iPhone.

The phone rang five times, then went to voicemail.

"This is Peabo. It's halftime and I'm getting reamed out by coach in the locker room. Leave me a message. I'll get back to you after we eke out a W."

Jesus, Janzek thought, *talk about a guy living in the past.*

He hung a left on Radcliffe, then a right on Smith, another

left on Warren, and skidded to a stop in front of Gardner's rental.

He jumped out, ran to the buzzer for Gardener's apartment, and pressed it for a full ten seconds. Nothing.

He buzzed again. Still no answer.

He grabbed the knob of the door that led to the upstairs apartments with both hands then yanked it as hard as he could. It didn't give an inch and Janzek looked again and realized, of course, the door opened inward. He lowered his shoulder, backed up, and crashed into it. The lock was a lot stronger than the wood door, which showed several cracks. He backed up even farther and slammed into it again. One of the upper panels of the door cracked.

Janzek rammed it with his left elbow, creating a jagged six-inch opening. He reached in and down, opened the lock, and pushed the door open, then ran up the steps to Gardner's second-floor apartment. The door was slightly ajar.

That was a bad sign.

He shoved it open and shouted. "Mr. Gardner, Nick Janzek, Charleston Police!"

Then he took a few more steps into the living room and saw Gardner lying on the dingy beige carpet, a pool of blood forming a burgundy halo around his head.

TWENTY-NINE

"WHAT THE FUCK?" RHETT SAID WHEN ME JACK MARTIN smiled up at him and Janzek and pried open Peabo Gardner's mouth: two inches of the victim's tongue had been cut off.

"That clinches it," Janzek said, turning to Rhett. "They're all related."

Rhett nodded.

"Can you hand me the guy's wallet?" Janzek asked the ME.

"Sure," Martin said. "Just leave me the hundreds and twenties."

Janzek wondered why all MEs felt compelled to be wiseasses at crime scenes. Was it buried in the fine print of their job description? Was it some compulsion to fend off the grisliness of a brutal crime scene? Maybe there was some noir movie they used as a training film. Or was it just that they needed to show you that they had been around the block a few times and were hardened to the sight of dead bodies in various stages of disfigurement, rot, and decay?

Martin reached into Gardner's back pocket and slid out a fake alligator-skin wallet.

He handed it to Janzek, who had slipped on latex gloves. He opened it and pulled out Gardner's driver's license.

"Just want to confirm something," he said.

"What's that?" Rhett asked.

Janzek pointed to the date of birth: "Killed on his birthday. I saw a post on his Facebook page, his sister wishing him a happy birthday." Janzek said. "Just like Swiggett and Landrum, killed and mutilated on their birthdays. So that's the end of the Three Musketeers."

"What?"

"That's what Gardner called them."

Rhett nodded as he looked down at Gardner's flabby white belly that hung out over his belt and below his buttoned shirt.

"Guy was a big time college ball player," Rhett said. "Wonder what happened?"

"Told me his downfall was that he was white," Janzek said.

Rhett shook his head. "Sounds like a guy looking for an excuse."

Janzek nodded.

Peabo Gardner had eighteen stab wounds in his stomach and chest.

Janzek had two reactions to Peabo Gardner's murder. The first one was that this had to be payback for something that had happened in the past, like maybe the rape incident that Benjy Kantrell had alluded to. Jamie Swiggett's Bobbitt job could have been a one-off. Whitredge Landrum's missing hands could have been due to the ravages of sea creatures. But all three in combination meant they had a single killer in common. A killer who liked to amputate body parts.

His second reaction was more a question.... Exactly how do you cut someone's tongue off? It didn't take long for one of the crime scene techs to find the answer to that: it lay under the stained blue sofa that Janzek had sat on when he first inter-

125

viewed Gardner. A shiny new pair of pliers with bloodstains on them.

———

IT WAS ten thirty at night. Janzek and Rhett had been at the crime scene for more than two hours. Now they were out in Janzek's car, their makeshift office, talking things over.

"Gardner told me Swiggett kept in touch with him and Landrum on a fairly regular basis," Janzek said. "Said they got together and played golf or had a beer every month or so. But that wasn't the case with Gardner and Landrum. They practically never saw each other."

"Sounds like you're thinking it might go back to something that happened back in high school?"

"Yeah, something I hadn't gotten around to telling you yet since we been going a mile a minute," Janzek said. "But I met with a guy named Kantrell who was in their class and he mentioned something about a gang rape. I called Gardner a couple of times to question him about it but got to him too late. I'm going to call this other classmate of theirs again. Find out what he knows."

Janzek opened the car door.

"Better do it quick," Rhett said, getting out of the car. "Way it's going, there's gonna be no one left from that class."

Janzek nodded and dialed Alex Smith's number. Smith answered and Janzek apologized for calling so late, then asked if he could meet him somewhere tomorrow. They agreed to meet at the Bull Street Market on King Street.

———

AT THE RESTAURANT, Alex Smith wore the same green

126

corduroys from Jamie Swiggett's funeral, as he sat at a table having lunch. Janzek wondered if they were the only pants he owned. Smith was eating a twelve-dollar ham and swiss that was too expensive for Janzek. Janzek settled for a plain yogurt and a bag of chips.

He launched right in.

"Mr. Smith, you probably haven't heard yet but Peabo Gardner was killed last night."

Smith's right hand snapped up to his mouth. "Oh, my God," he said. "You're kidding. What happened?"

"He was stabbed to death."

"That's just terrible. First Jamie and now—"

"And Whit Landrum. Did you ever hear of an incident where Gardner, Swiggett, and Landrum were involved in a rape?"

Smith's head jerked back like he had been zapped with a cattle prod. Carefully, he set his ham and swiss down.

"Yes, I did hear something about that," he said, "but I don't know any of the details. It wasn't like something they went around boasting about."

"What did you hear?"

"That Jamie and some other guys were down at his family plantation and something happened with a girl there."

"His family had a plantation?"

Janzek hadn't gotten the impression that Swiggett was from the landed gentry, at least based on his modest house out on James Island.

"Yeah, until his father lost all his money."

"How'd that happen?"

"Him losing all his money?"

"Yes."

"It's a very long story."

"Okay, well, what happened at the plantation?"

Smith brushed something invisible off his green corduroys. "Like you said, something with a girl."

"You mean a rape?"

Smith nodded, his head barely moving. "I guess. I mean, supposedly, they were all drinking and doing drugs—"

"Swiggett, Gardner, and Landrum, right?"

Smith nervously brushed his pants again and nodded.

"How do you know this?"

"I don't remember exactly, it was a long time ago," Smith said. "But I—I'm pretty sure Whit told me."

Janzek shook his head. "This plantation you mentioned, where is it?"

Smith didn't answer right away. Finally, he said, "Somewhere down in Georgia. I don't know exactly where. I've never been there."

"And the girl," Janzek asked, "what do you know about her?"

This time he shook his head quickly. "I don't know a thing about her."

———

JANZEK CALLED Camille Swiggett and got the name of the town where her husband's family plantation had been. When he said the word "plantation" he heard an almost audible gasp, like she knew something bad had happened there. She gave him the name of the town in Georgia: Thomasville.

He considered pursuing it with her, asking if she knew what had happened there, but then thought better of it. It would be better to get the perspective of someone who was *not* a family member. He could always double back to Camille, if necessary.

He Googled the town and with four clicks of the mouse

and ten punches of his cell was talking to Police Chief Todd Ireland. Ireland knew all about the Swiggett family. Apparently, they'd stopped coming to Thomasville seven or eight years ago.

Janzek asked him if he was aware of a rape that had occurred at the family plantation, possibly involving Jamie Swiggett.

"Possibly?" Ireland said in a tone drenched in irony. "How about *definitely*."

Janzek leaned back in his chair and listened to the chief recount the case.

A local sixteen-year-old girl and her mother had come to his station approximately fifteen years before—he wasn't sure exactly when—and the girl claimed that she had been raped by three boys: Jamie Swiggett and two friends, whose last names she didn't know. She was quite specific about what each boy had done to her, going into each sex act in exact detail. Her mother had kept her arm around her daughter the entire time and gasped frequently during the half-hour description of what had happened.

The sheriff proceeded to arrest the boys, but they had almost immediately been released on bail. Seniors in high school, they were allowed to go back to Charleston, where they were from, but required to attend their trial in the spring of their senior years. By that time, the boys had been accepted to colleges, and their colleges never got wind of what had happened.

"Long story short," Ireland said, "the defense attorney from Atlanta ran circles around our local prosecutor. No offense toward our guy but it was like the local Albany State University law school going up against Harvard Law."

"So they got off?"

"Got off? It was like that poor girl was the culprit. You

know how they do it—goddamn defense attorney made her out to be a two-dollar hooker turning tricks 'hind the Piggly Wiggly."

"Yeah, I've seen it before," Janzek said. "So what happened to the girl?"

"Her family got pretty tore up over it," Ireland said. "Parents got divorced within a couple months and she and her mother moved away somewhere."

"You don't know where?"

"No, sorry, down south is all I heard."

"And the father?"

"Glendon? He's still around."

"And what was the girl's name?"

"Jenny. Jenny Riles. God knows what ever happened to her," Ireland said. "Beautiful young girl, she was. Shame to have it happen to a kid like that. How's your life ever supposed be the same after something that brutal?"

THIRTY

AFTER GETTING GLENDON RILES'S PHONE NUMBER FROM Chief Ireland, Janzek called the man. Riles didn't seem eager to talk about his ex-wife Verna and daughter, but Janzek was able to get Verna's phone number out of him. She was living in Deerfield Beach, Florida, but Riles claimed he had no idea what had become of his daughter. Janzek also took Verna's address from Riles, who knew it by heart, since he was still sending her alimony checks in the amount of $113.67 every month.

Janzek called Verna Riles's number but it just rang and rang. He tried it again an hour later, then an hour after that. It just kept ringing.

He decided it was worth taking a trip to Florida and went straight to his chief's office and filled Ernie Brindle in. Given that all three murder victims had been charged with a rape together in Georgia fifteen years before, Janzek told Brindle that it was critical to try to find the victim and question her.

Brindle agreed and Janzek was on the next flight to Fort Lauderdale. He called Delvin Rhett right before his flight took off and told him about the rape that the three homicide victims were involved in. Rhett was excited that they might be on the verge of a break. *Finally*, was what he said a couple of times.

But Janzek knew they still had a long way to go.

DEERFIELD BEACH WAS 550 miles south of Charleston. It was twenty degrees warmer and a lot more humid.

Verna Riles had a small, neatly kept bungalow at the corner of Estes Kefauver Street and Duff Road.

He rang her doorbell and got the same response as when he called her: It rang and rang, and no one answered. He left to get something to eat, then returned and rang the doorbell again.

This time, a short woman in a gingham dress and dark hair that looked like chocolate pudding answered the door. She wore no make-up and reminded Janzek of an older version of Lily Tomlin's *Laugh-In* character.

"Hello, Mrs. Riles, my name is Nick Janzek. I'm a detective from Charleston, South Carolina, and I'm investigating the murders of three men up there. Would it be possible to come in and talk to you for a few moments?"

The woman eyed him warily. "What could this possibly have to do with me?"

"The murders have nothing to do with you," Janzek said. "I'm just hoping to get some information. Would it be all right if I came in? This shouldn't take more than five minutes."

Verna Riles turned inside, holding the door open for Janzek.

He followed her into a tiny living room that had very little furniture in it and nothing on the walls except one oval mirror and a picture of Jesus. He sat down in a ladder-back chair facing her, and she settled into a faded brown couch, from which she stared at him suspiciously.

"As I mentioned, I came down here to try to get some information about three men who were murdered in Charleston. They're the same three men who were arrested for raping your daughter fifteen years ago. Jamie Swiggett, Whitredge Landrum, and Peabo Gardner."

"All those men were murdered?" she asked quietly.

Janzek nodded.

"Oh, my God," she said. "The Lord works in mysterious ways."

"What do you mean?"

"Well, they were all evil, evil men," she said. "First, they gave my baby drugs, then they raped her, and then that Swiggett boy, he walked out of court after they got off and smirked at me."

"Mrs. Riles, I'd like to speak to your daughter."

"Well, so would I, but I'm afraid that's impossible."

"Why?"

Mrs. Riles exhaled. "Because she's dead, too."

THIRTY-ONE

VERNA RILES EXPLAINED THAT HER DAUGHTER HAD DIED in a fire outside of Philadelphia. Jenny had just graduated from the University of Pennsylvania at the time and the fire apparently had originated in the kitchen of her apartment.

Janzek asked a few more routine questions, then thanked Verna, offered his sincere condolences, and drove straight to the airport, calling Delvin Rhett on the way.

"So much for that," he said to Rhett. "The girl who got raped by our three vics died in a fire ten years ago."

"Shit. So, we're back to square one, huh?"

"Yeah...you found out anything about Peabo Gardner?"

"Nada, just what you already know. He was an ex-jock still living in his glory days. Apparently when he drank, he got a little nasty, but you could say that about a lot of people."

"All right, well, I'll be getting in late today," Janzek said.

———

JANZEK LANDED AT CHARLESTON AIRPORT, got to

his car, and headed south to Charleston. He decided to call Chief Ireland in Thomasville, Georgia and fill him in on what happened to Jenny Riles.

"Hey, it's Nick Janzek, the detective from Charleston. I met with Verna Riles down in Florida. Just thought you'd want to know, her daughter Jenny died in a fire up in Philadelphia about ten years ago."

There was a long pause on the other end. "Well, now, isn't that a coincidence."

"What do you mean?"

"The old Swiggett house here went up in smoke about ten years ago, too. It was definitely a torch. We found a couple of gas cans but never caught anybody. I always wondered if maybe Jenny and her mama snuck back into town and burned that sucker to the ground. You know, for old time's sake."

Janzek spent the rest of the ride to Charleston on his phone. After making several calls attempting to track down the ME in Philadelphia who'd investigated the fatal fire in Jenny Riles's apartment, Janzek finally got in touch with him. The ME remembered the case clearly. When Janzek asked him if there were any signs of arson, the ME said no, that had never come up.

"No signs of any accelerant or anything?" Janzek asked.

The ME again said no, but that the detective on the case— now retired—had theorized that an electric stove burner had been left on and had somehow ignited a roll of paper towels on the counter. When Janzek asked him if he knew how the detective came up with that theory, the ME said he had no idea.

The main reason the ME said he remembered the case was that the dental records of the victim didn't exactly match up.

"How far off were they?" asked Janzek.

"Well, as I recall, there were two fillings that weren't in the records of the victim's dentist back in Georgia. But that didn't particularly bother me 'cause I figured the new dental work was probably done later. Somewhere else."

"By another dentist?"

"Right. And besides, who else could have died in the apartment except the tenant?"

JANZEK GOT to the Charleston police station at six that night. Rhett was still there, talking on his phone. The two of them had a lot to go over. Janzek motioned Rhett to join him in his office as he walked past Rhett's office. Rhett came in a few moments later.

"So was that a big ol' wild goose chase?" Rhett asked.

"Maybe, maybe not," Janzek said. "Someone torched the Swiggett's family's house in Thomasville right after a fire allegedly killed Jenny Riles in Philly."

"Allegedly, huh...meanin' you ain't buyin' it?"

"Meaning I don't know yet," Janzek said. "Nothing suspicious about the fire so far, only about the alleged victim, Jenny Riles. The ME said her dental records weren't an exact match."

"So what do you think? She might be alive?"

"I think she went from a possible suspect to a dead suspect to a big question mark now."

"What are you planning to do?"

Janzek leaned back in his chair. "Try to find out if she died in that fire or not. Staring out my window at 35,000 feet gave me a lot of time to think. I started to wonder, for one thing, how does a girl whose mother clearly has no money graduate from an Ivy League university? She went to Penn."

"Uh...scholarship?"

"Yeah, except I called Penn and asked if she had one. They looked into it, called me back, and said no. Then I tracked down the company that owned the apartment she rented and found out it was a two-thousand-dollar-a-month space in a luxury building."

"You're kidding," Rhett said. "I think I paid something like five hundred a month for my dump at the Citadel."

"Yeah, exactly," Janzek said, "and this was back ten years ago."

"Sounds like what a rich girl would pay."

"Or maybe... the girlfriend of a rich man."

THIRTY-TWO

Janzek was thinking how much easier computers made the job. This, despite the fact that he was hopeless when it came to social media, had absolutely no interest in having a Facebook page, and figured he probably could get through life quite comfortably without ever having to communicate in 140 characters or less on Twitter.

Online, he'd gotten the name of the company that managed the building in Philly where Jenny Riles had been a tenant ten years before, then called to ask if they had a record, or copies, of her rent checks. He got connected to a back-office drone who he imagined was dying for a little human contact to add some excitement to her humdrum day.

"Her rent was paid by a Naomi Chernoff at Derbyshire Properties. Every check was written on the first day of the month," the woman said. "Derbyshire Properties, I'm pretty sure, is one of the biggest apartment owners in Philly. I think it's owned by the guy who owns the Flyers."

"The hockey team, you mean?"

"Yeah, I forget the name of the owner. I only know this 'cause my boyfriend is a hockey nut."

"Can you call him and ask him for the owner's name, please?"

"Sure. I'll try him on his cell if you want to hold on."

"Thanks a lot."

"Hang on."

Two minutes later she came back on. "His name is Seth Miller, the owner."

"Thank you very much," Janzek said. "You've been a big help. Thank your boyfriend for me, too."

"I wonder why they'd be paying her rent?"

He had a pretty good idea the answer was a three-letter word ending in 'x.'

———————

JANZEK DECIDED it was time to take an approach that had worked for him in the past. A guy up in Boston called it *Classic Janzek: make-like-you-got-the-goods-on-a-guy-when-in-fact-you-ain't-got-dick.* Janzek had used the technique successfully to get a confession from a man who he knew killed his wife's boyfriend even though he didn't have anything close to a smoking gun.

He Googled Seth Miller at Derbyshire Properties then went to work, climbing up the chain of command to speak to him on the phone.

He went from receptionist, to secretary, to personal assistant. And finally, the great man himself.

Janzek had told the first two employees that he was a detective who needed to speak to Mr. Miller "on an urgent matter." To Miller's more inquisitive personal assistant he added that he needed to speak to Miller about the "fire that killed Jenny Riles."

He figured odds were against Miller picking up. He was on hold for a few minutes and was about to hang up.

"Hello," a man's voice said, finally.

"Mr. Miller, my name is Detective Nick Janzek and I'm investigating the death of your friend, Jenny Riles, back in 2010."

"Who the hell is Jenny Riles?" Miller said.

"Someone who your wife and the Philadelphia newspapers might want to know about," Janzek bluffed.

A long pause, then, "Who are you?"

"I told you. Janzek. Violent Crimes, Charleston, South Carolina Police Department. I'd like to have a candid conversation with you."

It elicited the long, strained sigh he expected.

"Mr. Miller?"

"Yeah, I'm here."

"Can we have that candid Q & A now?"

"What do you want?"

"Answers."

"Ask a question."

"Did Jenny Riles die in that fire or was it someone else?"

"Ask the police or the medical examiner."

"I'm asking you," Janzek said. "You had the relationship with her."

Another long pause.

"Do you want me to open up the whole thing for everyone in Philadelphia to hear about?" Janzek asked. "Launch a new inquiry into it? Because I can and I will."

"Why would you want to do that?"

"Because I have a feeling the body that was found was not Jenny Riles. That she may have had another life after the one that supposedly ended in that fire ten years ago. I'll ask you again, do you want me to open up the matter again...very publicly?"

"No."

"Then, answer my question. Was it Jenny Riles, in the fire?"

Miller sighed deeply. "I don't think so."

"Then, who was it?"

"Sometimes she had a high-school friend come and visit her."

"From Florida, you mean?"

"Uh-huh."

"And this woman was staying there at the time of the fire, right, Mr. Miller?"

"She might have been."

"No, you know for a fact she was, right, Mr. Miller?"

Nothing.

"Right, Mr. Miller?"

Faintly. "Right."

THIRTY-THREE

JANZEK DIALED RHETT RIGHT AWAY.

"She's alive," was all he said.

"So what about the fire?"

"Seems like it was someone else, a high-school friend of hers, probably."

"So you think...she set it up? The fire?"

"That would be my guess."

"And you think she's in Charleston? Killing these guys...one by one."

"Yeah, I do," Janzek said, "I gotta make some more calls."

He hung up and dialed Verna Riles's phone number. As usual, it rang and rang.

He clicked off and called Torborg. "I got another police job for you."

"Why don't I just stop pedaling for a living and move into your police station?"

"That would be nice. A little cubicle with your name on it."

"Are you kidding? I'm a corner-office kind of a gal," she said. "What kind of a job did you have in mind?"

"The kind where I show you pictures of a woman at age twenty or so and you show me what she'd look like ten years later."

"That's not something I've ever done before."

"But I bet it's something you *could* do."

"I probably could."

"I *know* you could. Just throw in a few wrinkles around the eyes, make the skin droop a little."

"You jerk. Is that what you see when you look at me?"

"No, course not, you're—"

"Thirty years old."

"You don't look a day over...twenty-five."

"Don't try soft-shoeing your way out of this."

"Twenty-six at the most," he said, "I gotta go. I need to dig up some pictures of the girl."

"Okay, just email 'em to me. I can work from that."

Janzek hung up and tried Verna Riles again.

This time she answered.

"Mrs. Riles, it's Detective Janzek. I wanted to thank you for seeing me at your house. Can I ask you a favor?"

"If I can help, I will."

"Do you have any pictures of your daughter you could send me? From when she was a college student, maybe?"

"I think I have a few. What do you need them for?"

"Just part of my investigation."

"Of what?"

"Well, as I mentioned before, the murders of those men up here in Charleston."

"Oh, okay."

"If I give you a FedEx account number, would it be possible for you to overnight them to me?"

"Sure, I guess I could do that, there's a FedEx office not far from me."

"Thank you very much, Mrs. Riles, I really appreciate it," he said and gave her his shipping-account info and address.

THIRTY-FOUR

Sarah Rentschler, the buyer of the house on Atlantic Street, had really gotten on Billy Hobart's nerves. First, she had demanded to close on the house three weeks after she won it at the Coastal Conservation League auction. He kept telling her that it would take him two months to finish the work on the house, but she'd insisted on closing anyway. Then, when he agreed, she called him every day to bug him about getting the work done even sooner.

He was getting pretty close to telling her to go fuck herself but decided instead that to shut her up, he'd take a shortcut or two, something he never did. But now he wanted nothing more than to get the damned job done. Anything to get her out of his hair.

The next call he got from her was a clipped announcement that she had movers coming in two days.

He had never met a pushier person. The woman had clearly spent way too much time in New York.

He finally said okay, called up his plumber on his cell, and told him to wrap up the job right away—pack up his wrenches and pipes and whatever, and move on to the next one. The plumber hemmed and hawed and told him he never did half-assed jobs, but Billy told him he didn't want to hear it. Then he called his electrician, who was also working on the house, and told him to be out of there by the end of the day, that the cleaning crew was coming tomorrow morning. The man grumbled a little but agreed to do what Billy wanted.

BILLY CALLED Sarah Rentschler after the cleaning crew finished up the next morning.

"Sarah, it's Billy Hobart. You can move in now. My contractors have finished up and my cleaning crew just left. You can eat off the floors now, they're so clean."

"Well, it's about time," Sarah said, which was exactly what he expected her to say.

"I hope you enjoy your new life at 101 Atlantic."

"Thank you, Billy, I'm sure I will."

Ungrateful bitch.

WELL, as it turned out, she didn't. Enjoy her new life at 101 Atlantic, that is.

She spent a long day barking out commands to the movers, and that night was all moved in. She went and mixed a tall cocktail then walked into her lavishly appointed bathroom and turned on the water of her elegant, new two-person whirlpool tub, which actually had a name: The Indulgence.

She took off her clothes, climbed in and luxuriated in a frothy bubble bath for a solid half-hour. She would have stayed there for another half hour but was eager for her second cocktail of the night. She turned the brass faucet to let the tub drain, toweled off, then went to her massive walk-in closet and put on a full-length, snow-white, monogrammed, terry-cloth robe.

Then she walked down to the kitchen below and mixed another drink. She took a long sip, then went to the refrigerator and took out a wedge of gouda from the shop called *Goat. Sheep. Cow.* on Church Street. She pulled a knife from the drawer and brought the drink and plate of cheese into her spacious and impeccably furnished living room.

She sat down in a club chair and gazed across at the star attraction of the space: a one-of-a-kind Queen Anne cherry highboy desk. Once again, she had been the high bidder at an auction, this time at Sotheby's in New York. She took pride in having beat out a pudgy Kuwaiti sheik who had been way too sure of himself.

She cut a big hunk of gouda, spread it on a wheat cracker, then finished it in two bites. Then she took another sip of her drink.

Suddenly, out of nowhere, she heard a sound like nothing she had ever heard before. It was like the creak of an old boat combined with the muffled flush of a toilet and a gurgling sound. That was the best description she could come up with when she described it to a friend later. She looked up at the ceiling in the living room and knew immediately that some-thing was wrong—terribly wrong.

The ceiling, she saw to her horror, was suddenly bloated and bowed. As she stared up helplessly, The Indulgence came plunging through the floor in full free fall. Sarah watched as it landed on the Queen Anne Highboy and crushed the invaluable antique into a million tiny wooden pieces.

The plumber, in his haste, it was later determined, had not connected the drainpipe from the tub to any other pipe. So, water had sluiced into the space between the first-floor ceiling and the second-story floor. Fifty to eighty gallons of sudsy bath-water were looking for a home.

The electrician, also in a mad scramble to get the Atlantic Street job done, had installed electrical outlets not hooked up to actual wiring in the several rooms which he hadn't yet gotten to. There were a few other examples of incomplete construction. Rather than replace the termite-damaged floor in the den, the flooring man had simply put down three quarter inch plywood on top of it, then installed the hardwood. The roofer, who had also been told to wrap it up quick, had simply repaired sections of the roof that were visible from the street.

Sarah Rentschler's building inspector found other things, too, but those were the big items.

Her attorney drafted a five-million-dollar lawsuit naming Billy Hobart and Miranda Bennett as plaintiffs.

That would turn out to be an ill-advised move.

THIRTY-FIVE

Janzek got the FedEx envelope from Verna Riles and tore it open. There were three photos of Jenny Riles. Janzek's first impression was that she was a beautiful woman. His second was that she looked a little off. Haunted, troubled, something in her eyes...she looked a little tortured somehow. He only noticed it in one photo. She wasn't looking straight into the camera, but distractedly staring at something that must have been far, far away. Her eyes had that thousand-yard stare, a little like military vets sometimes had when they were dredging up some particularly horrifying war memory.

Janzek guessed Jenny might be flashing back to what happened on her sixteenth birthday.

He dialed Torborg. She picked up after the first ring.

"Hey," she said.

"Hey. So, I got the photos of the woman. I'm guessing she's nineteen or twenty when these were taken. Can I meet you?"

"Sure, I just dropped a couple off at White Point Garden. Want to meet me down here?"

"Yeah, that's good," he said, "the scene of the crime."

"Exactly."

THIRTY-SIX

SHEILA LESSING REMAINED A COMPLETE ENIGMA TO Janzek. He decided that while Torborg was busy adding ten years to Jenny Riles's face that he'd give Sheila a call.

He called her at her farm in Pasco, but the woman who answered said she was at her house in Charleston for the week. He tried her cell, which she answered, and asked if he could come to her house and talk to her about the Swiggett murder again.

"I got a better idea," she said. "Since we didn't get off on the best foot last time, I'll buy you dinner. How about we meet at the Ordinary tonight at eight? They have the most amazing oysters. I'm going to be there anyway 'cause I'm having drinks with a friend."

He hated oysters but accepted anyway. Before signing off, he insisted on paying. Lessing thanked him but said, no, it would be her treat.

THE FIRST THING Sarah Rentschler did when Sheila Lessing met her for dinner was show her a collection of pictures on her iPhone of the damage done to her new house at 101 Atlantic Street. Sheila commiserated and said Sarah was welcome to stay at her house on Tradd. Sarah thanked her but said she was ensconced at the Charleston Place hotel until the work was completed.

Despite her inauspicious start, Sarah was excited about becoming an official resident of Charleston. She explained that her husband was going to commute from his job as a hedge-fund manager in New York on weekends. She, however, would be looking for something to keep her busy, as she'd quit her job as head of Wealth Management at JP Morgan only a few weeks before.

Sheila agreed wholeheartedly. Charleston was not an ideal place for a dynamic, ambitious woman. "No way you want to end up with the ladies-who-brunch-bunch or on the bridge-and-book-club circuit."

Sarah sighed. "That's for damn sure. So, how's it going for you, making the College of Charleston into the Harvard of the south?"

"Pretty well, I'd say. I've poached eight professors from the Ivys, including a Pulitzer and a Nobel prize winner."

"Jesus," Sarah said, "how'd you do that?"

"Money, of course... speaking of which..."

And Sheila leaned across the table and, under her breath, told Sarah her bombshell.

Sarah's eyes lit up as she heard the news. "You're kidding!" she said so loud that someone at the next table spun around and stared at them.

"Shush. Jesus," Sheila said. "Obviously, you have to promise me you won't tell a soul."

"Of course."

"So I guess I gotta learn how to speak Korean, then," Sheila said.

Sheila told Sarah that, twenty-four hours earlier, she had inked a deal with Hyundai Motors to build a second U.S. manufacturing plant in—of all places—Pasco, South Carolina. How she had been seeing those ubiquitous little Elantras, Sonatas, and Tucsons multiplying on the streets of America like rabbits and had gone to Hyundai and basically pitched them the BMW story. That is, how—fifteen years before—she and the governor of South Carolina had approached BMW's CEO about locating a huge manufacturing plant in South Carolina when she had gotten wind that BMW was thinking about building a new factory in the States. And how the governor had ended up throwing a vast package of incentives at the Germans to locate in the Palmetto state. Fifteen years later, it was the phenomenally successful BMW plant located in the middle of Spartanburg, which was built at a cost of 2.2 billion dollars on 1,150 acres, and which employed ten thousand workers who cranked out two hundred ninety-seven thousand X3, X4, and X5s a year.

"Jesus, girl," Sarah said, raising her glass. "That's amazing. Congratulations."

Sheila clinked her glass. "Thanks. I gotta keep my hat in the ring around here. You know, when I moved, I think people up in New York figured I was done. 'Pushy bitch gonna ride off into the sunset' was probably what they were all thinking."

Sarah put her glass down and put her hands together. "Well, I'd say you disabused them of that notion pretty damn quick."

"Yeah but, then I took the job at the college and I bet they were wondering, 'What's that all about? One step up from the Department of Mosquito Control?'"

Sarah slapped Sheila's hand and laughed. "Yeah, well,

they're not saying that now," she said. "I mean, I doubt my kids are ever going to be able to get into the College of Charleston."

Sheila suddenly looked up and across the room. "Oh, here he comes."

Sarah turned and looked. "Oh, my God, what a hottie."

"I know."

Janzek walked up to their table. He was wearing his best tweed jacket from the Jos. A. Bank buy-one-get-one-free sale.

"Hello, ladies," he said, turning to Sarah and putting out his hand, "I'm Nick Janzek." Then he nodded to Sheila. "Hello, Ms. Lessing."

Sarah shook his hand and gave him an eye flutter she reserved for a special few. "Sarah Rentschler," she said, pushing back her chair. "Well, I've got to get going. Three's a crowd."

Sheila raised a hand to stop her. "Oh, come on, can't you stay for one drink," she said, not meaning it even remotely.

"I'd love to, but I've got three starving mouths to feed," Sarah said. "Nick, it's nice to have met you. Are you really a... policeman?"

"I really am."

"And an art collector," Sheila said. "He's got a Joe McGuirk and a Morton Riegleman."

"Good memory," Janzek said. "Not to mention a Ralph Eppsley."

Sarah smiled. "Well, you two have fun," she said, then to Janzek: "They have the best oysters in the world here."

"So I hear," he said, having no intention of getting one of those slimy suckers anywhere near his mouth.

THIRTY-SEVEN

Janzek sat down and turned serious.

"Ms. Lessing—"

"Will you stop with the Ms. Lessing? It makes me feel as old as a grandmother. I'm a vain woman who thinks she's only thirty."

"Sorry, *Sheila*," he said. "Okay, I'm just going to come right out with it. The more I look into the death of Jamie Swiggett, the more I hear your name. I just need you to level with me so we can have a nice, relaxed dinner."

She reached for her almost-empty wine glass and polished it off. "What do you mean?" she asked. "Hear my name, in what context?"

"I'll tell you. My partner is a badger. He dug around and got your phone records—" Sheila looked outraged, as Janzek raised his hands "—all perfectly legal. He found quite a few calls to Jamie Swiggett, going back a year or more. He went around to several restaurants with pictures of you and Swiggett and several said they had seen you there. He also found a picture in the *Post & Courier* of you two at a Spoleto event together. I mean, the list goes on."

"Okay, so?" Sheila shrugged. "We were friends."

"Last time, you said he was your lawyer."

"Is there a law against being both?"

He picked up the menu, looked at it, but didn't light on anything. "So you had... what? A platonic relationship with Swiggett?"

"That's exactly what we had," Sheila said, "Did your little badger of a partner find any hotel people who said Jamie and I checked in together?"

Janzek picked up the wine list. "No. Why would he? You have a nice house."

"Well, then," Sheila said, tapping her fork lightly, "I'm sure you had him talk to my neighbors. See if they saw Jamie sneak out in the morning."

"As a matter of fact," Janzek said with a smile, "I did that myself."

"I should have figured. And?"

"Nobody had."

Sheila smiled and tapped her fork again.

"It just seems strange," Janzek said.

"What? A fifty-year-old woman and a thirty-four-year-old man, you mean?"

"Fifty? I would have guessed forty-five, max."

She smiled. "Don't try to suck up to me, Nick."

"I'm not. Like I was saying, it just seems a little strange...a rich, fifty-year-old woman who purports to respect the marital vow, and a married thirty-four-year-old man who, clearly, did not."

"Now you're pissing me off," Sheila said, her eyes blinking rapidly. "I don't *purport* to respect the marital vow. I damn well do." Her eyes drilled into his. "You got it?"

Janzek raised his hands. "Okay, okay, I got it. Just asking questions."

"And your questions are getting *really* irritating."

He looked into her cold, steely eyes. "Sorry, but that kind of goes with the territory."

"I get that, but I'm done talking about Jamie Swiggett."

Janzek put up his hands. "Okay."

"Do you ever have normal conversations?"

"What's a normal conversation?"

"Exactly my point," she said. "You know, current events, the weather, stuff like that?"

Janzek realized it was time for a change of pace since the subject of Jamie Swiggett had been officially declared off limits. "Okay, let's have one. Let's start with the weather," he said. "My impression is that people in Charleston take weather a little too seriously."

"What do you mean?"

"Well, like last winter, I don't know whether you were here when we had that freezing rain and the whole city was paralyzed? Anyway, all the bridges were shut down, school was closed for three days, everyone stayed home. That was a joke. I mean, in Boston the weatherman wouldn't have even mentioned it. No one would have noticed it."

Sheila slowly shook her head. "So, I suppose that's why you Yankees won the war."

Janzek laughed. "Oh, God, what in God's name does weather have to do with *the Civil war*? And why is it that people here are still fixated on a war that took place a hundred-and-fifty years ago."

"A hundred-fifty-six," Sheila said. "But who's counting?"

Janzek smiled, took a sip of his drink then put it down. "This guy in my building was telling me about some guy who has a party every year on Robert E. Lee's birthday. Everybody sits around and talks about "that bastard Sherman" and after four or five cocktails they sing all five stanzas of 'Dixie.'"

Sheila brushed a strand of hair out of her eye and laughed. "Come on, Nick, that sounds like a bit of an exaggeration."

"Okay, only four stanzas," Janzek said. "And now that you got me started on this funky little burg of yours, what's with those signs you see on houses? I get that they're a protest against the cruise ships, but what the hell is the sign supposed to be of? It's a little abstract for me."

Sheila laughed. "You know what? I absolutely agree with you on that. You won't see one on my house."

"I mean, I look at it and have no idea what it means. And while I'm at it, how come you let golf carts clog up the streets. What's that all about?"

"You're really on a tear now, aren't you?"

Janzek leaned closer to Sheila. "Not to mention the fact that everybody drives eight miles an hour. I mean, in Boston they'd all be horned to death."

"Those are all tourists, gawking and rubbernecking."

"Whatever. And the couple of houses I've been to South of Broad. I gotta tell ya, pretty unimpressive." Janzek shook his head. "I mean, big, old houses from like two hundred years ago with all this frumpy furniture, paint peeling everywhere, walls covered with portraits of great-great-granddaddy and grandma looking all prune-faced."

Sheila shook her head firmly. "You really don't know what you're talking about now. Some of the houses here will make ones on your precious Beacon Hill look downright shabby."

"It's hardly *my* Beacon Hill. I lived in lowly Allston."

"Wherever the hell that might be. But, seriously, you don't like it here?"

"No, actually, I love it, it's just—"

" A funky little burg."

158

"Yeah, exactly." Janzek was on a roll and couldn't stop. "Then this other thing I heard about, foxes and hounds. You know, where riders on horseback go after foxes. Dogs chase 'em up trees or whatever?"

"Yes, Nick, I'm familiar with the practice."

"Well, someone was telling me that before they start out, they get a padre from the local church to come and perform some religious ceremony. You know about that?"

"Yes, I do. It's called the Blessing of the Hounds."

Janzek shook his head. "That is just so weird."

"I bet if I went up to Beantown, it wouldn't take me long to come up with weird things people do there."

Janzek nodded. "Yeah, about five minutes. But I'm pretty sure the local priest doesn't go around blessing a bunch of mongrels right before they chase a tomcat up a tree."

Sheila laughed. "You're funny."

Janzek smiled at her. "Why do you say that?"

"Because when I don't want to talk about what you want to talk about, you launch into a whole diatribe about Charleston."

Janzek smiled. "What's a diatribe?"

Sheila put down her drink and patted him on the hand. "Don't play dumb with me. You, the famous art collector and I barely graduated in place of Just cum laude graduate of Boston College."

Janzek shook his head. "Just cum laude. And as I said, I love Charleston... just not sure it loves me."

THIRTY-EIGHT

TORBORG DUBBED HER PAINTING ASSIGNMENT "TIME-advanced photo realism" and Janzek was amazed at how she had added years while not changing Jenny Riles's basic features. They were sitting in his office, looking over the painting on his desk.

"I think you've got a new career," he said.

"Oh, yeah, like people are going to come running and say, 'Oh please, Torborg, make me look older, will ya?' I'd guess that's a pretty small market."

Janzek scratched his head. "You could go the other way, make them look younger?"

"That's been done before," she said. "Starting with Goya."

Janzek nodded. "I can't believe you knocked it out so fast."

"You said you needed it in a hurry."

"Well, thanks, I appreciate it."

"Who is she, anyway?"

"A suspect."

"In the murders?"

He nodded.

"She hardly looks like a stone-cold killer to me."

"I know."

A text beeped from her pocket. She pulled out her iPhone. "Well, gotta get back to my day job." She stood. "It's been real, Nick."

Janzek walked around his desk and gave her a kiss on the cheek. "Great job. I'll get 'em to send you a check."

Torborg nodded. "Thanks, and good luck finding this chick."

JANZEK'S GAME plan was to make up fliers from Torborg's painting then have uniforms go door-to-door south of Broad St., concentrating on houses to the west of White Point Garden, initially. But first he took a photo of it, then put it in an email attachment and shot it out to every cop in the department. Almost immediately, another detective named Herman Smalls, who specialized in burglary, stopped by his office, iPad in hand.

"I'm lookin' into a brunette version of this woman," Smalls said. "She's a person of interest in the Faberge egg robbery."

Janzek motioned to the chair across from his desk. "Have a seat, Herm. You're talking about that egg that was stolen during a party, right?"

"Yeah, exactly. A benefit for the Preservation Society about a week ago. There was a photographer there from the *Mercury*, taking pictures of all the movers and shakers. This woman was one of the shakers."

Smalls slid his iPad across Janzek's desk. "Dead ringer," Smalls said, "except the hair color."

"Yeah, sure looks it. You talk to her yet... about the egg?"

"Haven't gotten around to her." Smalls said. "Don't even know her name yet."

"So, at this stage everyone who was there is a person of interest?" Janzek asked, handing back the iPad to Smalls.

"Yeah, basically. I was working my way down the list when I got this from you. But now she's goin' to the top of it. So far, I've done the caterers and the bartenders. About ten of them all together, and I already ruled them out. I was just starting in on the guests."

"You got the name of someone who can ID the guests?"

"I was just going to tell you," Smalls said, reaching into his pocket. "I got two, actually: Estelle Ripton, head of the Preservation Society, and a guy named Lucien Wiedemann, who hosted the party in his house. Between them, I was told, they know everyone who was there."

"Well, thanks for coming by, man. That's really helpful. I appreciate it. Can you make me a copy of that photo?"

Smalls stood. "No problem."

"Thanks."

"You got your hands full, huh? Seems like they're droppin' like flies around here."

THIRTY-NINE

No doubt about it, Tipton was in better shape than her trainer.

She had been working out at the MUSC gym for a long time and, on off days, did a hundred laps in the pool there. As a result, she had wide shoulders and eight percent body fat. She could also bench press twenty pounds more than the 130 she weighed.

A good portion of the workout crowd at MUSC were there for the chitchat as much as for the elliptical and treadmill machines, but Tipton was all business. By now, she knew a lot of the regulars by sight, but she never got into conversations, only smiled a lot and, said 'hi,' and kept pumping iron. Even with her trainer, she never got into the subject of real-estate or her social life, just barbells, aerobics, and plenty of stretching.

Guys tried to hit on her, both subtly and overtly, but she had no time for that. Instead, she'd smile politely and move on to her next set.

Today she got to the gym late—eight p.m.—and did a session without her trainer. On the drive over, she went through a litany of reasons to skip the workout—long day showing houses, a book she wanted to finish, it was dinnertime —but, as she always did, she sucked it up and went. You wouldn't find many people more disciplined than Tipton.

As she was walking past the front desk, on her way out, the woman working there looked up at her and smiled.

"Best part of the workout, right?" the woman said.

Tipton laughed and nodded. "Yup. When it's over and I'm walking out."

But she didn't really feel that way. She actually loved pushing herself hard.

Five minutes later, Tipton buzzed herself into her building and rode the elevator up to the penthouse.

BILLY HAD SET his alarm for 1:15 a.m. He went into the second bedroom, which he had converted into a dressing room, and changed into an all-black costume—tight black jeans, a black, collared, short-sleeved shirt, and a black baseball cap. Then he opened the front closet door and pulled out his North Face backpack.

He went down to the first floor, where all the storage units were located, and unlocked his unit. He pulled out the two gas cans he had bought earlier that day and slipped them into his backpack.

He walked over to Murray Street and took a left onto King. A car came along, and he turned his head away so the driver couldn't see his face. Then he cut through White Point Garden until he got to Meeting Street. On Meeting, he again looked away when two cars came toward him, hanging a quick right onto Atlantic.

The backpack with the cans was heavier than he expected, and he slid it off when he approached 1 o 1 Atlantic Avenue.

There were no lights on in the house. He looked up and down the street, then, seeing no one, opened the ornate, Philip Simmons wrought-iron gate on the right side of the house. He pushed it open and walked down the driveway into the back yard. Before going to sleep that night, he had thought about where he should douse the gasoline. He'd decided to start on the back porch, his plan being to break a living-room window, pour the remainder of the gas quickly into the room, strike a match, and toss it in.

Such a shame, he thought. That Sarah Rentschler.... What an overbearing, pushy bitch. Her lawsuit could really mess things up for him, among other things creating a rift between him and Miranda Bennett. Rentschler's chances of getting out of the house alive, assuming she was in there, were about fifty-fifty. It didn't much matter to him either way. Then he remembered all of her harassing phone calls and that pain-in-the-ass personality of hers. On second thought....

He went around the house and carefully stepped up onto the back porch. He unscrewed the cap of the red aluminum can, then turned it upside down. The smell was pungent, but he'd always liked the smell of gas. He reached into his pocket for a stick match, struck it on the door, and watched it hiss into a bright flame.

He took a few steps back, tossed it onto the porch, and watched it ignite.

He hurried to the other end of the porch and swung the second gas can against a living-room window, which shattered. He spun the cap off, emptied the gas onto the floor, tossed the can in with it, and struck another match.

As the room lit up with flames, he saw a really strange sight.

It was the seven-thousand-dollar Indulgence bathtub he

had personally ordered, lying in a bed of splintered dark wood and slabs of discolored, waterlogged plaster.

It was apparent to him Sarah Rentschler was not there.

Billy turned and ran like hell.

Ten minutes later, back in his pajamas on the top floor of the Fort Sumter house, he heard sirens coming from all directions. He looked down and the first thing he saw was the bench in White Point Garden. Then, five blocks beyond it, lapping, yellow-orange flames enveloping the house that he had worked so diligently to finish only days before.

The house had become a liability since Sarah had filed the lawsuit.

Well, Sarah, there's your evidence, hon...going up in a cloud of smoke.

FORTY

Janzek called Estelle Ripton at the Preservation Society at nine in the morning. She wasn't there yet so he got her cell number, called her directly, and asked if he could come to her house and run through a few quick questions.

She agreed, and an hour and a half later he showed her the photo of the woman Herman Smalls had given him. She quickly identified the woman as Tipton Hill and said she worked as a real-estate agent at Carriage Properties.

Janzek thanked her and drove straight to Carriage Properties on Broad Street. He parked in front of a fire hydrant and walked in.

"Yes, sir, can I help you?" the receptionist asked.

He pulled out his ID. "Yes, I'm Nick Janzek, detective with Charleston Police Department," he said. "I'd like to see Ms. Hill, Tipton Hill."

The receptionist looked suspicious. "Ah, sorry, but Tipton's not here at the moment," she said. "Would you like her cell-phone number?"

"Yes, please," Janzek said. "Do you know where she is?"

The receptionist handed him a card from one of the many cardholders on her desk that had Tipton's name and contact information. "Sorry, I don't, but you can probably reach her on her cell. Or else she'll call you right back, I'm sure."

A well-dressed woman in her forties came out of a room behind the receptionist.

"Hi," she said with a smile. "I overheard you. I'm pretty sure Tipton's at the gym. She lives there when she's not showing."

Janzek was halfway to the front door before he stopped. "Thank you," he said, turning. "Which gym?"

"MUSC," said the older woman.

Janzek walked out of the Carriage Properties office, hit his remote clicker, got into his cruiser, and cut a hard U-turn in front of a horse and carriage.

THE MOMENT JANZEK left Carriage Properties, the receptionist made a call.

Tipton Hill picked up right away.

"Hey, Tip," she said, "Just wanted to give you a heads-up. Some guy, a detective, is looking for you. He's on his way over to the gym if that's where you are."

Tipton thanked her, jumped off the treadmill and threaded her way quickly out of the main aerobics area.

She reached the front reception area and was about to exit through the turnstile when she changed her mind, instead taking the back exit down to the parking garage below.

Janzek didn't turn on the siren or his light but was going as fast as he could up Ashley Avenue. Sixty-five, to be exact. He crossed the double yellow line and passed two cars that were creeping along at the twenty-five-mile-an-hour speed limit. He caught the tail end of a yellow at Calhoun and skidded left, fishtailing. He stomped the pedal again and heard the Crown Vic Interceptor engine roar. He took a hard right at Courtenay Street, then—quickly looking both ways—rolled through a red light and powered left into MUSC. A silver BMW came out of the underground garage and slowly rolled past him.

Its driver, a woman, wore a neon green t-shirt, an Atlanta Braves baseball hat, sunglasses, and a dead-serious expression.

FORTY-ONE

FIVE YEARS AGO, TIPTON HILL HAD BOUGHT JAMIE
Swiggett's father's ocean cottage on Sullivan's Island in a foreclosure sale. The word cottage did not do justice to the house. It
was an eight-thousand-square-foot Georgian with six bedrooms
and seven and a half bathrooms. Not exactly on the scale of a
summer house in the Hamptons but, all in all, quite adequate.
It also had a pool and tennis court, which were both rundown
when Tipton bought the house. Since then she had spent a lot
of money restoring them, and they were now in exceptional
condition.

Tipton purchased the house—*Joliemer*—under the name of
"Sullivan's Island, LLC," and nowhere was her name on the
title. She'd hired a woman to manage the house. The manager
knew her only as Ms. Hill and received monthly paychecks
from the Sullivan's Island, LLC, trust account.

Tipton had been there only five times in the four years that
she had owned the house. She never seemed to have time for
tennis or for appreciating the gorgeous ocean view.

It would serve as her safe house, now that she knew a Charleston detective was looking for her.

She was fully prepared for this day and had stocked the house as if she had advance warning that World War III was coming. She had enough food to last a year and money in a Grand Cayman bank that would last far beyond that. In case of emergency, she also kept two hundred thousand dollars in cash in a wall safe in her master walk-in closet at *Joliemer*.

"DELVIN," Janzek said into his cell phone as he walked through the MUSC gym, "put out an APB on a silver BMW 760Li".

"Who is it?"

"Tipton Hill. Local realtor and the woman who got raped by our mutilated vics and maybe killed 'em all," Janzek said. "We gotta track her down and catch her *fast*."

"Okay, I'm on it."

"Last seen wearing a neon green t-shirt and a baseball cap," Janzek said.

"Who told you?"

"No one. She drove right past me. It didn't occur to me until too late."

"We'll find her," Rhett said.

At the reception desk at the gym earlier, he had learned that Tipton Hill had indeed checked in, but had left a short while ago. Just in case, he requisitioned three female employees who knew Hill to look through the two ladies' locker rooms, the pool areas, the big main gym, the yoga room, the separate weight rooms, the spinning room, aerobics...everywhere.

But she was definitely gone.

He returned to the reception desk and, with the help of the

receptionist, got the application Tipton had filled out eight years before when she first joined the club. It said where she worked. Where she lived. And what she drove, because she had a monthly permit for the parking lot underneath the building.

When he saw that her car was a silver late-model BMW, he knew for a fact she was the woman he'd passed coming in. He remembered looking into his rearview mirror and seeing the car accelerate faster than normal as it exited the MUSC parking lot. At the time, he hadn't thought anything of it.

He took another look at the address on the gym application and was surprised to see that she lived in the same building where Billy Hobart hung his hat: the Fort Sumter house.

FORTY-TWO

JANZEK DROVE UP TO THE FORT SUMTER HOUSE AND parked in the back. He went through the same drill as he had the last time he visited. Except this time, he was in a much bigger hurry.

He pressed the buzzer for the manager. The same tall, bald man came to the door and gave him a 'you again?' look.

"Remember me? Detective Janzek?" he said. "I need to go up to Tipton Hill's apartment. The penthouse, I believe."

The man just stared at him.

"This is urgent police business. I need to go up right now."

The man nodded with no urgency and they walked to the elevators on the far side of the lobby. The manager pushed the button and a waiting elevator opened up.

"Have you seen her in the last hour?" Janzek asked, getting in.

"No, not since yesterday."

"In case she's not there, or doesn't answer, do you have a key?"

The man scowled. "Do you have a warrant?"

The elevator stopped at seven.

"No."

"Well, maybe she'll be there," the manager said, leading Janzek down the hallway.

He stopped at a door and knocked three times.

They waited.

The manager knocked again, a little louder.

Janzek put his ear to the door. He couldn't hear a thing.

TIPTON PARKED in the garage of the house on Sullivan's Island and opened the door that led to the starkly modern kitchen.

She went straight to the stainless-steel Subzero, opened it and pulled out a bottle of white wine. She got a fancy-looking corkscrew out of a drawer and opened the bottle then reached into a cabinet and retrieved a crystal wine glass. She filled it a quarter full, paused, then poured another quarter.

She almost chugged it.

DELVIN RHETT CALLED Janzek as he was leaving the Fort Sumter house.

"Yeah, Del?"

"Where are you?"

Janzek was getting into his car in the Fort Sumter parking lot. "Just left Tipton Hill's apartment. She wasn't there. I'm gonna get a warrant to get in. What's up?"

"Think you'll find this interesting," Rhett said. "There was a fire last night at a house South of Broad. Arson. Used to be owned by your friend, Billy Hobart. He just sold it a few days ago to a woman named Sarah Rentschler."

Janzek stopped at a light on Meeting Street. "No shit. I met the woman. She's a friend of Sheila Lessing."

"One big happy family, I guess," Rhett said. "Everyone's connected to everyone. Whoever did it left a couple of gas cans there. CSU's checkin' 'em for prints, but I'm guessin' they'll come up with nothin.'"

"I need to have a conversation with Sarah Rentschler. Try to find out what this is all about."

"Maybe have one with Sheila Lessing, too?"

"Yeah," Janzek said, "I agree. Hey, do me a favor... will you get us that warrant to get into Tipton Hill's apartment? I'm going in about ten directions at once."

"Yeah, sure, I'll get right on it. You got your hands full, don't cha? Chattin' up all these chicks."

FORTY-THREE

Janzek dialed Rhett on his way to Sheila Lessing's house an hour later.

"Tipton Hill's definitely our perp," Janzek said when Rhett picked up. "I left four messages and went to her office again. She missed three showings she had for houses. Any luck with the warrant?"

"Yeah, got it, I'm going to email it to you."

"Good. That'll get us past the building manager. Anything else?"

"That's all I got, man. Busy as hell."

Janzek pulled up to Sheila Lessing's house on Tradd St.

"See if you can track down Sarah Rentschler, will you?" Janzek asked, parking his car. "Find out where she's staying now. Wonder how she got out of the burning house?"

"I don't know for sure, just know nobody got fried."

Janzek had called Sheila, saying he had a thousand questions. She said she had time for about three of them.

He parked in front of her house, hit the buzzer on the ten-foot-high wrought-iron gate, and was buzzed in.

He walked up the path through the impeccably manicured garden to the front door. As he was about to knock, it opened.

"Hello, Nick," Sheila Lessing said. "Come on in. I've missed you and all your probing questions."

He followed her into the living room. She motioned to a chair and they sat.

"So, I guess you've been pretty busy?"

"Yeah, sure have. Let me ask you the first of the three questions you've so generously provided me."

Sheila hiked her right leg over her left. "Fire away. I might even give you more than three, just 'cause you amuse me."

"Thank you, glad someone gets it. Okay, first, what do you know about a real-estate agent named Tipton Hill."

Sheila ran her hand through her hair. "I know who she is. Don't know her well, though. Just by reputation. And her reputation is she can be a piranha."

"In real estate, you mean?"

"Correct. To some people that's a bad thing, but not to me. I think it's a good thing. If you know what you're doing, that is. And apparently she knows exactly what she's doing."

"So, she's good at it?"

"Good? Oh, yeah. Supposedly makes over a million a year. That's real money in Charleston. Biggest producer at Carriage Properties, is what I've heard. What do you want to know about her?"

Janzek blinked, read her expression, and decided to play it down. At least until he was absolutely sure Tipton was his perp. "She's just one of several people I'm looking into. You know, flavor of the day. Like you were a while back."

"So am I off your radar now?"

Janzek chuckled and patted the arm of his chair. "No, you're still on it. You still haven't given me a good answer yet why you spent so much time with Jamie Swiggett."

Sheila blew out a long, slow, dramatic sigh, lifted her arm out of her lap and put it on the armrest of the couch. "It's my business, Nick. If I knew anything about what happened to Jamie that would help your case, I would have told you by now."

"Why can't you just tell me about your relationship with him?"

"'Cause it has nothing to do with your case."

"You don't know that. Clearly, you're holding back. If you told me, I wouldn't have to give you the third-degree every time I see you."

"Christ," she muttered, rubbing her eyes wearily.

Janzek waited.

"Just to get you off my back...." She sat up straight and pulled back her hair. "Okay, here goes...."

And with that, she suddenly seized up with emotion and the tears flowed.

"You okay?" Janzek said, leaning forward.

Sheila waved him off. "I'm fine," she said. "Okay, so a long time ago, before I got all holier-than-thou...back when I was twenty-two years old,

I—" she exhaled deeply "—had an affair with a married man."

Janzek nodded and opted to let her take her time. Cruise along at her speed.

"It went on for a while, and one day, lo and behold, I found out I was pregnant. So—" Sheila buried her face in her hands.

Janzek came around, sat down on the sofa, and put his arm around her.

She looked up, tears in her eyes, and smiled at him.

"Cops aren't supposed to do that. You're supposed to maintain your professional detachment."

He laughed. "Yeah, and titans of industry aren't s'posed to cry."

She laughed. "Okay...I'm going to get through this. See, this is the first time I ever told anybody about it. So...the married man—twenty years older than me—talked me into getting an abortion. At the same time, I found out his wife was pregnant."

She looked away. Her jaw muscles tightened, and her eyes seemed to dim. She looked unspeakably sad.

"His wife gave birth right around the same time I would have, if I had gone through with it," she continued, her voice faint. "She gave birth to a seven pound, nine-ounce, apple-cheeked boy named James Bryant Swiggett. When his proud father showed me the pictures, all I could do was think of the baby I never had."

It was suddenly crystal clear to Janzek now. Sheila had, not illogically, transferred her love for a lost baby to a kid who probably never deserved it. A kid who'd also figured out, as he got older, how to take advantage of it. Borrow money from her, for starters. Use her influence to his advantage, no doubt.

Janzek didn't know what to say.

"I—I'm sorry," he said and squeezed her shoulder.

"Thank you." She buried her head in his shoulder and wept.

FORTY-FOUR

A FEW MOMENTS LATER, AS IF NOTHING HAD HAPPENED, Sheila looked up at him and wiped away the tears. "Okay, enough of my soap opera. What did you want to ask me about Tipton Hill?"

Janzek removed his arm from around her shoulder.

Sheila frowned. "I liked it there."

He brought his arm back around her shoulder. "It's hard to ask tough questions when you've got your arm around the interviewee—"

"Too bad. You can do it."

"Okay, I'll do my best. So, what do you know about her personal or social life?"

Sheila shrugged. "I see her around. She seems to get out there. You know, goes to benefits and some of those dreadful black-tie things. I always get the sense she's doing it more for business than anything else."

"She date anyone, you know?"

Sheila tilted her head and thought for a second. "Not that I can think of. And she's definitely one of the best-looking women in town."

Janzek shrugged. "I only saw her briefly in her car. What else have you heard? She must do something besides selling houses, going to the gym and, showing up at the occasional black-tie thing."

Sheila thought for a few moments. "Nothing that I can think of."

"Okay, changing the subject. I heard about the fire at your friend Sarah Rentschler's new house. She's okay, right?"

Sheila nodded. "Yeah, she's fine, but that was the damnedest thing. I mean, who goes around torching a house in this neighborhood?"

"No clue. You heard any theories, anything at all?"

Sheila shook her head.

"I heard that a man named Billy Hobart used to own the house. I met him once," Janzek said.

"Yeah, he renovated it," she said, "and, according to the grapevine, didn't do such a hot a job."

"What do you mean?"

"Well, he's got a really good reputation for renovating high-end houses," she said. "But I heard on this one there were some things he scrimped on, took a few shortcuts, and there were some problems with the house."

Janzek looked away as he tried to figure out how to pose his next question. "Let me ask you about him. Billy Hobart, I mean. Is... he... maybe...."

Sheila laughed. "I know where you're going. Is he gay? Is that what you're asking?

"Well... yeah."

"Well, you *are* in Charleston, we've got a long tradition of gay people here. They add to the style of the place in a million different ways. As far as Billy Hobart goes, I got my money on *asexual*. Know what a walker is?"

"Something slower than a runner?"

"Funny," she said. "A walker is a man who takes out older women— often married and usually rich."

"Why?"

Sheila had no response at first. "You're the first person who's ever asked me that question... maybe because they're rich and they pay for things. Or maybe because they open doors...."

"So that's what Billy Hobart is? A walker who...flips houses?"

"Something like that," Sheila said. "A friend of mine once told me, 'He's a gigolo who doesn't jiggle.'"

Janzek thought that over. "I don't even know what that means."

Sheila laughed. "Well, let's just say I wouldn't put him at the top of my list of men likely to become fathers any time soon."

FORTY-FIVE

JANZEK AND RHETT HAD A WARRANT. JANZEK HAD TO LEAN on the front-door buzzer at the Fort Sumter house for a full three minutes before the tall, bald manager answered. It was like he knew it was them and wanted them to give up and go the hell away.

They rode the elevator with nary a word, walked down the hall, and the manager opened the apartment. The manager walked in first but Janzek brushed past him and went into the living room, pulling out a pair of latex gloves from his pocket, Rhett right behind him.

The first thing Janzek saw was the Faberge egg on a four-shelf etagere at the center of a wall in the living room. It was on the second shelf down and around it stood other pieces that looked rare and expensive.

"I'll be damned," Janzek said to Rhett, pointing. "That's the Faberge egg that, I'm guessing, was the same one stolen a couple weeks ago. Weird that she'd just leave it out in the open so anyone can see it."

"As far as I know, Ms. Hill never has visitors," volunteered the manager.

"Is that right?" He and Rhett walked up to the egg and studied it.

"That bad boy didn't come out of any chicken I ever saw," Rhett said. "How much do these go for, anyway?"

"Oh, like ten mill, give or take," Janzek guessed, scanning the room.

"I don't get it," Rhett said. "It's nice, but I bet I could make one almost as good in my shop."

Janzek just smiled.

Rhett followed Janzek into the bedroom as the manager stepped up to the etagere with his phone and snapped a few shots of the Faberge egg.

The bedroom was large and beautifully decorated, the centerpiece being a king-size bed with a beige Pratesi duvet and four puffy, monogramed pillows. Off to one side stood a small, antique printer's writing desk and a chair that had a nice view of White Point Garden.

Something on the desk caught Janzek's attention. It was a silver, leather-bound book which had the current year printed in embossed letters.

Janzek picked it up and opened it. Rhett came up behind him.

"Whaddya got?"

"Her daybook." Janzek said, turning pages. "Could be interesting."

"What are you expecting? 'Two a.m., June 12: kill Jamie Swiggett, cut off his dick, and dump him in the park.'"

Janzek turned to Rhett. "It wasn't dumped. It was carefully placed in a sitting position."

"Whatev."

Janzek set the book down on the desk and walked into the

bathroom. It, too, was large, immaculate, and fashionably decorated.

Janzek walked over to the antique claw-foot tub, then, holding the side of it with his gloved hands, got down on his hands and knees. His football knee popped again.

Rhett was right behind him. "What are you look—" Then, it dawned on him as he watched Janzek's eyes carefully scan the surface of the tub.

They spent a full three minutes examining it.

"Not even a speck," Rhett said, finally.

"Yeah, I'm not surprised," Janzek said. "I mean, imagine taking a bath where you just drained ten pints of blood out of a guy."

Rhett nodded. "If this is where it went down, I'm guessing she went through a couple cans of Scrubbling Bubbles."

"That's your brand, huh?"

"Yeah, works like a charm."

Janzek stood up and Rhett followed him back to Tipton's desk, where he picked up the daybook again. He leafed to the page from the day before.

"What are you looking for?" Rhett asked, looking over his shoulder.

"To see what she was up to when Peabo Gardner bought it."

"Gotcha. Well, she had a busy day," Rhett said. "Showing a bunch of houses, looks like."

"Yeah, except for between twelve and two," Janzek said, pointing. "Coulda been a long lunch, I s'pose."

"Or a quick sandwich, then go cut a guy's tongue out," Rhett said. "A tongue sandwich, maybe?"

Janzek turned and looked at his partner. "Come on, man, get serious." He flipped back through pages to the night Jamie

Swiggett was killed. Tipton's last entry was for a five o'clock showing with someone named Donald Knott.

Janzek kept turning the pages. "I'm seeing the name John Paine every Thursday at six."

"Yeah, I noticed."

"I'm guessing a shrink."

Rhett nodded. "Could be."

"I think a conversation with him might be in order."

"Good luck," Rhett said. "Doctor-patient confidentiality."

"I know, but maybe we can get him to make an exception. Particularly if we tell him his patient is going around lopping off guys' body parts."

"Yeah, maybe."

Janzek looked over at the manager, who was pretending not to overhear. "How many penthouse apartments are there in the building?"

"Three."

"And so the one next door is—"

"Morehead Cato's on the right... Billy Hobart's on the left."

FORTY-SIX

Tipton was sure she had covered her tracks with her house on Sullivan's Island. Only her lawyer knew that Sullivan's Island, LLC, was solely owned by her, and he was the most tight-lipped man she'd ever dealt with. Of course, if the word got out that the police were looking for her for murder, he might feel pressured to come forward and tell them she was the owner.

That prospect sent a shiver up her spine. In that moment, she decided to sell the house. Quick as she could. Put a price on it so it would sell fast, then get the hell out of town for good.

BILLY CALLED UP COTTIE MAXWELL, a broker who specialized in Sullivan's Island beachfront houses, and said a friend of his had an awesome house there and wanted to sell it quick. He made up a story about how she was in contract on another house out of town and was eager to sell her Sullivan's Island property in a hurry, close in two or three weeks if possible. Cottie said she knew the house—the old Swiggett house, she referred to it—and said how it had "great bones" but she couldn't make any promises about selling it that fast.

"What if we put a below market price on it?" Billy suggested.

"That would definitely help," Cottie allowed.

"All right, then, do your comps, figure out the value then list it for twenty percent less."

"That should do it," Cottie said. "When can I see it?"

"Hell, right now. The owner'll leave it open for you."

"Are you sure that's okay?" she asked.

"Absolutely. Get back to me with a price later today, then start calling up your buyers."

When Cottie asked if she could meet with the owners to get them to sign the listing, Billy told her it wouldn't be necessary—he had the owner's power of attorney.

JANZEK WAS in the office of Carriage Properties meeting with the owner. Martha Jones-Jones was an all-business woman with absolutely no light touch at all. Or maybe she wasn't used to having a detective in her office, barraging her with questions.

She had already told Janzek that Tipton had been the biggest producer for Carriage Properties over the last seven years, having started there ten years ago. No one worked harder or was more dedicated to her job, she said. Buyers and sellers alike liked her, and Tipton knew Charleston houses and the local real-estate market cold. Jones-Jones said she wished she had ten more agents just like her.

Janzek wasn't sure she'd feel that way once the Faberge-egg discovery went public.

Jones-Jones also volunteered that Tipton had a network of people who referred buyers and sellers to her.

Janzek asked how that referral system worked and she explained that typically an agent pays a "referral fee" for a buyer referral. But it didn't always work that way, she explained, because in some cases referrals are made, but no fee is paid.

"Why wouldn't a referral fee be paid in every case?" he asked.

She smiled. "That's a very good question. I'll give you an example: Tipton has a good friend named Billy Hobart. He's one of her best sources for buyers—and we never cut a check to him." Jones-Jones shrugged. "I'm not quite sure why, to tell you the truth."

Janzek perked up at the mention of Hobart, who was at the top of his list of people to see. He'd figured Hobart might know something about Tipton Hill since they lived in adjoining penthouse apartments. Now he realized they shared a business connection too.

The owner frowned deeply when Janzek asked her if any sellers had ever reported any possessions missing from their house after Tipton had been there.

"Why would you ask that?"

He took out his iPhone and let a photo of the Faberge egg in Hill's apartment answer the question.

Beads of sweat formed instantly on her upper lip, and Jones-Jones started to stammer, but "Oh, my God," was all she could get out. She was no doubt envisioning a future of negative articles in the *Post & Courier*.

"Does Tipton have another house somewhere else? Besides her condo?"

Jones-Jones, clearly still rattled, shook her head. "Not as far as I know, anyway." Then she put up a finger. "No, wait a second... Come to think of it, I heard she's building a vacation place down in Georgia somewhere."

He wrote that in his murder book. "Could you tell me who Tipton's closest friends are, besides Billy Hobart?"

Jones-Jones shrugged. "Not really...all she ever does is work. And work out." Once more, she raised a finger. "Actually, she does have a friend named Kitty. Savage is her last name." She shrugged. "I don't know anything about her, though."

Janzek wrote that down too, stood, and thanked her.

Jones-Jones had a look on her face that suggested she'd soon be going into extreme damage-control mode.

Janzek found Kitty Savage's number on the internet, called her, and was a little surprised when she answered right away. He asked if he could come over and see her about a police matter.

"Sure," she said. "But my house is a little messy."

On his way to see her, Janzek got a call from Delvin Rhett.

"So it seems like half the stuff in Tipton Hill's place is stolen goods," he said.

"Yeah, like what else?"

"Like everything. Those blue and white figurines? They're called Delft and they're rare and expensive. Stolen from a house in Ansonborough during an open house for realtors. I spoke to the owner and she said her broker had like fifty agents come through her house that day."

"So Tipton figured there'd be fifty suspects and she'd get away with it?"

"I guess. And remember those little boxes—there were five of them all in a row?"

"Yeah, I do."

"They're called tea caddies. Same deal: they all disappeared during open houses when there were either lots of agents or lots of buyers going through a house. I found out that real-estate agents who host open houses have a book that everyone's supposed to sign. But sometimes people don't. I'm betting our girl didn't."

"Pretty easy pickings," said Janzek.

"Yeah, plus some for-sale houses just have those lockboxes on them, so any agent can get in at any time. Hell, man, fill up a shopping cart with shit. Nobody'd ever know who it was."

"Wow, I wonder why this doesn't happen more often?"

"I guess most agents aren't kleptos," Rhett said.

"And most sellers don't leave their family jewels in the house they're selling."

"That too. Anyway, the most expensive doo-dad is that egg."

"Doo-dad?"

"Good a word as any."

"A thing you could make in your shop, right?"

"Well, maybe not quite as elaborate," Rhett conceded. "I also found out the owner of the egg was trying to get Chubb, his insurance company, to pay him twelve million for it."

"You're about to make a lot of new friends, Delvin."

"How's that?"

"Tellin' 'em you found their lost shit."

"I don't know about that. Judging by the owner of the egg, guy named Lucian Wiedemann, they might be happier with a nice, fat insurance check."

"I hear you," Janzek said, stopping in front of Kitty Savage's house on Lamboll Street. "Okay, Del, I'm at this woman's house now, friend of Tipton's. Talk later."

"I'm very jealous."

"Why?"

"You're always hangin' at some woman's house?"

KITTY SAVAGE LIVED in a Charleston single that had all the classic exterior details from another era—the 1780s, in this case. Her decorating, however, came straight out of the 1950s. As she led him through the house, he noticed a profusion of pastel-painted rooms—mint green, turquoise, and pale yellow were only three of the colors. The dining room featured vinyl chairs and a chrome-legged table. Something told him she had gone for retro-chic but, to his mind, fallen woefully short. The Formica-top table in the living room cinched it.

They went out to her overgrown backyard and sat in rickety teak chairs that looked ten years older than Kitty Savage herself, who Janzek guessed was in her early 30s. She wore a tight black gym outfit and yellow Nikes.

"Why do you want to know about Tipton?" she asked.

His stock answer to questions like that always went something like: *I'm interviewing as many people as possible about a case of mine.* He took out his murder book and chose to go with a variation on that theme: "I just have a few routine questions about a case."

"And what case is that?" she asked.

"Several homicides, actually."

"That means murder, right?"

Oh, God, really?

"Yes. A woman at Carriage Properties said you and Ms. Hill are very good friends. When did you see her last?"

"Just yesterday. We take a yoga class together."

"And when is it? The class?"

"Seven in the morning."

He wrote it down. "And, Ms. Savage, what can you tell me about Ms. Hill's past? You know...where she grew up, went to school, stuff like that."

Kitty Savage scratched her head and stared blankly at a Spanish-moss-covered tree. "You know, for someone I consider one of my best friends, I don't really know that much about her. I mean, she's smart as a whip, beautiful—obviously—and is a really good friend, but unlike most women I know, she doesn't talk about herself much. Hardly at all, in fact."

Janzek wasn't surprised. "Do you know where she grew up or went to college, by any chance?"

"Sorry, I couldn't tell you. A good one, though, I'd say, 'cause she seems to know a lot about a lot. She mentioned growing up in a small town a couple times. In the south somewhere, I think."

"Georgia, maybe?"

"Could be Georgia, though I don't remember her ever saying that."

"So, she never mentioned building a vacation home in Georgia?"

Kitty shook her head. "Not that I remember."

Janzek was ninety percent sure but still sought confirmation that Tipton was the same woman—girl, actually—who had been raped by the three boys fifteen years before. Tipton Hill and Jenny Riles became the same person. He knew it. But he still didn't have conclusive proof.

He sat up straight in the uncomfortable wooden chair. "In the time that you've known her, has she had a boyfriend or a man she went out with?"

Kitty put her hand on her chin and leaned forward slightly. "Are these really routine questions? They strike me as kind of... *unusual.*"

She wasn't as dumb as he thought.

"I'm just trying to get a complete picture of her."

Kitty nodded, clearly skeptical. "She went out with men. But I'm not sure about the rest of the equation...if you know what I mean."

"You mean, had sex with them?"

193

Kitty's head snapped back. "Well, yes, in so many words. I don't get the idea that she's super interested in *that.*" Suddenly, his witness seemed to be gathering conversational steam. "I kind of got the sense that there was maybe a little of the...wounded bird to Tip."

"Interesting," he said. "Any idea where that might have come from? I mean, did she ever talk about anything...traumatic?"

Kitty shrugged. "No, she didn't. She's just so damned private."

Janzek turned away from her and looked up at the steeple of a nearby church. "Would you say she got along with men? I mean... she didn't have a problem with men generally speaking... did she?"

Kitty waited for him to look back at her. "Those sound like shrink questions."

He smiled. "I guess I ask all kinds. Did she?"

"No, she got along fine with men. I mean, you can't be the best realtor in town and *not.* Right? Maybe the right guy just hasn't come along." She shrugged again. "I honestly don't know."

"Did she ever talk about her family?"

"Just her brother once in a while."

Janzek's eyes bored into hers. Verna Riles had never mentioned anything about a son.

"Her brother? What was his name?"

"I forget. Something common like Richard or William, I think." Kitty said. "You know, I'm a little uncomfortable telling you all this about Tipton. I'm not sure I'd like it if she was telling you all this about me. In fact, I know I wouldn't."

Which was okay with Janzek because he had gotten all he needed. Besides, he was dying to call Verna Riles now. He got to his feet. "I understand, Ms. Savage. And I really appreciate you meeting with me on such short notice. If Ms. Hill calls you, will you call me right away? I really need to speak to her."

"Sure. I'll be seeing her at spin class tomorrow morning if I don't speak to her before."

Don't count on it, Janzek thought.

FORTY-SEVEN

BILLY HOBART WAS CLEARLY NOT THRILLED TO GET A CALL from Janzek. He told Janzek he was really busy, had no time to spare.

Janzek said he only needed five minutes, which was bull-shit because he planned to question him for a lot longer than that.

Billy responded with another person-of-interest classic: "Why can't we just do it on the phone?"

Janzek explained that he had some pictures and needed to see if Billy could identify them. Also a lie, because the only photos Janzek had were of the things in Tipton Hill's apart-ment, which he was now 100% sure were stolen.

Janzek had two reasons for wanting to see Billy in the flesh: First, to look him in the eye as he answered his questions and see if he could spot a tell. Second, to see whether he could coax any intel out of Billy face-to-face. He was less optimistic about the latter.

Billy finally sighed and gave in. "Okay, I'm on a treadmill at the gym in the Fort Sumter house. Why don't you come on over now?"

Janzek thanked Billy, tempted to ask if he could meet him at the front door so he didn't have to deal with the cranky manager again.

On the way to the Fort Sumter house, Janzek dialed Verna Riles. As usual, it rang and rang but, a second before he was about to hang up, she answered.

He came right out with it and asked her if she had any other children besides her daughter Jenny. Verna said no, Jenny was an only child. He thanked her and asked if she knew whether Jenny had had any dental work done after leaving Thomasville. Verna said she didn't think so because her daughter really had a thing about being touched by doctors or dentists. Well, actually, anybody for that matter, she added. He thanked her and parked around the corner from the Sumter House.

The manager came to the door with his trademark humorless expression. "I don't know, detective," he said, "maybe you should start paying rent here."

The cranky, old bastard actually had a sense of humor. Feeble though it was.

"Yeah, I probably should," Janzek said. "I'm meeting Mr. Hobart in the gym."

"Follow me," the manager said. They went inside the lobby, turned a corner, and the manager pointed to a closed door. "In there."

"Thanks," Janzek said and went in.

The bare-bones gym was in a small room, the kind you'd see in medium-sized hotels. It had two elliptical machines, two treadmills, a few mats on the floor, and some free weights that didn't exceed twenty pounds.

Billy Hobart was working up a pretty good sweat on a

treadmill. He saw Janzek, nodded and turned off the treadmill. It slowed then stopped and he got off it, grabbed a towel off the arm of a nearby elliptical, and swabbed his face.

Janzek couldn't help remembering his conversation with Sheila Lessing. For a walker, gigolo, or asexual man—whatever Billy was—he was in phenomenal shape. He had quite a large chest, though Janzek couldn't see much definition because Billy was wearing a loose-fitting sweatshirt, but his legs were chiseled and sculpted beneath his basketball shorts. It also occurred to Janzek that Billy's legs were hairless. He wondered if maybe that was a walker thing....

Billy caught him staring.

"Okay, detective, I really am in a big hurry. Your five minutes just started."

"What can you tell me about Tipton Hill?"

Billy toweled the back of his neck. "What do you want to know?"

"The owner of Carriage Properties told me that you refer a lot of people to her."

"Yeah, I do. So what?"

"Why do you do that?"

Billy tilted his head and looked mildly irritated. "Well, no offense, detective, but that's kind of a dumb question. I recommend her because she's the best real-estate agent in Charleston. And 'cause we make money together."

Janzek nodded. "But you don't get a referral fee for referring her."

"No, I don't, 'cause she makes up for it in other ways," Billy said. "See, for one thing, she tells me right away about houses that have just come on the market. Which means I get first look. She also advises me, tells me sometimes not to buy a house when I've got my checkbook out and am ready to pull the trigger. Or, the other way around, tells me sometimes to make an offer when I'm not that psyched about a house. I guess you could say she's my real-estate consultant."

"I understand. Have you seen Ms. Hill recently?"

"No, not in a few days. What is this, detective? First, I'm your murder suspect until it turns out your key eyewitness is a raging alcoholic. Now it's Tipton?"

"I didn't say anything about her being a suspect. I just want to talk to her."

Billy nodded and smiled a knowing smile. The man had cheekbones and teeth like a runway model.

"Have you ever met her brother?" Janzek asked.

The smile disappeared and the muscles around his mouth tightened. "Brother? Since when does she have a brother?"

"I just heard she did."

"I don't know anything about a brother. Weren't you going to show me some photos?"

Janzek reached into the breast pocket of his jacket. "Oh, yeah, thanks for reminding me," he said, unfolding the picture of the Faberge egg for Billy. "Have you ever seen this before?"

Billy moved his head closer. "Yeah, actually I have."

"Where?"

"On the front page of the *Post & Courier*. That's the egg that got stolen a week ago, right?"

"So you never saw it anywhere else?"

"No."

"Not in Tipton Hill's apartment?"

"No."

"You sure?"

"'Course I'm sure, 'cause I've never been to Tipton's apartment."

"But it's next door to yours."

"So? I've never been to the guy's on the other side either."

"I just figured—"

"Look, our relationship is strictly business. Everything we do takes place at her office or on the phone. Now, no offense, detective, but I want to finish up here."

"Okay, thanks for your time. You ever go to the gym at MUSC?"

"Nah, this place is good enough for me," Billy said.

Janzek nodded and turned for the door, wishing his building had a gym. Even a lame one like this.

FORTY-EIGHT

BACK AT THE STATION, AS JANZEK WAS WALKING PAST Rhett's office, Rhett, who was on the phone, gave him a wave and motioned him into his office. Janzek walked in and sat down. A few seconds later, Rhett hung up the phone.

"Holy shit, man," Rhett said, all jacked up. "So I'm looking into this Sarah Rentschler business—you know, the woman who had the fire at her house?—and find out a whole bunch of crazy shit."

"Define 'crazy shit,' Delvin."

Rhett stroked his Fu Manchu. "First, Rentschler's lawyer filed a lawsuit alleging that MiraBill Properties, LLC, sold her a house that had all kinds of problems. MiraBill Properties turns out to be, guess who? Billy Hobart, along with some society bimbo."

"Yeah, I know who you mean," Janzek said, putting his feet up on Rhett's desk. "Sheila Lessing mentioned it."

"But with Exhibit A burned to the ground, now Rentschler can't prove anything."

"I hear you," Janzek said. "Seems like a pretty drastic solution to a problem, wouldn't ya say?"

"Yeah, but think about this," Rhett said. "If Sarah Rentschler wins the lawsuit, Billy Hobart's reputation and business go up in smoke... so to speak."

"Yeah." Janzek nodded. "That's pretty interesting. What other crazy shit you got?"

"So in the course of my usual incredibly thorough investigation, I also found out Sarah Rentschler's been active in the real-estate biz in more ways than just buying herself a new house."

"Oh, yeah, what else?"

"On the Charleston County website I found out that an entity called SYR Properties not only took title to that house on Atlantic but, lo and behold, bought up about ten other houses in Charleston. So, I poked around a little more and found out that they're all smack in the middle of the Colonial Lake area."

It didn't click with Janzek. "I don't get it."

"Think about what's goin' on over there, Nick."

It clicked. "Smart," he said. "She's capitalizing on Sheila Lessing donating all that money for the development of Colonial Lake. Really smart, actually, 'cause once all the work's done there, those houses are gonna be worth a hell of a lot more."

"Exactly," Rhett said. "So I dug a little bit more and found out that's not all she bought. She also bought and closed on—really, really fast—two big parcels in a little hole-in-the-wall hamlet called Pasco. Couple thousand acres there, in fact, and guess who owns the land right next door?"

"I don't need to guess. I know," Janzek said. "Sheila Lessing."

"Bingo bango."

"But, the question is, what the hell'd Rentschler buy that Pasco land for? I mean, I've been down there and all they got are a bunch of strawberry fields and good old boys drivin' around in beater pick-ups."

"Don't be such a Yankee snob," Rhett said. "That's God's country."

"God's briar patch," Janzek said. "You did some good diggin', Del. Anything else?"

"Jesus, isn't that enough?" Rhett said. "How about you? What you got?"

"At this point, just exhaust fumes…a suspect who blew town in a hurry."

Rhett nodded.

"No sign of her car, nobody knows much about her, and she could be anywhere now. A million miles away or holed up a few doors down."

"So what do we do?"

"Well, I got Craven and Dutton out at the airport, getting copies of her picture out to the TSA people and cops there, and Bridges went to the train and bus stations, though I don't see Tipton pounding the hound. Aside from that, I've been going around talking to people and keepin' an eye out for a woman in a baseball cap drivin' a silver Beamer."

"She'll turn up," Rhett said.

"I don't know, man." Janzek said. "I got a meeting with that shrink of hers. See if I shake something out of him."

"Good luck."

"I'll need it."

JANZEK CALLED RHETT LATER.

"You were right."

His conversation with Dr. Robert Paine had lasted less than five minutes. He started by telling Paine that his patient,

Tipton Hill, was a suspect in the killing of three men in Charleston and possibly a woman in Philadelphia twelve years before.

Paine couldn't have been more polite but said he could not, and would not, divulge anything about any conversation with any of his patients. End of story.

Janzek had simply thanked him and left.

"Well," Rhett said, "I guess you'll be gettin' a bill for two hundred bucks. Hope it was worth it."

FORTY-NINE

THE CASE WAS STONE COLD. LIKE A GRAVESTONE IN A Boston winter.

Rhett was in Janzek's office, talking it over.

They didn't know what more they could do besides go house-to-house to every residence within a hundred miles of downtown Charleston. They figured a hundred miles was as far as Tipton would get by car before realizing there would be a BOLO—be on the lookout for—posted with every law enforcement agency in South Carolina. If she'd left by car, she'd know they were looking for her, and she wouldn't be driving the silver BMW for long.

They ran through other scenarios. One was that she could park the BMW in a garage near a car rental place and rent a car. But they ran a search for her name and license, and nothing showed up. They guessed she wouldn't be flying, because chances were good she'd either be spotted or her name would pop up. That left escape by sea. Possible, they agreed, but not probable.

Which meant, chances were, she was holed up somewhere.

Janzek got a call on his cell. It was Sheila Lessing.

"Hi, Sheila."

"So what's this I hear about Tipton Hill?"

"I don't know. What do you hear?" Janzek put her on speaker, so Rhett could listen in.

"One, you're trying to find her, and two, a small fortune of stolen stuff was found in her apartment," Sheila said. "Actually make that a *large* fortune. That missing Faberge egg, among other things."

"You got good sources. Can I come over and talk to you? I also found out something else that I think you're gonna be very interested in hearing."

"Of course. I've missed our little chats, and it's been two whole days without your relentless badgering."

"Oh, I'll make up for it," he said. "Okay if I stop by after lunch?"

"Why don't you stop by *for* lunch. I'll whip up something."

"Okay, thanks. Is twelve thirty good?"

"Perfect, see you then."

Rhett gave him a little smile and leaned back in his chair.

"Girl's got a little sneaker for you, Nick."

"Oh, please."

"*Oh Nicky, I've missed our little chats....*"

"Cut the bullshit," Janzek said. "And she didn't say, *Oh Nicky.*"

Janzek, fighting a smile, got up and headed for the door.

Rhett chuckled. "Go have a nice cucumber sandwich... with your lady friend."

JANZEK FIGURED Sheila would want to know about her friend Sarah Rentschler's land purchase in Pasco.

She was more than interested; she was in total disbelief and shock.

"You gotta be kidding."

"Nope. She closed on one parcel a week ago and the other one just two days ago."

"That is *in-credible,*" Sheila said, shaking her head. "You know, when you think about it, what she did is kind of like insider trading." Janzek nodded. "I told her I was donating a bunch of money for the Colonial Lake development, like, three months ago. Way before the news went public."

"Which gave her plenty of time to buy up everything she could get her hands on around there," Janzek said. "My partner found out she used an agent who basically went door-to-door for her, to every house in Colonial Lake, asking owners if they wanted to sell."

"And she bought how many houses?"

"Ten, I heard."

Sheila shook her head. "The agent she used...it wasn't Tipton Hill, was it?"

"No, someone from Daniel Ravenel."

"Then she does the exact same thing in Pasco," Sheila said, shaking her head. "Which actually makes sense, now that we know her game. I told her about the big Hyundai deal before it hit the papers. Obviously, she figured land there would be a hell of a lot more valuable after the news broke."

"She figured right. Right?"

Sheila nodded.

"Smart woman," Janzek said.

"Unethical woman. Sleazy woman. Who knew? I never sensed that side of her."

"So what are you gonna do?"

"Cross her off my list of friends."

"That's it?"

"What else can I do? She didn't do anything illegal. She just exploited a friendship. You don't go to jail for that."

"Have you heard anything more about the arson at her house?" Janzek asked.

"I was just going to ask you the same thing."

Janzek shrugged. "I've just heard the guys workin' it haven't come up with anything yet. A theory or two, but nothing solid. No suspects either."

"You and your colleagues sure have been busy lately."

Janzek snorted a laugh.

"What?" Sheila asked.

"Colleagues. That has a nice ring to it, but isn't that what lawyers call each other?"

"Uh, yeah."

"Well, don't throw us in with that pack of jackals, *please*."

FIFTY

Rhett called Janzek in the middle of the night.

"This better be good, Del," Janzek growled.

"They found Tipton Hill's car."

"Where?"

"Abandoned in the middle of the Ravenel Bridge."

"You're shitting me," Janzek said, clicking on his bedside lamp and looking at his clock. It was ten past three.

"I don't make crank calls at this hour, Nick."

"I'll meet you there in fifteen."

"Okay," Rhett said. "But what do you think?"

"Shit, I don't know, man, I was in the middle of a really good dream. But my first reaction...she faked it."

"Yeah, me, too."

WHEN JANZEK ARRIVED a little before 3:30 a.m., he saw black and whites from both Charleston and Mount Pleasant plus two helicopters below the level of the bridge, hovering with search lights covering wide circles of the choppy, black water. A small orange and white Coast Guard craft was searching the waters directly below the bridge.

Janzek drove up behind Rhett's car.

"They find anything?" Janzek asked as they walked over to the edge of the bridge.

"I saw a guy in the boat fish something out of the water."

"Not a body, though."

"No, something small. Don't know what."

"What is it, like two hundred feet to the water?" Janzek asked.

"Yeah, right around there," Rhett said. "I think there've been like ten or twelve jumpers since they built it back in 2005. One or two survived."

"Anybody see anything?"

"I talked to the first guy on scene—a Mount Pleasant cop. He said no."

Janzek turned and walked toward the silver BMW. People wearing crime-scene jackets and gloves were inside the car— one in the front, two in back. The area was taped off, though there weren't going to be too many gawking pedestrians at this time of night.

Janzek flashed his ID to a Mt. Pleasant uniform outside of the car. "I got a warrant for this woman. Was there a note or anything?"

The uniform shook his head. "Not that I know of."

"And nobody saw anything?"

"The guy who phoned it in said he saw a woman get out and head for the side of the bridge."

"Yeah, then what?"

"He said he pulled over and put the call in to us," the uniform said. "By the time he looked again, she was gone."

"But he didn't see her jump?"

"No."

"And no one else did?"

The uniform shook his head.

TWO HOURS LATER, all the Coast Guard had found was a neon canary yellow Teva sneaker that had gotten caught along the edge of the Cooper River just downstream of the bridge. It turned out that the Mount Pleasant police had jurisdiction covering the southbound lanes of the bridge and Charleston police the northbound lanes. An hour later, having found no body and no car keys in the ignition, they towed the car. Then all the cops and crime-scene techs left, and they reopened the bridge.

Janzek asked the tech who had bagged the sneaker if he could borrow it and return it to her later that morning. She started to balk, so he laid on the Janzek charm. She finally agreed and asked him to get it back to her by ten that morning.

A half hour later, Rhett was following Janzek to the Fort Sumter house on King Street. It was 6:30 a.m., so they had made a quick pit stop at Dunkin' Donuts along the way.

Janzek parked in front and Rhett pulled up behind him.

Janzek reached for the bagged Teva sneaker on the passenger seat along with their Dunkin' Donuts purchases, got out and waited for Rhett. Rhett exited his car and walked up to him.

"Manager's gonna be real happy to see our smiling faces at this hour," Rhett said.

"That's why I got him the jelly donut," Janzek said. "The way to all men's hearts."

Janzek pushed the button for the manager. A minute later

the tall, bald man appeared. He saw Janzek and Rhett and rolled his eyes. But, at least, he opened the door.

"Top of the morning to you," Janzek said. "I got this for you."

He opened the bag, "Thanks," the man said, smile-free. "But I had breakfast."

"You sure?"

"Yeah," he said, eyeing the bag with the sneaker. "What can I do for you this time?"

"Gonna need to get into Ms. Hill's apartment again," Janzek told him.

The manager spun on his heel and led them to the elevators. Inside, the manager turned to Janzek.

"I might as well give you a key to the building," he said.

His feeble humor was back.

"Might as well." Janzek smiled.

The three of them got out, walked down the hall, and reached the door of Tipton Hill's apartment. The manager opened it and the three went in.

In the bedroom, Janzek opened the walk-in closet. He crouched, picked up a white Nike, and compared it to the yellow Teva sneaker. They looked to be the same size. He looked inside one of the Nikes: seven and a half, exactly like the Teva.

He looked up at Rhett, who shrugged and smiled. "If the sneaker fits, you must convict."

FIFTY-ONE

Janzek and Rhett walked out of the Fort Sumter House. It was six forty-five a.m.

"What do you make of the whole bridge thing?" Rhett asked.

Janzek didn't hesitate. "I think she tossed the sneaker over the side and beat it out of there on foot."

"But nobody saw her walking off the bridge."

"Yeah, I know, but nobody was looking for her, either. And it was three in the morning," Janzek said. "Someone dressed in black, in a hoodie or something, walking down that bridge would be pretty invisible."

"Yeah, I guess. Plus, there was only the one witness who passed by around that time. Smart woman. Where do you think she went?"

"If she was on foot, I'd guess back to wherever she's hiding out," Janzek said. "Hey, by the way, did you put a trace on her credit and debit cards like we talked about."

"Sure did. Nada. Probably got a stash of cash."

Just then, Janzek saw Torborg in running clothes coming

down King. She saw him a block away and waved. He waved back.

"What little I know about Tipton Hill," Janzek said, "is she's sure not the profile of a suicide."

Rhett nodded as Torborg huffed and puffed up to them.

"Hey, boys. Out fighting crime at the crack of dawn, huh?"

"Never stops," Rhett said, "How's it going, Torborg?"

"Good, thanks," then to Janzek, "I think this is where I left you last time I saw you."

"Yeah, never left," he said with a grin.

"All right," Rhett said, turning toward his car. "Well, I'm outta here. See you back at the station, Nick. Nice seeing ya, Torborg."

"Same," she said, as Rhett walked away. "So, how are you?" she asked Janzek.

"Busy. Got a wake-up call at three o'clock this morning."

"Oh, God, really?"

Janzek nodded.

"So that's your excuse for not calling?"

"Sorry, it's just been non-stop," he said.

"Well, you know how to reach me." She leaned forward and kissed him, "Gotta run...literally."

Janzek watched as she ran past the bench where Jamie Swiggett's body had been found, then over the macadam until she disappeared into the trees of White Point Gardens.

She even ran sexy.

FIFTY-TWO

SECURITY CAMERAS DEFINITELY MADE THE JOB EASIER.

In this case, they were called 'tag readers.' Cameras positioned on the Charleston side of the Ravenel Bridge to do exactly what the name said: read the license plates of cars as they went over to the bridge to Mount Pleasant.

Only problem was, from the hours of midnight to three AM on the morning when Tipton's Teva sneaker was found, her license plate, B114S, was not one of the ones identified by the tag reader.

That could only mean one thing: Tipton came from the Mount Pleasant side of the bridge. Sure enough, after going through two hours of license-plate scans from that side, Janzek finally came across B114S. The timestamp said 2:14 AM. His first thought was that she had gone over the bridge from the Mt. Pleasant side, then U-turned and went back over from the Charleston side. But since there was nothing on the Charleston tag reader, he deduced that she must have just backed down the bridge in the breakdown lane.

That narrowed the search area for her hideout, but not by

much. Mt. Pleasant was not only a big area—fifty square miles with more than twenty thousand "housing units"—but beyond it, you could access the rest of South Carolina and, for that matter, the rest of the country.

Sometimes there were no shortcuts and no one else you could trust to do your investigative grunt work. Rhett had his hands full at the moment, so Janzek decided the only thing to do was to go through the tedious process of looking through every strategically positioned tag reader on the Mount Pleasant side of the Ravenel Bridge. The two feeds onto the Ravenel Bridge were from Coleman Boulevard and Johnnie Dodds Boulevard, also known as Route 17. So, the first question was, from which of the two did Tipton Hill come onto the bridge? With the help of the Mount Pleasant police, Janzek gained access to the DVR machines and went through them one license plate at a time.

After four long hours of looking at license plates, he hit the jackpot and spotted Tipton's plate. She had driven onto the bridge via Coleman Avenue. That narrowed things down a little.

Janzek theorized that a woman who made a million dollars a year was most likely hanging her hat in one of the more toney neighborhoods. The most logical ones would be the Old Village in Mount Pleasant or Sullivan's Island, both accessed from Coleman Boulevard.

Janzek struck out with the Old Village but lucked out on the short bridge over to Sullivan's Island. Tipton's license plate had registered on the tag reader. The time stamp said 2:02 AM. Janzek thought he had just narrowed his search to 2.4 square miles and fewer than a thousand houses until he realized that there was another bridge that connected Sullivan's Island to Isle of Palms. The good news was, yet another tag reader showed that Tipton Hill's silver BMW had never crossed the bridge from Isle of Palms.

Janzek dropped in on the Sullivan's Island police chief at their headquarters behind the fire department on Middle Street.

Dale Cooper was a big man who reminded Janzek of his partner up in Boston. Deliberate and restrained, a man of few words.

When Janzek showed him a photo of Tipton Hill, Cooper had no recollection of ever having seen her and knew he had never met her.

"And she's someone I'd definitely remember," Cooper said. "So you're saying she was the jumper?"

"No, I'm saying she's the *alleged* jumper, but she never jumped. She faked it."

"Really? But they found something in the water?"

"Yeah, a sneaker, but no body or other clothes. I got a strong suspicion she's somewhere on Sullivan's right now."

"Well, I'm ready to help you any way I can, but we got over a thousand houses, condos and apartments here and just six uniforms and one detective," Cooper said. "You're not lookin' to do a house-to-house, are you?"

"No, man, nothing like that," Janzek said. "I just wanted to give you and your guys some photos of her. Just be on the lookout for her, keep a photo in your squad cars maybe."

"Yeah, sure, no problem. What did she do, anyway?"

Janzek put his hand on his chin. "What we know she did? Or what we think she did?"

"Both."

"We know she stole a bunch of really valuable stuff. Millions of dollars' worth. Probably been doing it over the course of a couple of years. What we *think* she did…. Well, let's see: Strangled a guy to death, beat a guy to death, stabbed a guy to death."

Cooper whistled. "No shit. Sounds like a hell of a dangerous woman."

Janzek nodded. "Oh, I forgot one: burned a woman to death up in Philadelphia."

FIFTY-THREE

CHIEF DALE COOPER SAID HE'D BE HAPPY FOR SOME HELP from Charleston PD when Janzek proposed it. Janzek had gotten Ernie Brindle to let him sprinkle a handful of undercovers around the streets of Sullivan's Island. They made the rounds from food stores to restaurants to gas stations, showing photos of Tipton Hill. They also positioned themselves at stop signs and red lights in case Tipton Hill had another car she was driving around in. Not long into the search, a shopkeeper and a checkout clerk at Publix reported having seen Tipton a few days before, but neither had any idea where she lived.

It was a start, anyway.

Janzek himself had staked out a corner on Sullivan's Island. It was at Jasper Boulevard and Route 703. He logged four hours there. He had seen a lot of drivers not come to full stops, one gentle fender-bender, and a dog almost get clipped by a car, but no Tipton Hill.

As it started to get dark, he was starting his cruiser and ready to call it a day when he looked up and saw Billy Hobart in a black Mercedes at the stop sign. Billy was looking straight ahead, lost in thought.

As Billy pulled away from the stop sign, Janzek decided to follow him. Billy went straight for five blocks, then turned left where the street dead-ended. He drove three blocks with the beach on his right, then swung into a driveway on his right. The house had a For Sale sign that said Handsome Properties. Janzek drove past and punched the name and number of the real-estate agent into the memory on his phone.

It flashed through his mind to knock on the door of the house... could Tipton Hill possibly be holed up there? If so, Billy Hobart would demand to see a warrant and he didn't feel he had enough for probable cause.

So, he pulled over and called the Handsome Properties agent. As she was launching into a long-winded explanation why the six-bedroom, four-and-a-half-million-dollar house on the ocean would no doubt be perfect for him, he cut her short and told her he was a single cop. She was clearly disappointed by that news and claimed she didn't know who the home's owner was. A man named Billy Hobart had power-of-attorney and was acting on the owner's behalf, she explained.

Janzek called Rhett and asked him to go access the Charleston County tax records and look up the owner. Meanwhile, Janzek needed to go back to Tipton Hill's apartment at the Fort Sumter House to check something out. Yet again.

He drove off of Sullivan's Island, through Mount Pleasant, over the Ravenel Bridge, and into Charleston. He parked in front of the King Street building and pressed the buzzer for the manager. Another man opened the door—the assistant manager, evidently. Relieved, Janzek showed him ID and explained that he needed access to Tipton Hill's apartment. The man didn't balk; they rode up the elevator and he let Janzek in.

As he went inside, he got a call on his cell from Rhett.

"Yeah, Del, what's up?"

"Can't help you with the name of the owner of that Sullivan's Island house," Rhett said. "All I got is Sullivan's Island, LLC."

"Is there an address or anything?"

"Just a p.o. box."

"That's no help," Janzek said.

"But, in the meantime, I might have something just as good."

"What's that?"

"James Livingston Swiggett sold the house to Sullivan's Island, LLC."

"Well, I'll be damned," Janzek said. "As in, the father of the recently deceased James Bryant Swiggett?"

"Yup. That's the guy."

THE ASSISTANT MANAGER said he'd wait until Janzek was done to lock up Hill's apartment and went and sat in the living room. Janzek went into Hill's second bedroom/home office and found what he was looking for after a fifteen-minute search. It was an unmarked file at the very back of a file drawer. In it was a contract from a few years back for the purchase of Jamie Swiggett's father's Sullivan's Island house.

In another file next to it were documents for another real-estate purchase. The file was marked Thomasville Property, LLC. Once again, James Livingston Swiggett was the seller. It was dated six years before and documented the purchase of 543 acres of land. Janzek filled in the blanks: she bought only the land because the majestic plantation home on it had burned to the ground the year before. Janzek also realized that the seller—James Livingston Swiggett—had no idea who the buyer was because the title for the land had been taken in the name of Thomasville Property, LLC.

Janzek dialed Rhett.

"Okay, I just went through Tipton Hill's files," Janzek said. "She bought Jamie Swiggett's old man's house on Sullivan's. But get this: she also bought his plantation land down in Thomasville, Georgia."

"Ho-ly shit."

"Yeah," Janzek said. "Hey, do me a favor, get me a warrant to get into the house on Sullivan's, will you? Call me as soon as you get it. I want to go there right after I see Sheila Lessing."

"You got it."

"Good. I'll meet you there."

"You think she's at that house, Nick?"

"Could be," Janzek said. "Maybe her friend Billy Hobart, too." He clicked off and walked out into the living room, where the assistant manager was reading a magazine.

"I'm just going to use the bathroom for a second, then I'm done," Janzek said.

The assistant manager nodded as Janzek opened a door. But, as Janzek knew, it did not go to a bathroom.

Instead it opened up into a large living room, which he recognized because he'd been there twice before.

It was Billy Hobart's living room.

Suddenly, all the pieces fell into place.

FIFTY-FOUR

SHEILA LESSING SAID SURE, COME RIGHT OVER, BUT SHE had to be at her office in an hour. A conference call, she said.

Janzek pulled up to her house on Tradd St. five minutes later.

"Hey," she said, opening the door, "You look like you just won the lottery."

"What do you mean?" Janzek asked, following her in.

"I don't know," Sheila said, "Your eyes are all lit up."

"That's from seeing you."

Sheila turned and smiled. "You are smooth, Nick. I'll give you that. Want to sit?"

"I can't. Sorry, I've got to get somewhere," he said. "Let me get right to the point."

"You always do."

Janzek smiled. "Billy Hobart. I have a few more questions about him."

Sheila scrunched up her eyes for a second. "I thought we covered him."

"Just a few things we didn't talk about. How would you describe him?"

"Well, I'd describe Billy as...one of Charleston's many oddities."

"How so?"

Sheila ran her hand through her hair and looked out the window. "I would have said, he's one of the most clever people around at making flawed houses into masterpieces...until that whole thing with Sarah Rentschler. But, actually, I take that back; I think the problem there was Sarah, not Billy. What I heard was that she was all over him to get the job done and he had to take a few shortcuts. So, I'm sticking with what I said: he has an incredible knack for making silk purses out of sows' ears."

"Okay, but I'm not hearing the odd part yet," Janzek said.

"I was just getting to that."

"Before you do, I have a strange question for you."

"What's that?"

"Have you ever seen Billy and Tipton Hill together?"

Sheila laughed. "You're right. That *is* a strange question."

"But have you?"

Sheila thought for a second.

"I'm probably not the person to ask. I kind of travel in different circles. But why—"

"Do you know why Jamie Swiggett's father sold his house on Sullivan's Island?"

"Jesus, Nick, you're giving me whiplash, switching from one subject to the next."

"Sorry, but why?"

Her eyes circled the room and came back to him and, slowly, reluctantly at first, she told him the story.

Jim Swiggett, the father, had lost all his money. Gone from a rich man to one who had to live with his son, daughter-in-law, and their children in a nondescript Tudor house in a so-so neighborhood on James Island.

Swiggett had been senior partner in an old, prestigious law firm started by his father, when he was charged with having sex with an underage girl—sixteen years old, to be precise. He and his wife—their children had grown up and moved out—lived in a large house on the water on Sullivan's Island and their cook and housekeeper lived on the third floor with her young daughter.

One day, when Swiggett's wife was away visiting her sister in Savannah, the girl's mother contacted the police and said her daughter had been molested by Jim Swiggett on numerous occasions, but most recently, when she had gone out to get groceries. Upon questioning, it came out that Swiggett had been allegedly molesting the young girl for a long time. The police found a drawerful of little blue boxes from Tiffany in the girl's bedroom. Jim Swiggett had also given her rings, diamond earrings and clothes from King Street shops.

It was a story that had a long shelf life in the *Post & Courier*, as details leaked out one by one.

Almost immediately, Swiggett's law firm, Swiggett & Weekes, started losing clients. Several of their attorneys quit, including three who were highly profitable for the firm. Within six months, the firm had lost ninety percent of their billings and Jim Swiggett was a haunted, hollow, tortured man. Then, his plantation in Georgia was burned to the ground, some thought by someone who didn't want a pedophile living in their town. Then his wife left him. Several months after that, the bank foreclosed on the Sullivan's Island house, where he was spending his days watching soap operas on TV and drinking Jim Beam while awaiting trial.

But eight months later, it was revealed that the girl, sixteen at the time, had made the whole thing up. It was all a colossally sadistic, elaborate lie. A young woman, thought to be in her late twenties, had approached the girl's mother and offered to pay her fifty thousand dollars—which she subsequently did—if the woman would coach her daughter to tell the sordid story in vivid detail to the police and then a jury. The girl's mother told the police she had no idea who the young woman was, and she was never found or identified.

Exoneration had finally come to Jim Swiggett. But it didn't matter.

He was not only broke, he was broken.

FIFTY-FIVE

Janzek thanked Sheila and left quickly. He ran to his car and dialed Rhett.

"Did you get it?" Janzek asked when Rhett picked up.

"No, man," Rhett said. "I'm having trouble tracking down the judge."

"Shit," Janzek said, pounding his steering wheel. "Well, keep trying. I'm gonna go to the house on Sullivan's Island. Oh, and Del? For the record, Tipton Hill and Billy Hobart are the same person."

BILLY HOBART'S Audi was still in the driveway of the Sullivan's Island beach house with the For Sale sign in front. Janzek got out of his car and went and pressed the buzzer on the front door. He waited for a minute, then knocked on the door. Nothing. He pressed the buzzer again but got no response.

He walked around the house, looking into windows, but didn't see a thing. The back yard opened up to a jaw-dropping

227

view of the ocean with a tanker in the far distance. So, this was what $4.5 mil got you in Sullivan's Island, he thought.

Pretty damned nice.

He knocked hard on the back door. Again, nothing.

He put his hand on the doorknob and turned it. It was not locked.

He opened it a few feet.

"Charleston police, anyone home?" he called.

No response.

He stepped inside and heard a rustling sound behind him, then felt a sharp pain to his head.

Then everything went black.

FIFTY-SIX

Janzek's eyes opened to a pair of dark purple Wellies. He knew they were called Wellies because his wife had had a pair. They sat two feet away from him, on the floor alongside a pair of yellow Nikes and L.L. Bean boots. He realized he was in the mud room of the house he had entered. Tipton Hill and Billy Hobart's home.

His head was killing him as he struggled to get up, then looked out the window at the ocean. He reached for his Sig Sauer but realized it was not in his shoulder holster.

Not good.

He walked through a swinging door into a massive kitchen. All high-end stainless-steel appliances and beige lacquered cabinets. Then he walked into the living room. It had fourteen-foot ceilings and was flooded with light but sparsely furnished.

He reached into the breast pocket of his jacket for his iPhone. It had a long, zig-zag crack in the screen and when he dialed, nothing happened.

Also, not good.

He looked at his watch. Its second hand was moving. That

was good. It was 3:15. He had been out cold for about twenty minutes, and Hill/Hobart would be long gone. He looked around the living room for a landline and saw a white phone on a coffee table. He went over and dialed it.

"Hey, Nick," Rhett answered, "I just got the warrant."

"I don't need it anymore. I jumped the gun and went to the house on Sullivan's. Billy Hobart's car was there so I went around back. Door was open and I walked in. Next thing I know it was lights-out."

"You're shittin' me."

"No, got whacked on the head with something. Put out a BOLO for a late-model black Audi A7 with a thirty-year-old blond man or woman at the wheel. He... she's only been on the road for about twenty minutes, so they can't have gotten very far. Subject, presumably, armed and dangerous," Janzek said, then lowered his voice. "Got my damn Sig, too."

"Jesus, man."

"Only good news is, I got a hunch where she might be headed." Janzek said. "I'm going over to the station now to get another piece. See if you can get something on that Audi?"

"You got it," Rhett said. "I'll get eyes on all major roads within a hundred-mile radius of the house on Sullivan's."

"Yeah, do that, but my guess is she's gonna dump that Audi pretty quick."

THERE WASN'T anything more humiliating to a cop than getting their weapon stolen and having no back-up. But that was the case with Janzek. Ernie Brindle refrained from rubbing it in, and told Janzek he didn't expect to be getting into any shootouts in the near future so Janzek could borrow his Glock G30S. Janzek had always been a Sig Sauer guy, but a Glock was a pretty good stand-in. He figured choosing between a Sig P226 and a Glock G30S was kind of like choosing between a BMW and a Mercedes. In this case, a well-made Swiss piece and a well-made Austrian one. Both had their share of fans. Navy SEALs used P226s and lots of cops used G30Ss. It was a toss-up. Then again, there were plenty of guys in law enforcement who swore by Smith & Wessons, H & Ks, and Berettas.

Turned out the Glock fit into Janzek's empty holster just as well as the Sig.

He thanked Brindle, got into his car, and headed south on Highway 17.

FIFTY-SEVEN

TIPTON HADN'T BOTHERED TO PACK. SHE HAD GONE straight to her car and now was on Highway 17 South, doing seventy. She didn't dare go too fast and risk getting stopped. She also didn't want to have to shoot a cop... but she would if she had to. She wondered how long Janzek would be unconscious. How long would it take him to pull up Billy's license plate number and get it out to every cop in the state. She had hit the detective pretty hard, but you never know....

She pulled off of Highway 17 at a town called Hardeeville and looked for the parking lot of a big-box store. She found a Publix, drove in, and parked the Audi right in the middle of it, then walked around, peering into driver's side windows. After ten minutes, she hadn't found any keys left in the ignition. She got back in the Audi and drove to a nearby CVS and started prowling the parking lot. As she was about to give up, she saw the keys in the ignition of an old, dented Volvo. The two front windows were rolled down, too. Apparently, the owner didn't think anybody would bother stealing the dilapidated beater; or they figured, if it did happen, they'd be better off getting the insurance money.

Tipton opened the door, started the engine, and looked down at the gas gauge. She could have expected as much: almost empty. She went to a gas station a mile away, filled up, paying cash, and got back on the highway.

As she drove the noisy Volvo, she considered what the police had on her and guessed what they'd most likely do.

They'd be able to connect the dots pretty quickly.

Go to the apartment in the Fort Sumter House, turn the apartment upside down, and find the contract for the sale of the Thomasville plantation.

Tipton exited the highway, turned around, and headed in the opposite direction.

JANZEK WAS LISTENING to Carl Hiaasen's *Bad Monkey* as he powered down 95 toward Georgia. The story was pretty funny...Hiaasen's over-the-top, bizarre characters winding up in outrageous situations. Good way to pass the time at eighty-five miles an hour. His GPS said it would take him five and a half hours, but it was probably figuring on a driver doing the 70-mph speed limit.

Four hours and forty-five minutes later, he drove down a long allée of live oak trees and pulled up to what was clearly a brand-new house. He had called the Thomasville sheriff he'd talked to before and had gotten directions from him. As he got closer to the house, he saw the little stickers on the windows that indicated they were brand-new. The house was Georgian-style and smaller than Janzek expected, but then why build it any bigger if only one person was going to live in it? He noticed the new landscaping around the house could use some water.

There were no cars in sight, but he figured if Tipton had come back, she'd be parked around back.

He got out, unholstered his Glock, and walked around the house. He found nothing behind it except an old guesthouse which, clearly, had not been burned down when the mansion had been. He noticed recently planted trees and a big swath of lawn that looked like it had just been sodded in.

Even with her half-hour head start, Janzek figured he'd beaten Tipton to the house, if in fact, that's where she was going. She wouldn't be driving as fast as he, for fear of getting pulled over. Also, Tipton would need to ditch the Audi at some point, and that would take time.

He went back to his car, got in, and drove it around back, parking it behind the guest house, where nobody could see it. He got out and walked up to the porch of the guest house and turned the doorknob. It was locked. He peered through the sidelight and saw an old pool table in the middle of the room next to a foosball game, then walked back toward the main house, looking for a place to lie in wait.

On the other side of the driveway, across from the main house, was a free-standing enclosed gazebo with a red tin roof. *Perfect.* It had a two brand-new wicker chairs, with tags still on them. He sat in one and dialed Rhett.

"Where are ya, man?" Rhett asked.

"Thomasville, Georgia. Sitting in a nice, little gazebo. Just swattin' flies, waiting for my girlfriend to show up."

"Or boyfriend."

"Exactly. You got anything?"

"I was just going to call you," Rhett said. "We found the Audi. It was headed in your direction, at a little shopping center right before the turnoff to Waltersboro. She boosted an old, blue Volvo, tag number ITL354. Might be rolling up the driveway any minute now."

"The welcoming party is ready," Janzek said, writing the license plate number on his wrist.

"All right, man, well, we got a jail cell here with her name on it," Rhett said. "Just bring her up."

Janzek clicked off and saw a blue car turn in and start down the long allée. He dropped to his knees and watched the car drive up, his eyes just above the top of the enclosed wall of the gazebo.

It was old but it was not a Volvo. It was an ancient El Camino and a man who looked to be in his forties stopped in front of the house. He took three boxes out of the back of the El Camino and carried them over to the porch of the house. Then he got back into the El Camino and drove off. Janzek could see the name Kohler on all three boxes and knew they were plumbing fixtures. Man was probably a plumber.

He sat back in the wicker chair and stared down at the road for the blue Volvo.

An hour later, he was still staring.

FIFTY-EIGHT

Tipton's first thought had been to go to the airport, but she quickly nixed that idea. The cops would have called the TSA and put them on high alert. Her second thought was to head back down south again and drive to Miami. It would take her about six to seven hours depending on traffic. She could get on a boat and go somewhere. Anywhere. That's when she had a brainstorm. She pulled off of 95, parked in a residential neighborhood, got out the burner she had purchased the day before, and looked up Carnival Cruises.

FIFTEEN MINUTES LATER, Janzek was still in the gazebo.

Agitated and edgy now.

Things weren't working out the way he'd planned.

Finally, he called the Thomasville sheriff.

"Got a question for you, Sheriff," he asked. "Is there a Best Buy or something around here?"

"You come all this way to buy a new TV, Nick?"

Janzek was in no mood for humor. "Is there?" he asked impatiently.

"No, but in Tallahassee. Forty minutes south," the sheriff said.

He gave Janzek directions and Janzek got in his car and gunned it.

An hour and a half later, he was back.

He was not the best handyman, but he was able to hook up the $114 D-Link Surveillance Camera and attach it to a tree where nobody would spot it right away. It was either that or ask the sheriff to check the plantation every hour or so for signs of life. He figured the security camera would serve its purpose just fine.

He got back on the road, set the cruise control, and pushed in tape six of *Bad Monkey*.

Hiaasen did wonders for his shitty mood.

TIPTON BOOKED a ticket online at the Carnival website. Fortunately, it gave her the option of paying in cash right before she boarded. She got lucky with the timing since the five-day cruise to the Bahamas departed at five that afternoon. It was the last thing in the world she'd ever dream of doing, had she the choice. Get on one of the tacky cruise ships with every fatso in the south stuffing their faces all day long, burping and farting their way to Nassau.

Then, she read through the specific events and features of the 5 p.m. cruise. It was hideous. Passengers had their pick—depending on the date—of tribute bands doing the moth-eaten hits of REO Speedwagon, Olivia Newton-John, and .38 Special. And if a boatload of sound-alike has-beens weren't enough, the ship was hosting something called the Hasbro

Game Show, followed by DJ Imre emceeing all the karaoke you could stomach.

Then there was a comedian apparently channeling George Lopez, who Tipton just knew would be riotously un-funny. Other entertainment was being offered, guaranteed to tickle the funny bone, so Tipton decided the cruise would be a perfect opportunity to catch up on her reading. Plus, Carnival couldn't mess up a simple massage. Could they? On second thought, maybe they could.

FIFTY-NINE

Sheila was having dinner with Sarah Rentschler at Lucca, where the owner/chef who fancied himself as being in the same league as Bobby Flay, decidedly was not.

Still, it was a good menu, and the wine selection was above average.

Sheila was setting her trap. Slowly, methodically, and carefully. So far, the two women had talked about everything except what Sheila had invited Sarah to dinner to discuss. Finally, it was time.

"Did you hear about the new tech start-up?" Sheila asked Sarah, baiting the trap.

Sarah leaned in close. "No," she said, wide-eyed, "do tell."

"I figured with all your contacts it would have hit your radar screen by now," Sheila said. "Anyway, I'm sworn to secrecy on the company name, but suffice it to say, one of the top tech companies in the country is going to be turning Gallivants Ferry into Silicon Valley East."

"Where in God's name is Gallivants Ferry?"

"A charming little mecca on the Little Pee Dee River, up in Horry County."

"You're making these names up," Sarah said.

Sheila shook her head. "Swear to God, it's not too far from Myrtle Beach." She paused to take a sip of wine. "Anyway, they apparently just put fifteen hundred acres under contract. I heard it from a guy named Natty Holyfield, a broker friend of mine. That's more land than the BMW plant and Boeing together. Apparently, the company liked the location because there's a pretty well-educated labor force in and around the area."

Sarah looked like she was about to explode with excitement. "Come on, tell me who the company is."

"I can't. I promised the head of the board," Sheila said.

"That is amazing. So, the governor gave them a big tax-incentive package, I assume."

"Oh, yeah, huge," Sheila said. "California's losing a lot of businesses—first, big players in the film industry went to Atlanta, now this. It's definitely going to put Gallivants Ferry on the map."

"I bet it's Microsoft," Sarah said, trolling.

"I said I wasn't going to say," Sheila said. "My lips are sealed."

"Oracle?"

"It'll all be public in a month or so," Sheila said.

Sarah looked like she was wracking her brain. Probably thinking that a month gave her plenty of time to get in touch with this real-estate guy, Natty whoever, and buy a big chunk of Gallivants Ferry real estate.

Fifteen minutes later, Sheila gave Sarah a big double-cheeker, headed for the door, and walked to her car.

She slid in, pulled out her cell phone and dialed ten numbers. A man answered.

"Natty, that you, darlin'?"

"Oh, hello, Ms. Sheila," Natty Holyfield said. "So good to hear from you, ma'am."

"Thank you," she said. "You know that big, worthless piece of land my husband bought ten years ago?"

"Sure do, ma'am," Natty said, " down by the Little Pee Dee."

"That's the one," Sheila said. "What's it worth, anyway?"

Natty went silent for a second. "Um, maybe five hundred an acre...on a good day."

"Okay, here's what you're gonna do," Sheila said. "Put a price of twenty thousand an acre on it and be expecting a call from a Ms. Sarah Rentschler. She's gonna be thinking that's a really good deal with all the new industry coming to town."

Natty was silent again. "And just what new industry is that, Ms. Sheila?"

"The new industry that I made up," Sheila said, "but that's our little secret, Natty. Don't take a dollar less than seventeen-five an acre."

Natty laughed. "You got it."

Yes, she sure did.

SIXTY

JANZEK DROVE OVER THE LEGARE BRIDGE INTO Charleston. He wasn't much of a fisherman, but it reminded him of when he went fishing on Delvin's boat once and went a whole afternoon without a bite. He kept checking the surveillance feed from the camera he'd rigged up in Thomasville but not one car had rumbled down the long driveway to *Bellevoir* plantation.

So that was a waste of a hundred fourteen bucks, he thought, though he figured he could convince Ernie Brindle it was for a good cause and get reimbursed.

He looked at his watch. It was seven p.m. He was coming back to Charleston empty-handed—a cop up against a suspect who had outsmarted him. He was tired and he was thirsty and there was nothing more he could do about Tipton Hill at the moment.

He dialed his cell and Sheila Lessing answered after two rings. He wondered, not for the first time, how a woman as busy as Sheila always seemed to have time for him.

"Hi, Nick," she said.

242

"Hi, Sheila, feel like a cocktail?"

"Does a bear...live in the woods?"

Janzek laughed. "That's not how it goes."

"Yeah, I know, I cleaned it up a little," she said. "Why don't you come here? I don't feel like going to a bar and spending happy hour with a bunch of my students."

"Sounds good," he said. "How's your rum supply?"

"Strong. Gosling, Diplomatico, Don Papa, Mount Gay, Myers—"

"An all-star line-up. I'm going to swing by my place, take a shower, then I'll head over to you."

"See you in a bit."

HE STOPPED by his apartment and showered, figuring he had a lot of road dust on him. He changed into a pair of khakis and a blue-striped shirt and drove over to Sheila's house on Tradd Street.

Sheila opened the front door looking drop-dead gorgeous.

Janzek just stared.

"What?" she said.

"Nothing," he said, "you just look so damn good."

She wasn't wearing anything special. Just loose-fitting silk pants and simple beige top.

"So does that mean I *didn't* look good last time you saw me?"

Janzek laughed. "No, just this time you look... flat-out smoking *hot*."

"That's a phrase usually reserved for younger women," she said. "But I'll take it."

"You should. Can I come in or are we just going to stand here and swap snappy banter?"

Sheila stepped aside and ushered him in. "Go on in and mix yourself a stiff one."

"Man, do I ever need it," he said. "Which way's the bar?"

She pointed to the far end of the living room.

"What do you want?" he asked.

"I'll have a Belvedere and soda."

He walked over to the well-stocked bar, made drinks then went over to where she was seated and handed her a vodka and soda.

"Cheers," she said, raising her glass.

"Cheers," he said, clinking glasses.

"So, what do you want to pick my brain about this time?"

He smiled. "Believe it or not, this time I don't."

She looked surprised. "Come on, Nick. I don't mind. I'm actually kind of flattered that I'm your go-to girl."

"Well, that's nice, but this time I just came to see you."

"Well, I'm flattered about that too," she said, taking a sip of her drink. "So what's new with your case? Last I heard, it sounded like Tipton Hill faked a suicide off the Ravenel Bridge. Any sign of her since then?"

"No, she's.... God knows where. We've got probably the biggest manhunt in the history of South Carlina goin' on and nothing to show for it. It's pretty frustrating."

"I can imagine."

"I'm sick of talking about it, sick of thinking about it, too. What's new with you?"

"College of Charleston just got named fourth best college in the south."

"No kidding? That's great. Right up there with Duke, Virginia, and UNC, huh?"

"Yeah, exactly, but I want it to be better than them."

"My guess is no one ever called you a patient woman?"

Sheila shook her head and smiled. "How patient are you about finding Tipton Hill?"

He laughed. "You got a point there."

Sheila stood up.

"Where you going?"

"Over to you," Sheila said, sitting next to him in the couch.

She looked up at him and smiled.

He leaned down and kissed her.

"You cougar, you."

"Damn right. Somebody's gotta teach you young pups new tricks."

He kissed her again, but this time he put everything he had behind it.

It quickly became clear that Sheila Lessing could kiss younger women under the table.

His cell phone in his breast pocket rang. She reached in, pulled it out and held it up so Janzek could read the number.

"My partner. This'll just take a second."

He clicked it on. "Yeah, Del?"

"We found her car."

The stolen Volvo.

"Where?"

"Right here. Hasell and East Bay." That was about fifteen blocks away.

Janzek got to his feet. "See you there in ten minutes."

Sheila slowly shook her head and scowled.

"This is the hardest decision I've ever had to make, Sheila."

She shook her head and laughed. "Really? Is that why you almost threw your back out springing off the couch?"

"Tipton Hill's car was found close by."

"Okay, Nick, go get her. But you owe me... *big.*"

SIXTY-ONE

Tipton had no idea how she had turned into such a snob. She was, after all, the daughter of a man who trained dogs, mucked out stalls, and said, 'Yes, sir' to a man who was having sex with her mother. Look up blue-collar—with a tinge of redneck—in the dictionary and you'd find her family. But this was America, and with a little intelligence, drive, and ambition you could change your stripes almost overnight, even if it had taken Tipton more than ten years.

One thing was sure: There wasn't much of the South-of-Broad-Street crowd on board the cruise ship. It was a paunchy and friendly group that didn't seem to care how they looked; they just wanted to be fat, dumb, and happy and eat five meals a day.

———

AS HE GOT out of his Crown Vic at Hasell and East Bay, Janzek pulled on a pair of plastic gloves and walked up to the

Volvo that Delvin Rhett was standing beside. He laid the back of his gloved hand on the hood of the engine.

"Cold," he said to Rhett, "been here a while. But you already know that."

Rhett nodded. "Question is, why would she dump it here?"

"I got a theory," Janzek said.

"Let's hear it."

"Tipton figured we'd have the roads crawling with staties looking to bag her for triple homicide. Figured we'd have the airport, train stations and bus terminals covered, too. So, what mode of transportation is left?"

It suddenly hit Rhett, and he nodded excitedly. "She decided to take a little cruise, huh?"

"You got it. Just a hop, skip, and a jump down to the Caribbean."

Janzek looked up Carnival Cruise's 800 number and dialed it. He listened for a few moments, looked down at his watch, then clicked off.

"The *Fantasy* takes off in exactly thirty-five minutes," Janzek said, then smiled. "I could sure use a vacation, Del."

"Hate to tell you, bro, but this is going to be a *working* vacation." Rhett hit the button on his key and his car doors unlocked. They both got in and Rhett started up the engine. "Also, man, you got no clothes...no nothing."

"I'm sure they got a store on board," Janzek said. "Maybe get me some nice madras shorts and a shirt with a little alligator on it."

Rhett shook his head. "Fashionista, you ain't," he said as he gunned the cruiser. "More like a cargo shorts, strappy T-shirt kind of guy."

Janzek shrugged. "What can I tell you? I like pockets."

Rhett turned to him. "What if it turns out she's not on board?"

Janzek shrugged again. "Guess I'll have to jump overboard and swim to shore."

"Seriously, man?"

"I just have a strong hunch she is."

Three minutes later they pulled up to the huge Carnival ship. Janzek didn't know for sure but guessed it was taller than any building in Charleston.

Rhett screeched to a stop as close as he could get to the ship.

"All right," Janzek said, "Assuming I can get on, I'll call you. No idea how cell service will be, but I'll figure something out."

Rhett pulled out his wallet, scooped out all the cash he had and handed it to Janzek. "Here you go. Go crazy. A couple of Mai-Tais and a few rounds of Blackjack."

"Thanks, man, I owe you." Janzek opened the door and ran for the building marked 'Carnival Cruise Line.'

He owed everyone now.

THE CARNIVAL PEOPLE had apparently hosted last minute walk-ons before, but probably no one without any luggage at this late an arrival. Four different Carnival people asked him what he was bringing with him and looked both dumbfounded and suspicious when he told them not a thing. One even asked him how he planned to brush his teeth. Like what kind of a hygienically deprived slob was he?

It was a legitimate question, Janzek thought, but none of the guy's damn business.

He showed a few of the Carnival employees Torborg's picture of Tipton but none of them remembered seeing her.

He paid by credit card and stepped on the ship five minutes before it started to move.

SIXTY-TWO

HE HAD AN INSIDE CABIN, WHICH WAS ABOUT THE SAME size as the inside of a small U-Haul truck. Literally ten seconds after he opened the door to his cabin, an announcement came over the ship's intercom directing all passengers to participate in a fire drill in ten minutes, as mandated by U.S. maritime law and, yada, yada, yada.

Well, he thought, a perfect opportunity to spot Tipton Hill.

As he scanned the small cabin, he came to the conclusion that he had definitely slept in worse places. Nevertheless, not having a window or any source of natural light in his 200-square foot space was a little depressing.

A knock sounded on his door as Janzek was checking out his cell-size bathroom. He opened it.

"Welcome aboard, sir," said the short, smiling Carnival employee. "My name is Sobani, and it will be my pleasure to serve you on your cruise. If I can do anything for you, please don't hesitate to ask."

"Well, thank you," Janzek said. "Actually, I do have a question. Where can I find a shop that sells clothes... along with stuff like toothbrushes and razors?"

"Yes, sir, deck 8, the Promenade. It's called the Style Shop," Sobani said. "I'm sure you'll find everything you want there."

"Thanks, I appreciate it."

Sobani nodded. "You're welcome. Oh, and don't forget the fire drill, sir," he said, then turned and walked down the narrow corridor.

A minute later, Janzek walked down the corridor, headed for the theater on the Promenade deck where the fire drill would take place. He positioned himself way back in the room and behind a big steel beam so he couldn't be spotted by Tipton take out or Billy.

It turned out to be little more than a demonstration of how to put your life jacket on in the unlikely event that the *Fantasy* hit a rogue iceberg in the tropical Caribbean waters. Janzek was disappointed but not surprised to find that no one even remotely resembled either Tipton or Billy.

He went to the store and, five minutes later, walked out with a new Crest toothbrush and toothpaste and wearing an oversized, white Carnival baseball-style cap with, 'All for fun, fun for all,' emblazoned in bold, red lettering above the brim.

He decided it was time to go exploring, take a tour of the boat and get the lay of the land. The boat had twelve decks, all serviced by two different elevator banks. He had read somewhere that there were seven hundred employees on board and two thousand passengers.

And all he had to do was find one of them.

The first question was, would Tipton be playing herself or disguised as Billy Hobart? It didn't seem to matter much either way, since he knew what they both looked like.

It was a little past noon as he walked past one of the many bars on the ship. It was knee-deep in drinkers and he flashed to something a cynical friend had once said about low-end cruises: how they were all about eating and drinking, with a generous dollop of low-stakes casino gambling thrown in. Janzek watched a man take a heavy pull on a Michelob Ultra bottle. Tempting, but it was a little early.

On the top deck of the boat, he checked out the spa and the gym. The gym had fantastic views of the green sea and white-caps. It was well-equipped with Nautilus machines and free weights and had a room for yoga and stretching. He wasn't expecting anything nearly so nice and large, not to mention, immaculately clean. Based on what he had heard about Tipton's near-obsession with fitness, he suspected she'd spend time here if she went about her normal activities. It would be a tough place to disguise herself, too. Not that she would neces-sarily feel she had to, unless, of course, he got sloppy and she spotted him.

After he left the gym and spa, Janzek worked his way down from the top of the ship, walking out onto the deck where the pool, hot tub, and rows of chaise lounges graced the Lido deck. He was surprised by how many people were there already—most of them, it appeared, in their twenties and thir-ties. It hadn't taken them long to strip down to their bathing suits and stake out tanning spots. He walked along the length of the pool, then past something called the Mongolian Rotis-serie Grille, and reached the aft section of the ship, which hosted various buffet options. Long lines of eager eaters had already arrived—the longest line being at the stern, where cooks were doling out pizza and a deli was serving up hot sandwiches.

Janzek watched one of the chefs slide a Reuben sandwich onto a man's plate, then another, then a third. Man, it looked good. Janzek got right in line.

He planned to take his plate and park himself in one of the

few available deck chairs and simply observe...while eating his Reuben and knocking back a Michelob Ultra. Yeah, it was time.

He couldn't remember either one ever tasting better. As a testament to his lack of will power, he went back and got another Reuben, then settled in and observed for more than an hour. No Tipton. No Billy. But he did see quite a few pretty women in their twenties, thirties, and forties swimming in the pool and climbing in and out of the hot tubs. Buffed-out, tattooed guys clustered nearby were keeping them company, or moving in for the kill—so they hoped, anyway.

Janzek decided to walk down to the deck below. He was going to walk everywhere—unassisted by elevators—in anticipation of his newly increased eating consumption. His eating style had always been...*If it's there, I will eat it.* That could be a good thing or a bad thing—depending on what was in his refrigerator. The fact was, most of the time it was meagerly stocked. So, the benefit was, if it wasn't on the shelves of his Frigidaire 18, he couldn't eat it. But every month or so, Janzek would go on a bender. Toss his willpower out the window and fail to resist the two-for-one sale in the freezer aisle at Harris Teeter. The culprits were usually Breyers Heath Bar Crunch and Reese's Peanut Butter something. The two half-gallons would last about five straight nights; this included numerous second helpings and occasionally—when his willpower was at a really low ebb—a third. He only hoped he could hold himself back and not try to beat the two-Reuben record he'd just set.

He took the stairs down one flight onto what turned out to be the main entertainment deck. First thing he came across was a wi-fi area where you could hook up to the internet. Next came an unmanned library, about the size of his cabin that had —no exaggeration—twenty books that were laid out on a table. Despite the slim pickings, he spotted a Harlen Coben book he hadn't read yet, and took it with him.

Janzek moved on to yet another bar, where a singer was warbling a fair to middling version of a Cat Stevens tune from an elevated platform behind the busy bartenders who were shaking and stirring eight-dollar drinks.

Next after the bar came the Electricity Dance Room, a cavernous karaoke space that echoed with the tones of woefully off-key Beyonce wannabes and Mick Jagger imitators. Beyond it was the casino, no doubt one of Carnival's major profit centers. It had five blackjack tables—with an affordable six dollar minimum—a craps table, and a roulette table. In addition, there were tables for games he had never heard of: 3-card poker and one called Fun Blackjack—which was only fun, he suspected, if you won. He had a hunch that those lesser-known games— probably invented by Carnival upper management—were for the hardcore suckers.

Another game caught his attention. It was a plexi-glassed-in square that housed stacks of cash. Turned out the stacks were ten-dollar bills, and the object of the game was to operate a mechanical hand in such a way as to pick up a stack and drag it into your possession. It looked easy enough, but during his time in the casino, he only saw one woman hoist a stack into her hot little hands. The casino was not open yet because the ship was just shy of the three-mile limit, but there was a trio of eager looking older women with large plastic cups filled to the brim with quarters, destined to be swallowed up by the slot machines, eagerly waiting at the casino door.

After the casino came yet another bar, then a large room— not open—that looked about half the size of the karaoke room. Janzek peered through the darkened glass door and saw that the walls were covered with paintings. The ship's on-board art gallery featured paintings of big-eyed girls and garish psychedelic ones perhaps inspired by the artist Peter Max. Janzek flashed to the mostly bare walls of his apartment but knew he'd be better off without any of these Carnival masterpieces.

He continued walking and saw ahead yet another bar. He was losing count. This one was set up as a sports bar with big screens everywhere.

As he watched three men following a college basketball game, he had an urge for another Reuben and a Michelob Ultra. The sandwich was free, after all. Not to mention, really good. But this time, Mr. Willpower, resting daintily on his right shoulder, spoke up and drowned out Mr. Glutton on his left shoulder.

SIXTY-THREE

TIPTON NOT ONLY HAD A WINDOW BUT ALSO A SMALL balcony off of her cabin. She hadn't left it yet, not exactly dying of curiosity to find out what the *Fantasy* had to offer. Also, not eager to meet any of its two thousand passengers or lip-sync in the karaoke lounge. Instead, she'd read 300 pages of her book and had taken a long nap.

She had also spent time fine-tuning her plan. And though it wasn't fully developed, she was pretty content with it, especially considering that it was 100% spur-of-the-moment and hardly a plan at all.

She'd disembark in Nassau and fly from there to the Cayman Islands. She had more than a million and a half dollars in her account at the Cayman National Bank in Georgetown. Hardly enough to retire on at age thirty, but she planned to kick back for a while there while deciding what her next move was. She would have loved to live out her days in her newly built dream house on the old Swiggett plantation, despite the one horrific memory, but she realized with sadness that that was out of the question now. Such a shame....

She thought about selling it—particularly the logistics of receiving the money from the sale. She wondered whether the cop she had hit over the head at the Sullivan's Island house would be smart enough to find out about *Bellevoir* and follow the money to the Caymans and eventually to her. She had to refine the plan a little—or maybe the risk was too great. It might be best to let it go—let it turn to weeds, vandalized copper, stolen appliances, and, ultimately, end up a foreclosure.

She looked out her window and saw nothing but the vast green ocean. She'd left Charleston, and America, behind, maybe for the last time. The thought made her sad, but the reality was, she was now a hunted murderer and always would be. She had no idea whether they knew how many times she had killed—once, twice, three, four times—but once was enough.

Without meaning to, she flashed to the faces of her four victims. First was Jennifer, her best friend from Fort Lauderdale Community College. She truly felt bad about Jen, but it was something that just had to be done. To cover her tracks so she could invent a new life. Then came the boys who had assaulted her so brutally. Their attacks had gone on for two agonizing hours that felt like a week in Hell. She remembered the three at trial, smug, clean-cut, and claiming how sorry they were for what they'd done. They weren't, and she knew it. They were pigs who deserved to die, and she'd done the slaughtering in the most appropriate way possible. Cut off the hands of Whit Landrum for violating her with the pool cue and, if that weren't enough, the bottle of Mount Gay rum that she'd fetched specifically for Jamie.

Then there was Peabo Gardner, who had performed oral sex on her while watching her with those depraved eyes as she wept in horror.

And finally, the ringleader himself, Jamie Swiggett. She

knew none of it would ever have happened if it weren't for him. Her family's disintegration, her personal disgrace and ignominy, her mother's torturous decline into an impoverished life alone in a two-bedroom bungalow on a bleak street far from home. At least Tipton had made things better for her mother—presumably, anyway—when she anonymously FedExed her $100,000 in cash. It had been no big deal, really, simply her commission on the sale of one house on lower Meeting Street.

An eye for an eye, she thought. She had ruined the Swiggett family just as hers had been destroyed, the casualties staggering on both sides.

Stop, she told herself, *focus on the now*.

It was time to concentrate her efforts on getting away with it all. What good would it be if, in the end, she got caught? Yes, they'd all still be dead, but her life would be over, too.

SIXTY-FOUR

JANZEK HAD BEEN ASSIGNED TO A TABLE FOR DINNER. He was the ninth wheel. His table mates consisted of four couples, all in their mid-twenties. Two of the couples were traveling together. He was clearly the odd man out. Older and without a significant other.

He'd decided his cover would be a salesman for Dick's Sporting Goods.

"You guys have a really great selection of golf shoes," one of the young guys, Dan, said after Janzek told him what he did for a living.

"Yeah, we do," he said. "I'm actually in racquets, myself."

Dan thought for a second. "Oh, you mean, like tennis racquets?"

"Yeah, exactly. But also racquetball, squash, pickleball...we even carry badminton racquets."

"Wow," Dan said. "Badminton, huh? Anybody ever ask you, 'Hey, what's your *racket?*'"

Oh, God, Janzek thought. *Spare me.* Was that going to be the humor level?

He fielded a question from another guy nicknamed, "Whitey."

"Who is Dick, anyway?" Whitey asked.

Janzek was ready for that one. "Guy who started the company. Started out as a little bait and tackle shop up in Buffalo, New York." *Though, come to think of it, it might have been Binghamton.*

The reason Janzek had chosen Dick's as his cover was that he had just read an article about the company online and the facts were pretty fresh, plus he could wing it pretty well when the subject was sports.

The rest of the dinner conversation consisted of talking about what the others did for work, followed by what they planned to do on the cruise, how small their cabins were, the usual. On a scale of one to ten, his pork chops were a six, his peas and mashed potatoes eights, and the Caesar salad a two.

At a little past eight, two of the couples excused themselves from the table—they said they were headed to a show at the Punchliner Comedy Club. Janzek checked the schedule sheet in his pocket and noted that it was not the "Adult" show, but rather "General Audience." He figured the R-rated version would be more fun.

Alone again, he decided to try his luck at a game of chance. He walked up from the Jubilee banquet room to the entertainment deck, three flights above, using the stairs. He still had a dessert and a half to work off. It was creme brulee and he gave it a 9.

Inside the casino, he pulled his cap down so he would be harder to recognize, then cashed a hundred dollars' worth of chips—compliments of Delvin. He expected it to last him the rest of the 4-day cruise. Janzek was not a wildly aggressive player but knew the basics—split eights and aces, double down when you have a decent edge on the dealer. He mainly liked the game for the idle chit-chat and interplay with the other players. There were always one or two yakkers who had something amusing to say, or who you could commiserate with if the dealer went on a hot streak and hit twenty-one three times in a row.

This time he just went straight downhill from the get-go, like a big stone dropped from deck 13 into the Atlantic. It wasn't so much the dealer's cards as his own. He should have known it was gonna be bad when his first four hands added up to sixteen, fourteen, fifteen, and twelve. He busted on every one of them with face cards. Three and a half minutes in, he was down thirty bucks and having a lousy time. There wasn't even any player chit-chat to lighten the load.

Meanwhile, he watched other players at the table hit on eighteen and get a three, or split tens and get an ace and a queen—players clearly who had no clue. Yet his stack of chips dwindled while theirs grew.

He played another hand and finally won one when the dealer busted, but then lost four more straight. He was down close to fifty bucks and still hadn't had one pleasurable interaction, let alone even eye contact, with anyone at the table. He gathered up his chips, nodded at the impassive dealer, and slunk away from the table, feeling like a man whose best pick-up lines had been laughed off by every woman in the joint.

He went from wallowing in self-pity to chiding himself for not doing his job. He wasn't there to break the bank but to find a killer. He pulled his Carnival cap down again and stepped into the bar that seemed to have the most foot traffic going by it. He looked at his watch. It was 7:15 and there were lots of other men nursing drinks. He pulled the first-day schedule out of his pocket which said, '7:00—40+ Singles Meet-up at Rascals bar, deck 11.' Still stinging from his blackjack losses and feeling totally inadequate as a rascal, he forced himself to shuffle up to the bar.

The only woman in the place was the bartender.

He ordered a Planter's Punch, then immediately realized that it would be too sweet and have about a tablespoon of rum in it. It was and it did. So far, he'd had two Mich Ultras, two glasses of mediocre red wine at dinner, and a subpar Planter's Punch.

So now he was drinking a lot and still having a lousy time, and he didn't have even a slight buzz to show for it.

He watched passengers file past the front of the bar, but none bore the slightest resemblance to Tipton Hill or Billy Hobart.

Screw it. He ordered another Planter's Punch.

SIXTY-FIVE

Tipton had not slept well.

How could she? She had spotted the cop or detective or whatever he was.

It happened after the late dinner sitting while she was walking past the casino. She spotted Janzek hunkered down at a blackjack table. Even in the lame hat, he was recognizable. He'd seemed totally absorbed in the game and his cards. She raised a hand up to cover her face, in case he suddenly looked up, and walked quickly to her room.

Though he had met her only as Billy, she was sure that, in the course of his investigation, Janzek had probably turned up pictures of her. They could have come from her Facebook page, from the Carriage Property website, her ID-card picture at the MUSC gym, or any number of other sources.

So much for going to the gym, or to the wi-fi location on Deck 8, or one of the trivia games on Deck 9 that she thought might be fun. So much for getting a couple slices of pizza at that place on the Lido deck. And so much for checking out another book from the pathetic library.

It looked like room service three meals a day in front of a tiny TV with a serious dearth of channels.

Fuck!

What was she going to do for the next...she quickly calculated...110 hours?

IT WAS seven thirty in the morning and Janzek was hung over. It would have been one thing if he'd had a good time or brought a woman back to his glorified jail cell, but he had absolutely nothing to show for the wracking pain in his temples. Why the hell had he been drinking those vomitous Planter's Punches in the first place? Worse, why had he squandered thirty bucks trying to pick up the stacks of cash with the mechanical hand? Was he fucking nuts? He'd gimped back to his cabin at ten-thirty p.m., pissed at having been touched up by the devious Carnival hustlers for an additional two hundred bucks. He now had lost all the money he'd thought would last him the whole trip.

Fuck!

Upon returning to his cabin the night before and hitting the light switch, he'd glanced down at his bed and had seen two things. First, a pair of little chocolates wrapped in red foil. *Wow*, he thought, *something for nothing. Incredible!* Then, at the bottom of his bed, lay a white object that seemed to be made of washcloths or small towels. As he looked closer, he realized that someone—Sobani, maybe—had made a crude sculpture of a rabbit out of the cotton material. A Carnival trademark, he guessed. Those upper-management guys, at it again.

Now, in the harsh light of day, the rabbit seemed to be casting a scornful, mocking, glare at him. Well, to be fair,

Janzek was the bungling schlub who couldn't even get three cards to add up to twenty-one. He reached down, picked up the towel rabbit, and hurled it against the far wall. It was a short flight.

He got out of bed and lurched a step to his left as the *Fantasy* seemed to rock. Or maybe it was the booze.

He squeezed into the tiny shower that had a taut string in the back to dry clothes on. It delivered a sporadic jet of water as he brushed his teeth and soaped himself up.

He planned to stake out two or three places that day and wait for Tipton Hill to come along. First stop would be the deck adjacent to the large pool and not far from the main buffet. The buffet would be serving breakfast now. He could picture the stacks of pancakes, trays of eggs, and piles of tangled and—no doubt—woefully undercooked bacon. He planned to have a little of each. He'd throw in a half grapefruit and maybe some strawberries as an unenthusiastic concession to eating healthy. He didn't expect the twenty-something hard-bodies—and big bellies—to show up there until later, the nine to ten shift. He also planned to bring along his Harlan Coben book, then hang out on the open-air deck. Then he'd swing by the gym, do a not-too-taxing workout, and show the attendant a picture of Tipton. He'd slide her a few bucks to call him if she spotted his quarry.

He was also thinking about making contact with the ship's captain. Tell him that he was there to arrest one of his passengers. A murderer, to be exact. He was not sure how this would play with the captain: knowing that a Charleston police detective was scouring his seventy-thousand-ton ship in search of a killer. In fact, the more Janzek thought about it, the more he figured it might be a really bad idea. He knew there was no way Tipton or Billy had used their real names, so the captain wouldn't be of any help finding him/her. Better to keep the captain out of the loop.

Which raised a whole set of questions: What authority did he have to arrest someone on the high seas? What would he do with Hill once he arrested her? Was there a jail cell on the ship or would he have to cuff her up in his tight, little cabin? And what was Sobani going to make of *that*? Assume Janzek had captured a sex slave?

He decided his next stop after breakfast and his stint on the Lido deck would be to park himself in a high-traffic area of Deck 10, the Promenade.

Twenty minutes later, he looked down at his plate: waffles, pancakes, eggs, and a tangled pile of bacon. Sure enough, undercooked. He'd left zero room to squeeze even one straw-berry—or anything else healthy—onto the plate. *Oh, well.* He went over to one of the deck loungers, set his tray down on the table, and pulled the chair behind a column in a shaded area where he couldn't easily be spotted.

Then he sat down in the deck chair, looked down at the steaming breakfast, and promised himself—just as soon as he made room on his plate—that he'd pick up a half-grapefruit or a slice of melon.

What he ended up doing instead was return to the buffet for more syrup because the pancakes had completely absorbed all that he'd initially poured on the stack. He ate everything on his plate except for one extremely mushy slice of bacon. Then, after finishing off a third cup of muddy coffee, he set the tray down on a nearby table and leaned back in his chaise, glutted. He reached into the breast pocket of his shirt, fished out his Wayfarers, and put them on. Between them and his Carnival cap he'd be unrecognizable.

Five minutes later, he heard a voice. "Hey, Nick, you're up early, man."

It was Whitey, from dinner the night before. Janzek's disguise clearly needed work.

"Hey, Whitey," Janzek said. "Yeah, figured I'd beat the rush."

Whitey looked over at Janzek's plate. "I hear ya," he said. "How was it?"

"Good," Janzek said. "If you like a two-thousand-calorie breakfast."

"Matter of fact, I do," said Whitey, pushing off. "Well, catch you later, bro."

"Yup. See ya," Janzek said.

He pulled his deck chair a little farther back in the shade, tugged his cap lower, and watched people walk past him for the next two hours.

None of them was a killer. Well, at least not *his* killer.

SIXTY-SIX

TIPTON HAD ORDERED A PLAIN OMELET, A SLICE OF cantaloupe, an English muffin, a glass of orange juice, and tea. She didn't finish the English muffin.

She looked at her watch and calculated that she now had ninety-four-and-a-half hours left on the un-*Fantasy*.

She walked to her door, opened it, and looked in the hall for the cabin boy. No one was there. But a few seconds later, a man in a white uniform came down the hallway.

"Excuse me," Tipton said, take out taking the tray. "Can I ask you a huge favor?"

"Sure, ma'am. What can I do for you?"

Tipton glanced down at his name tag. It was Ronick.

"I need a book or two from the library," she said.

"Of, course, ma'am. Anything special?"

"They don't have anything special."

He laughed knowingly.

"Hold on a sec," Tipton said, going back into her cabin and picking up her wallet from the small desk. She pulled out a twenty and went back to her door.

Ronick was waiting.

"If you could get me two, please," she said, handing him the twenty.

"Yes, ma'am," he said. "You have a favorite... author?"

She started to say, no Danielle Steele or anything with vampires in them, then decided to spare Ronick the trouble. "Nope. Whatever looks good. I trust you."

"Yes, ma'am," said Ronick.

He came back in five minutes and handed her *Confessions of a Wild Child* by Jackie Collins and *Power Play* by Danielle Steele.

She wanted her twenty bucks back.

Instead she handed him another twenty. She needed a loyal retainer for the remainder of the hell ride, and forty bucks was a small price to pay.

"Thank you very much," Ronick said. Clearly, he didn't get a forty dollar tip every day for ten minutes' work.

"No, thank *you*," she said, taking the books from him. "I appreciate it."

"You're very welcome," Ronick said. "Well, happy reading, ma'am."

JANZEK WAS ANTSY. He had been sitting in a couch between the Electricity Disco and the casino on the Promenade deck, watching the traffic going to the Grand Spectrum dining room, the Twenty First Century bar, and the photo studio. The photo area was especially popular; there were, by Janzek's count, at least eight photographers employed by the ship in stationary set-ups that featured lavish, photorealistic, backdrops of Bahama island scenes and what looked to be living rooms in twenty-million-dollar homes in Palm Beach.

The idea was to lure starry-eyed couples from western Kentucky or eastern Alabama into the studio and photograph them as if they were actually in the exotic locations so realistically pictured.

Janzek allowed himself a cynical thought: *That's as close as they'll ever get.*

He was still wearing the Wayfarers and the Carnival cap but was now holding his hand over his mouth and chin to further ensure that he wouldn't be recognized by Tipton Hill.

But after hours of reconnaissance with nothing to show for it, Janzek realized it was time to get proactive.

He decided he needed a look at the ship's manifest, just on the off chance that Hill or Hobart had used their real name. Once again, he thought about approaching the captain; and once more, thought better of it.

Earlier in the day, he had developed an eye-contact thing with what he guessed was a Russian woman at Special Services. Special Services was where, among other things, you changed cash into little plastic cards that you used to buy things —stuff like Dramamine, duty-free booze, or drinks at one of the eleven bars on the ship (Janzek's unofficial count). He had passed by Special Services a second time and—sure enough— she'd given him the eye and smiled.

All right, he thought, *might as well give it a shot.*

He walked up to Special Services and waited for the Russian woman to be done with another passenger. When she was done, he approached the window. He caught her name on her badge: Ulyana.

She smiled up at him. "Hello, Mr..."

"Janzek. Hi, Ulyana," he said. "I wonder if you could do me a huge favor."

"If I can. Sure." It came out as "chewer".

"I have a friend on the ship I'm trying to find. She never

gave me her cabin number and, you know, with two thousand passengers I haven't run across her yet...."

Ulyana nodded.

"So I wondered if it would be possible to check the ship's manifest, or maybe better, to ask you to look up a passenger by the name of Tipton Hill... or Billy Hobart, that's her boyfriend."

A trace of a frown appeared on Ulyana's face. "I am very sorry, Mr. Janzek, but we are prevented from doing that," she said. "It is a confidentiality policy of the ships. I'm sure you can understand."

He thought about trying to bribe her. *Baksheesh*, they called it in her part of the world.

"Well, thank you, anyway," Janzek said, "I appreciate it."

"I am so, so sorry," Ulyana said. "But I hope you understand."

"I do," he said and walked away, thwarted.

As he walked past an older couple in twin electric wheelchairs, he had another idea. It meant a lot of walking.

He took his wallet out and removed a folded-up piece of paper. It was one of the copies of the painting that Torborg had done of Tipton. He had completely forgotten about it. He looked at it again and, for the first time, noticed how Torborg had captured a look of faint anguish on Tipton's face. It was like a wince of pain, nothing major, more like she had just stubbed her toe.

He decided to start on the bottom of the ship and work his way up to the top. He began on what was called the Riviera deck, which was the fourth level. Something told him that there were no passenger cabins below Riviera, but he decided to check with Ulyana to be sure. He turned around and walked back to Special Services. She looked up, saw him approaching and smiled.

"I just can't stay away from you," Janzek said, and she laughed. "Can you tell me what floors the passenger cabins are located on, please?"

"Sure. Empress is on the 7th deck. Then, going down, Upper is on the 6th, Main on the 5th, and Riviera on the 4th."

He started to thank her, but she stopped him.

"Wait, I forgot Verandah. Another forty cabins, maybe, are on that level. That's deck 12."

"So are those considered the best?"

"Yes, I suppose so...they have the best views."

"Thanks. And below that are the crew's cabins?"

"Yes, exactly," she said, pushing a strand of hair behind her ear.

"I'm going to go knock on every door until I find my friends," Janzek said with a straight face, then he smiled. "Just kidding."

She laughed like she wasn't so sure he was kidding.

"Well, thanks again, Ulyana," he said, turning, then swiveling back around. "So how many cabins are there all together?"

"I don't know exactly. Maybe fifteen hundred?"

"Okay, well, thanks again," he said and walked away.

He briefly toyed with the idea of actually going door to door and knocking on all of them. But he figured there was no way in hell that Tipton Hill would ever answer an unexpected knock.

Not to mention the bloody knuckles he'd end up with, rapping on more than a thousand cabin doors.

SIXTY-SEVEN

IN THE END, JANZEK FIGURED THAT MONEY TALKED.

Especially if you were a cabin boy making thirty to forty grand a year.

He started on the Verandah, deck 12, knowing it was considered the best and that Tipton Hill would *not* be slumming it like he was. His plan was to walk down the narrow corridors and find a cabin boy going about his daily duties— making beds, taking away trays, whatever. The first cabin boy he came across was a bowling ball of a man with a megawatt smile. Janzek said hello and showed the man the picture of Tipton.

"Have you seen this woman?" he asked. "She's a friend of mine and I'm not sure what cabin she's staying in."

The man looked closely and scratched the back of his head. "No, sorry, sir. I haven't seen the lady."

"Well, if you do," Janzek said, "please let me know. I'm in cabin M41, on the Main Deck. I'll give you three hundred dollars if you tell me what cabin she's in."

The man's face lit up like he'd hit all six Powerball numbers. "I will definitely be on the lookout, sir."

"Great, thanks. Hope to hear from you..." Janzek said, looking down at his nameplate. "Nelvin."

Nelvin thrust out his hand. "Me, too, sir."

Janzek spent the next two hours cruising the corridors of all five decks. He didn't keep a count but figured he'd spoken to at least twenty-five cabin boys. There was Bayani, Rainer, Sanjaya, Jericho, and his favorite named King Arthur, all quite eager to keep their eyes peeled for the attractive American woman.

His legs and feet were tired, and he had worked up an appetite. Again. A check of his watch showed it was a little past one and he rationalized that all the walking must have burned off at least three hundred calories or so, earning him the right to take the elevator up to Lido deck.

The Mongolian Rotisserie Grille was a stone's throw from the pool and hot tub. The drill at the Mongo, as Whitey had referred to it, was you put raw ingredients—Janzek chose chicken strips along with lots of raw vegetables topped with a soy sauce—into a bowl and let the attendant mix it up in a wok, and thirty seconds later it was ready to go. Janzek walked into the pool area, stir-fry in hand, and sat at a table. He took a bite and deemed the Mongo meal pretty damn good.

After a few more bites, he looked up and saw a woman walking along the other side of the pool. She was wearing a classic disguise—big black sunglasses and a beret pulled down so low you couldn't see her hair. She was also wearing sneakers, tight blue jeans, and a short-sleeved shirt with some kind of logo on the left pocket. Not exactly how you expected to see someone dressed when it was eighty-five degrees out. The sunglasses were okay... but no way anyone would be wearing a beret and blue jeans on a hot day like this. She was tall, as well

273

—at least five-nine or ten, Janzek guessed—and didn't seem to have an ounce of fat on her.

Suddenly she turned her head and her eyes met Janzek's; she spun on her heels and started walking in the opposite direction.

Janzek sprang out of his chair, bumping the table with his hip, and watched as the woman shoved open a door that led to the four elevators and stairways that connected the ship's many decks. Janzek burst through the door and reached the elevator banks in seconds, but the woman was nowhere to be seen. His first thought was that she had gotten on a well-timed elevator, but then he leaned out over the stairway rail and caught sight of her black beret one flight below.

He raced down the stairs, taking three at a time, and entered the next deck's hallway. To the right he saw nobody. He looked left and there she was, walking a little faster now. He ran down the corridor and got to within fifteen feet of her.

"Hold it!" he shouted.

She turned. He knew immediately it was not her. This woman was at least forty. Granted, a fit forty, but minus Tipton's high cheekbones and dazzling blue eyes.

"Can I help you?" she said in a distinct Midwestern accent.

He held up a hand. "I'm really sorry, I thought you were someone else."

The woman looked him over and smiled beguilingly. "Sorry I'm not."

SIXTY-EIGHT

A KNOCK CAME ON TIPTON'S DOOR AT THREE IN THE afternoon. She was on Chapter Four of *Power Play* and didn't want to put it down.

"Who is it?"

"It's Ronick."

She folded down a corner of a page, put the book on her bedside table, got up, and opened the door.

"Hey. What's up?"

"Just something I thought you'd want to know, madame. A man approached me a few hours ago and showed me a drawing. He said he would pay me...five hundred dollars if I told him what room the woman in the drawing was staying in," he said, inflating the three hundred to five hundred.

Her mind was going in six directions, but she had to stay cool. "Yes, and?"

"And the woman in the drawing was you."

She laughed. Ronick looked surprised.

"Oh, God. He actually did it."

"Excuse me, madame?"

"What did he look like? This man."

"He was about six feet tall, dirty blonde hair, a little scar—"

Janzek.

She shook her head. "He's my old boyfriend. We broke up and.... Why am I boring you with this? Anyway, thank you for telling me. We need to keep where I am our little secret. Okay?"

Ronick didn't speak nor did his expression change.

She got what his hesitation was about. "Hold on," she said, turning and going back into her cabin. She went to a pocket of her suitcase, pulled out a wad of cash, and walked back to the open door where Ronick stood. She counted out five hundred-dollar bills and handed them to him. He didn't take them.

"I was thinking," he said. "Five hundred dollars to tell you he was looking for you and another five hundred dollars *not* to tell him where you are."

She shook her head, counted out five more hundred-dollar bills, and handed them to him. "You're a goddamn thief."

He laughed. "Just trying to keep you properly informed, madame."

She went back in her cabin, lay on her bed, and stretched out. For the next two hours, she stared up at the ceiling, which was lower than the ceilings she was used to by several feet. The first thing she decided was that she couldn't just wait in her room until the cop somehow figured out where she was. Besides, Ronick, who seemed entirely capable of playing both ends against the middle, clearly had his price. It wouldn't take him long to figure out that he could go to the cop and extract an even better price for revealing her location.

For a while, she entertained the idea of luring Ronick into her cabin and killing him. The problem was, he'd be missed much more quickly than Janzek. And what would she do with the body?

Finally, she reached the inevitable conclusion—the cop had to go.

SIXTY-NINE

So far, Janzek had covered the Verandah, Riviera, Main, and Upper decks, and was halfway through Empress. While doing so, he had realized that he needed a cover story. He'd decided to say that Tipton was a friend of his cousin, and that his cousin—upon learning Janzek was taking the same cruise as Tipton—had suggested he look her up.

Okay, the story had a few holes in it—for instance, wouldn't his "cousin" have the woman's phone number or e-mail?—but it wasn't like Janzek was going to be put through a vigorous cross-examination by some badgering defense attorney. So far, the best lead Janzek had come up with was a woman passenger he'd talked to who was pretty sure she recognized Tipton from being ahead of her in the line to board the ship.

He finished off the Empress deck and decided to go back to his cabin—1605 on Riviera—because he was hot and wanted to change out of his long-sleeved shirt and into a short-sleeved one before he went back and started all over again on Verandah. He slid the card into the slot in his door and opened it when he saw the flashing green dot. He walked in, pulled open the top drawer and took out a brand new short-sleeved shirt he'd purchased at the Style Shop. He put it on and was about to walk up to the Verandah deck when a knock came at his door.

He opened it and recognized the man as one of the cabin boys he had spoken to earlier.

"Hello, sir, my name is Ronick. Remember me? You asked me if—"

"Yes, yes, I remember. So, have you seen my friend?"

Ronick looked down the corridor to his left then his right. "Well, I may have," he said. "I am not absolutely certain it is the same lady, but it could be."

Janzek pulled the folded-up sketch of Tipton out of his pocket and showed it to Ronick. "Take another look. She's taller than average, five ten or so, and pretty slender. Big shoulders, though."

Ronick put his hand on his chin. "I'm pretty sure it's her."

"Well, tell me what cabin she's in," Janzek said, reaching for his wallet and taking out a slew of twenty dollar bills. "Like I said, I'll pay you three hundred dollars if it's her."

Ronick took his hand off his chin and cocked his head. "See, that's the thing. I could lose my job if I told you. My boss is very strict about discretion, and I believe they might deem this indis—"

"Wait. How is it indiscreet if you tell me what cabin a friend of my cousin is in?" Janzek asked, trying to look appropriately indignant.

"But, sir," Ronick said, "what if you were a stalker or—"

"For Chrissake, I'm not a goddamn stalker. I just want to find the woman."

Then it dawned on Janzek. This was a hold-up. The guy wouldn't have come knocking if he wasn't prepared to tell him where Tipton Hill was staying. He just wanted to milk the situation for everything he could get out of it.

"How much do you want?" Janzek asked.

"Well, please understand, sir, if I am going to risk my job—"

"How much?"

Ronick leaned in closer. "One thousand dollars, sir."

"Are you crazy?" Janzek said, louder than intended. "That's outrageous."

Ronick put his index finger up to his mouth. "Please, sir, as I said, discretion is critical."

"Listen, my friend," Janzek said, lowering his voice. "I know the cabins you're in charge of are on the Riviera deck. I could just knock on every door on that deck until I find her. So, I really don't need you at all."

"Yes, sir. And I could—right after I leave here—go tell that woman that a man from the Charleston Police Department is looking for her."

The squirrely little bastard's good, thought Janzek.

Ronick shrugged. "There's no rush, sir, you know where to find me." He turned to go. "I take cash or check."

"Okay, okay, give me a few minutes. I need to get the money at Special Services," Janzek said, starting to close his door. But he was curious. "How'd you know about—"

"You being a policeman?"

Janzek nodded.

"When you opened your wallet," Ronick said proudly, "I saw your badge."

SEVENTY

Tipton, who had created a long-range plan days ago, finally had come up with a near-term plan.

Unfortunately, it required the services of Ronick, the wiry, little bandit.

He was usually easy to find, or maybe he just liked to hover around her cabin because she seemed to have plenty of cash on hand. In any case, she needed him. She cautiously opened her door a crack and saw him diagonally across the corridor with an armful of sheets.

He spotted her. "Oh, hello, madame, is there something I can help you with?"

"As a matter of fact there is. Can you come into my cabin?"

He looked both ways down the corridor, clearly unaccustomed to getting an invitation like that from a beautiful female passenger.

He put down the sheets on a large, portable pushcart and walked into her room.

"How can I be of service?"

She studied him closely. She had a few inches on him and

guessed they probably weighed about the same. She could probably overpower him if she had to.

"Ma'am?"

"Do you have a pass-key?" she asked, showing him the keycard to her room. "You know, one of these that opens all the doors on the ship?"

He smiled his *it's gonna cost you* smile. "No, I'm afraid not."

"But you're able to open all the doors. I've seen you."

Ronick pulled a plastic keycard from his pocket. "This is only for cabins on the Verandah deck."

She suspected it was a lie and that his keycard opened every cabin door on the ship.

Tipton tapped her toe and thought for a second.

"I think there *might* be a card for all the cabin doors," Ronick said, setting the trap, "but I don't know how to get it."

She looked him in the eyes and couldn't get a clear read. "If I paid you another five-hundred dollars, could you find one?"

Ronick exhaled as if he'd been insulted. "Madame, you're asking for so much...and offering so little."

"Five-hundred dollars is 'so little?'" She tried to meet outrage with outrage.

"Yes, it is for a woman who is no doubt a very successful real-estate broker in South Carolina."

How the hell did he know that? Then she guessed he had seen her South Carolina real estate license when she opened her wallet last time. The "successful" part—just a guess.

"I'll give you a thousand."

"I was thinking two thousand."

She shook her head in disgust.

But paid him two thousand dollars.

SHE SET her alarm for four in the morning. Even the most hard-core revelers would be in bed by then. She checked and confirmed that the casino closed at two and the various night-clubs and bars shut down well before that. She just didn't want to bump into anybody who could later describe her in the tight hallways.

She was wearing a dark blue hoodie and black jeans as she walked down the corridor. She went up the stairway two flights and turned to her left. She started down the long corridor, which looked exactly like hers two flights below. She followed the numbers to 1605.

She took the card from the pocket of her jeans and started to insert it in the slot. She was shaking badly, her right hand trembling. She heard a toilet flush behind her and freaked. She slipped the keycard back in her pocket and walked back down the corridor. She turned to where the stairway was and started to go down it.

Then she stopped. She had to do it. The cop was going to find her sooner or later. He'd tracked her to the house on Sullivan's Island, after all, and she still hadn't figured out how he'd patched together enough clues to find her there. Must have been the car. Whatever it was, he'd done it. And he'd do it again.

She turned around, climbed the stairs, and walked back down Janzek's corridor. She moved quickly to the door and pulled out the plastic card. She was still shaking but not as bad as before; she heard the rush of her pulse in her ears. The last time she'd felt this way was when Jamie Swiggett had started pawing her and trying to kiss her at her apartment on King Street.

She slipped the key into the slot and saw the blinking green light.

She took a deep breath and slowly turned the knob. Then

she pushed it open and took four quick steps to the side of the cop's bed. Without warning, she started slashing with the same knife she'd used on Swiggett and Peabo Gardner. Her blade hit something soft, then something hard, then she heard a shout, then a groan, then what sounded like the air going out of a tire.

She turned, exited the cabin, ran down the corridor, turned to her right, and raced down two flights.

Back in her hallway, she stopped and calmly walked to her door. She opened it, took off all her clothes, hid them under the mattress at the end of the bed, and picked up where she'd left off in her Danielle Steele novel.

SEVENTY-ONE

JANZEK FIGURED THAT HARLEN COBEN HAD SAVED HIS life.

Or more accurately, the hardcover copy of his novel *The Stranger* had. What happened was, he had been reading and dozed off, and the book had fallen to his chest. When he was attacked, the book had taken two blows. One of the knife marks had penetrated the hard cover and made it all the way to page 174. Janzek's shoulder had sustained a knife wound, but fortunately the blade had caught the outside of his right shoulder, a superficial wound, even though it had bled a lot.

Right after it happened, Janzek's first instinct was to chase his attacker, who could only be Tipton Hill. He jumped out of bed, clad just in his boxers, took the few steps to the door, pulled it open, and looked both ways down the corridor. It was then that he saw the blood streaming down his arm. He went back in, grabbed a towel, and, holding it to his shoulder, ran down the corridor and turned to the stairway. There was no one in sight and he knew Tipton Hill was long gone, probably back in her cabin already.

Bleeding and clad only in his boxers, he retreated to his cabin, sat on his bed, and put pressure on his shoulder. As he did, he got more and more enraged by the attack. A few minutes later, he lifted the towel and saw that the bleeding had stopped. He looked at his watch: 4:17 a.m. Screw it, he wasn't going to wait to let the powers-that-be know someone had tried to kill him. He put on clothes quickly and walked out into the corridor. Near the end of it, he practically collided with what appeared to be a drunken couple staggering, he guessed, to their cabin. With no clear destination in mind he walked to the Special Services office, where he found an industrious deck-hand swabbing the deck in front of it. He saw a sign that said the office didn't open until seven. He wandered around for the next twenty minutes but found no other sign of life. He looked at his watch again—4:38—and went back to his cabin, resigned to waiting a few hours.

He took the bloodstained bed clothes off his bed, tossed them into a heap on the floor, got into bed, and tried with difficulty to read his wounded Harlan Coben book.

———

A LITTLE OVER two hours and ninety-four pages later, he felt a bump and initially feared it might be the return of Tipton Hill. Then it dawned on him, it was the *Fantasy* docking in Freeport. He had read on the itinerary that passengers would wake up in Freeport and were free to go ashore for the day, starting at nine. He got out of bed and put his book in his recently purchased backpack, thinking it might turn out to be evidence. Then he took a shower and got dressed. He went down to the Riviera deck, looking for Ronick. It didn't take him long to find him. Sporting a grin, the cabin boy walked behind his pushcart of towels, washcloths, linens, and soap. He saw Janzek coming down the corridor and the grin disappeared.

"Good morning, sir," Ronick said cheerfully. "A new day on the high seas."

"Yeah," Janzek said, glowering and getting in his face. "I need you to take me to the cabin of that woman... *right the fuck now*."

"But, sir, what about our...arrangement?"

Janzek took a step closer to Ronick and got in his face. "Fuck the arrangement. I'm a detective looking for a killer."

Ronick took a step back. "But, sir, it is my understanding of maritime law that you have no jurisdiction here. The ship is of Panamanian registry and laws of Panama apply. You're not a detective from Panama, are you, sir?"

Janzek took a step closer and Ronick backed up against a wall. "Don't be a wiseass, dirtbag. Where is she?"

Ronick put his arms up. "Okay, okay," he said, eyes darting around like a trapped rat. "She's on the other side R...R-52."

Janzek took a step back. "Thanks. I'll put a good word in for you in the customer survey," he said with a sarcastic snarl.

He turned and walked down the corridor. He took a right and passed the stairway on his left and the bank of elevators to his right, where he began looking at room numbers. The first one was R-80. He kept going until he got to R-52, an outside cabin.

He knocked on the door.

"Who is it?" came a woman's voice.

He didn't answer and simply knocked again.

"Hold on," the voice said.

The door opened. A sixty-year-old woman with curlers in her hair frowned out at him.

"Yes?"

"Sorry, I have the wrong room."

She closed the door in his face.

Janzek turned and ran down the corridor, almost plowing into two teenage girls. He raced past the elevators and stairway, then back down the corridor where Ronick had been.

But Ronick wasn't there. He saw another steward farther down the hall and walked down to him.

"Where's Ronick?" he asked. "He was here five minutes ago."

"Sorry, sir," the man said. "He said he was sick and went to his cabin."

"Where's his cabin?"

"Sorry, sir, I do not know."

Janzek wasn't going to play games anymore.

It was time to go to the top. The captain.

It took him twenty minutes to track the man down.

It wasn't as though you just went up to the *Fantasy*'s bridge and found him steering the ship.

It was just past eight and Janzek and the captain were seated in the Forum aft lounge, which didn't open until noon. The captain had chosen the location, no doubt, because no one else would be there. To reach the man, Janzek had gone to Special Services and told them that he needed to speak to the captain about an "urgent matter." The person he met with in Special Services did his best to get Janzek to divulge what the urgent matter was, but Janzek didn't reveal it.

Captain Morelli, a short man with bushy eyebrows and a comb-over, got right to the point in an accent that sounded like something between Italian and Russian.

"I understand you have an urgent matter you would like to discuss with me, Mr. Janzek?"

"Yes, I do," Janzek said, reaching for his ID and showing it to Morelli. "It's Detective Janzek and I'm a homicide cop from Charleston. I followed a murder suspect onto the

Fantasy, and she tried to kill me earlier this morning. I need your help."

Morelli reacted like Janzek had tossed a bucket of ice water into his face. "Someone tried to *kill* you?" he asked in apparent disbelief. "That is not possible on my boat."

Janzek knew that Morelli was a man whose goal would be to bury any situation that reflected badly on him and his ship. A man intent on not having an incident on his ship make the news.

"Trust me, it happened. The woman who did it is named Tipton Hill," Janzek said. "The thing is, she may be disguised as a man. In any case, I'm sure she didn't use her real name when she made her reservation on the ship."

Morelli put his hand on the table and thrummed his fingers. "What is it you would like me to do, detective? How do you expect me to find her if she used a fake name?"

"I showed this sketch—" he reached into his breast pocket and pulled out the sketch of Tipton "—to quite a few of your stewards. One of them recognized her, but when I asked him what cabin she was in, he steered me to a cabin that was not hers."

"What deck was that on, and do you remember the steward's name?"

"Riviera and his name is Ronick. Do you know him?"

The captain stopped thrumming and shook his head. "No, but you must remember that I have over nine hundred crew members," he said. "I still do not know what you would like me to do."

"Speak to Ronick and find out where the woman is."

"And then what?"

"And then I would like to arrest her."

The captain shook his head emphatically. "You can't do that. You have no authority here."

"Well, then *you* arrest her."

"For what? I can't arrest her for suspicion of committing a crime on the mainland."

"Well, then arrest her for trying to kill me four hours ago," Janzek said, pulling his shirt down to show the stab wound on his shoulder. He wished it were a little longer and a little deeper.

Morelli looked at the cut. "What happened?"

"Like I said, she attacked me. At about four this morning. I was asleep in my cabin. She attacked me with a knife."

"And how do you know it was her?"

"It had to be. Who else could it have been?"

"But did you see her face?"

"No, for chrissakes, it was dark."

Morelli grimaced. "Detective, as I'm sure you realize, you don't have much of a case." He glanced back down at Janzek's shoulder. "And though I don't mean to treat your wound lightly or be disrespectful, it looks like you'll survive."

SEVENTY-TWO

ASSHOLE, THOUGHT JANZEK, RESISTING AN OVERWHELMING urge to wring the dip-shit captain's scrawny neck. As he left the lounge, he realized his only recourse was to come up with a plan wholly independent of Morelli and his crew.

His first step was to make a call. His cell service had been nonexistent when the *Fantasy* was at sea, but he now had four bars. He dialed, figuring it would cost him a fortune in roaming fees, but Chief Brindle would be okay with that. Assuming, of course, that he dragged Tipton Hall back to Charleston.

He dialed Delvin Rhett's number.

"Yo, Nick, what's up in *Fantasy*-land?"

"You mean, aside from the fact that Tipton Hill tried to stick a knife in me last night?"

"You're shittin' me."

"No. Hey, do me a favor: Look into what I gotta do to arrest her on board, will ya? Legally, I mean. Also, what I can do in the Bahamas. Freeport and Nassau, specifically."

"Okay. Where are you now?"

"Freeport."

"Can't you just get... the captain of the ship to arrest her?"

"I just went down that road. Had an audience with the great man. He was worried about there being an incident. You know, negative press, someone tweets somebody else and suddenly it's all over the news."

"He tell you that?"

"Nah, but I could tell."

"So you gonna have cell service for a while? Be reachable?"

"Yeah, at least 'til eight tonight. Then we go back out to sea again."

"Okay," Rhett said. "I'll try to get you some answers to all this jurisdictional stuff. Meantime, watch out for that girl. As we know, she's pretty handy with a knife."

JANZEK WAS SCOPING out how passengers disembarked from the Fantasy, which turned out to be similar to how they came aboard. They inserted their plastic cards into a machine manned by two vigilant-looking crewmen, then walked down a slanted gangplank to Bahamian soil.

The *Fantasy* was scheduled to stay in Freeport until nine o'clock that night and the passengers were required to be back on board by seven. Janzek's assumption was that the brain trust of Carnival management had learned—the hard way, no doubt —that having a certain element, i.e., the young and the wild, cruising local bars all night long, or finding their way to the local house of ill-repute, might be detrimental to the sterling Carnival reputation. And in extreme cases, that might mean behind bars—and not the drinking kind.

A steady stream of passengers were filing off of the *Fantasy* in ones, twos, and larger groups. According to the schedule sheet, there were all kinds of ways to spend your time and money in Freeport. Janzek had the sheet in his hand and was studying the activities available to *Fantasy* passengers. There was something billed as a "dolphin close encounter," reef snorkeling, deep-sea fishing, a two-hour cruise in a glass-bottom boat, or sightseeing by Segway, kayak, dune buggy, or Jeep.

Janzek would have loved to have signed up for the reef snorkeling but his hands were full. He flashed to a vision of Tipton Hill attacking him underwater with a glistening knife.

Looking back at the disembarking passengers, he watched a tall, skinny woman move down the ramp in an oversized straw hat and Ray Bans. His eyes went to her legs. They were too heavy and untoned to be Tipton Hill's.

Next, what he assumed were three generations of a family descended the gangplank. A couple in their sixties came next, followed by another couple in their mid-thirties or so, a bored-looking teenage boy, and a shy-looking girl around thirteen texting on her cell phone, no doubt racking up the rip-off roaming charges.

Janzek was hoping he'd spot Tipton walking down the gangplank but was fully prepared to pursue her until he tracked her down on the island of Freeport.

TIPTON REALIZED she had failed in her mission of killing the cop. Ronick had hit her up yet again for another five hundred dollars to reveal that Janzek was hot on her trail. Aggressively on her trail. That had been right before Ronick disappeared to his cabin with an unknown ailment.

That meant Tipton was a sitting duck on the *Fantasy*. She decided to accelerate her game plan. Rather than leaving the ship and going AWOL in Nassau, she would do it right here and now in Freeport. She knew Nassau had flights to the

Caymans because she'd looked into it but had no idea whether Freeport did. It didn't matter; she'd find a way to get to Nassau if necessary.

The trick was to get off the ship without the cop recognizing her and coming after her. Not that he could arrest her legally, but she'd dreamed up plenty of scenarios in which he took her back to the States and, officially, arrested her there. One method was to take the law into his own hands: find her, handcuff her, go to the local airport, charter a plane, and fly back to Charleston. It would cost him, but to book a suspect who'd killed four people, Janzek's superiors would probably have no problem with the money.

Tipton was dressed and ready to flee, trying to figure out the best way to escape detection.

Her sense was the cop would be looking for a single woman. More specifically, a heavily disguised single woman. A pair of Jackie-O's, a big, floppy hat that covered her hair and half her face, or a veil even.

Then she remembered Janzek questioning her at the Fort Sumter house...when she was Billy Hobart. So Janzek would also be on the lookout for a handsome, slightly effeminate, five-foot ten-inch man.

She had one set of men's clothes and a pair of men's shoes.

She thought for a while longer then stripped down to her underwear. She took the sharp knife out the pocket of her suitcase, went into her bathroom, held up a big hank of hair, cut it off, and dropped it into the wastebasket. She spent the next ten minutes repeating the process until she'd cut off all of her hair.

When she looked in the mirror, she saw what reminded her of a female Marine recruit. It made her smile.

She turned on the faucet, put her hands under it, and splashed water onto her quarter-inch hair. She took a razor out of her toiletry case and spent the next fifteen minutes shaving her head as well as her eyebrows. Good thing she'd brought three razors, because the first two got dull after a few minutes.

She looked at the mirror and smiled even wider. She was only halfway done but already pretty sure the cop would have no clue.

When she was done, she went back into the cabin with her knife. She cut up the sheets and covers into neat six- and eight-foot strips, wrapping half of them around her waist and tying them up. She went back into the bathroom and looked at herself in the mirror. She had successfully added four to six inches to her waist.

Then she went back into the cabin, sat on the bed, picked up one of the pillows, and with the longer strips of cloth tied it to her waist. She used the four remaining strips to flatten her breasts, leaving her with what looked like an average man's chest.

She reached into her suitcase and took out the blue, long-sleeved men's shirt. She put it on and, with difficulty, buttoned it over her newly increased body mass. It had fit loosely on her back when she was Billy Hobart.

Now in the mirror she saw an albino fat man. The only thing that remained of Tipton Hill were the azure eyes.

She reached for her sunglasses and put them on.

Now she saw an albino fat man wearing shades.

SEVENTY-THREE

As Janzek watched the ragtag passenger groups stream off the *Fantasy,* it suddenly dawned on him that he was wasting time. Tipton Hill would never look anything like how she did in the photos of her. She would know by now that she hadn't killed him, and she also knew perfectly well that Janzek could identify her as either Tipton Hill or Billy Hobart. The woman had a long history of being competent at two things: one, disguising herself; and two, cutting up men—even though she'd come up short with Janzek.

So, what he'd been doing for the last hour—trying to spot her as either Tipton or Billy—was a giant waste of time. In fact, she could have already disembarked without him giving her a second glance.

He got up from the deck chair and went to track down a certain steward, who hopefully, was no longer feigning sickness. Ten minutes later, he spotted Ronick in the narrow hallway on Riviera, pushing his cart. When Ronick saw him, he looked like he wanted to bolt, but there was nowhere to go.

"I could get you fired," Janzek said, "and thrown in jail for a whole lot of things. For starters, giving a key to someone who tried to kill me."

Ronick held up his hands. "I had nothing to do—"

"Can it, numb-nuts. Just open her room for me and I'll forget we ever met."

Ronick didn't have to hear any more. He left his cart where it stood. "Follow me."

Janzek was envious of Tipton Hill's cabin. Compared to his, it was the difference between the presidential suite at the Belmond Charleston Place and the cockroach suite at Motel 6. The good thing was that no one had gotten around to cleaning her cabin yet. Janzek found what he was looking for right away: a few strands of blonde hair in the sink and a lot more in the wastebasket. The bedding situation was curious, and it took Janzek a while to figure it out. A few long ribbons of slashed-up sheets remained, and a pillow seemed to be missing. He tried to visualize what the new Tipton Hill would look like.

Very different.

SEVENTY-FOUR

AT 10:52 A.M., JANZEK WALKED DOWN THE GANGPLANK.

One of the vigilant crew members smiled up at him. "Gotta be back by seven, you know."

"Oh, don't worry," Janzek said, but what he was actually thinking was, *I doubt you'll ever see me again.* "By the way, did a chubby friend of mine with a shaved head leave the boat? Would have been by himself. About this tall? Five-ten or so?"

"I do remember a guy like that. Blue long-sleeve shirt and shades, right?"

Janzek nodded. "Yeah, probably," he said. "Hey, by the way, how's cell reception in Freeport?"

"Pretty good. Way better than out at sea."

Janzek nodded. "Alright see you a little later." *Highly unlikely.*

He turned and made for the T-shirt shops and other island tourist traps.

At the first one he reached, an Aunt Jemima-sized woman was sitting in a cerulean blue Adirondack chair outside the door to the shop. She shaded her eyes as he approached and flashed a dazzling smile, showcasing her snow-white teeth and one gold incisor.

"Morning, ma'am," Janzek said, no time to waste. "You know anyone who wants to make $200 for a day's work?"

"Cash money?"

"Yup," Janzek said, pulling out a new wad of hundreds that he had taken out at Special Services.

"I got my husband and my boy in the back." She turned and shouted, "Hey, Rodney, Marquis, get out here."

A husky man with slab-like arms came out first, followed by a boy with dreadlocks who was texting on his cell phone.

"Yeah, hon?" said the man.

"This man—"

Janzek stepped toward them. "I'm Detective Janzek."

The man stuck his hand out. "Rodney," he said. "This is my son Marquis."

Janzek shook their hands. "You got a car, Rodney?"

"Yeah, ain't much to look at."

"But it runs, right?"

"Oh, yeah. Doesn't go much over sixty, though."

"That's all right. It doesn't need to. I'll give you a hundred to rent the car and two hundred each for the day. And the good news is the day's almost half over."

Rodney looked like he had just won the lottery. "You got a deal. What we gotta do?"

Janzek decided not to say, *Take down a dangerous killer*, saying instead, "We just need to find someone."

"So, we're like your...deputies?" Rodney asked, giving his son a wink.

"Something like that."

THE CAR WAS a 2002 Chevy Nova and, as Rodney said, it wasn't pretty. Rusted out and sunbaked, it, nevertheless, started right up. Rodney drove with Janzek in the passenger seat and Marquis in back.

"Okay, first stop is the airport," Janzek said, as Rodney slipped the Nova into gear.

"No problem, mon," Rodney said. "About a ten-minute drive."

Janzek nodded. "So, we're looking for a woman dressed as a man. About five-ten, shaved head, kinda chubby and wearing a blue, long-sleeved shirt. At least, he was." Then it occurred to Janzek that she could easily shed her disguise. "Or a tall woman wearing a hat and sunglasses."

"Wow, that's a big difference," Rodney said, clearly bewildered.

"Yes, it is," Janzek said. "And we need to be careful."

"Why?" asked Rodney.

"She's pretty handy with knives."

Rodney's eyes bugged out. "Oh, lordy."

Janzek took out his cell and was about to dial when it rang. It was Rhett.

"Yeah, Del?"

"So, I was in touch with a guy named Quinn McCartney, deputy chief of the Central Police Station in Freeport. I apprised him of your situation, and he wants to get in on the arrest with you. That's probably normal protocol but my guess is he wants to make the front page of the local paper."

"Okay, that's fine with me. Call him back and tell him I'll call him when I got Tipton in my sights. No sense dragging him around 'til I do."

"Makes sense. In the meantime, he's going to write up an extradition warrant for her arrest."

"Sounds good. Got the guy's number?"

"Yeah, name again is Quinn McCartney." Rhett recited the number for Janzek.

They were approaching the Freeport airport, which didn't look nearly as grand as its name—the Grand Bahama International Airport—suggested.

"Okay, boys, here's the plan: This man...or woman, wants to get off the island as quick as possible. Unless you tell me otherwise, there're only two ways to do that—by plane or by boat."

Rodney and Marquis nodded.

"So, first we're gonna see if she's at the airport. If not, I'm going to leave one of you here to keep an eye out for her."

They nodded again.

"Marquis, let's you and me go in and look around. If we don't see her, I'm gonna leave you here as my eyes and ears." Janzek looked at the boy in the rear-view mirror. "You see her, you don't do anything except call me right away and keep an eye on her. But be careful she doesn't know you're following her or paying too much attention to her. Got it?"

"Yes, sir," Marquis said, clearly amped up.

He turned to Rodney. "If she's not here, you and me are gonna hit the local marinas and try to find her. It's possible she may have taken off already. We all clear, fellas?"

"All clear," said Rodney.

Marquis nodded. "Could you describe him...and her again, please?"

Janzek did. Then he parked the car, and Marquis and he entered the airport, leaving Rodney in the car. The facility, a large pink stucco building, which Janzek expected to be third-world, pleasantly surprised him. It was modern, clean, and nice and cool inside. The first thing Janzek did was go to an airport store and buy another hat. It had a blue brim and a white crown and said, *Hey, Mon, No Problem,* then, below it, *Freeport, Bahamas.*

"Lookin' dope," Marquis said approvingly as Janzek pulled it low on his head.

"Well, thanks. Let's go find our girl."

"Or guy."

Janzek nodded.

But they didn't. They cruised the airport for the better part of thirty minutes. No luck.

"Okay," Janzek said, "I'm gonna leave now. Just keep walkin' around. You see anyone fitting one of those descriptions, call me right away."

"Yes, sir," Marquis said.

Janzek clapped him on the shoulder, walked through the airport and back to the car.

Rodney looked up from something he was writing. "Nothin', mon?"

Janzek shook his head and saw Rodney was writing on the back of an envelope. "What are you writing?"

"The names of the different marinas our suspect might go to." Rodney pointed at Janzek's cap and floated his eyebrows. "I like your lid."

"Thanks. So how many you got? Marinas?"

Rodney scratched his head. "Well, here's the thing. I tried to put myself in the head of a taxi driver...."

Janzek nodded. "Keep going."

"See, drivers get a little...tip if they recommend a hotel, a restaurant, or a marina when they pick up someone at the airport."

"Got it. And you're thinking what marina a driver would recommend?"

Rodney nodded.

"You'd make a good detective."

302

"Thank you, sir," Rodney said, keying the Nova's ignition. "So, top on my list are the Port Lucaya Marina, the Grand Bahama Yacht Club, and Flamingo Bay."

Janzek shrugged. "Okay. Which first?"

"Grand Bahama," Rodney said, pulling away from the airport.

They struck out at the Grand Bahama and Flamingo Bay and hadn't heard a word from Marquis forty minutes after leaving him at the airport. It was almost two by the time they reached Port Lucaya Marina. They got out of the Nova and walked past a life-sized sculpture of two dolphins and a shark. Rodney waved to a man stepping off an older-looking sport fishing boat. The man waved back and approached them.

"Hey, mon, how ya doin'?" Rodney said, giving the man a bear hug.

"Long time no see, brutha."

"This my friend Nick," Rodney said. "He's a detective from the States."

"Hey, Nick. Renwick Burr's the name."

He and Janzek shook hands.

"So, question for you," Rodney said. "You been here long?"

"Yeah, three, four hours. Why?"

"Have you seen—"

"Either a chubby, white man with a shaved head wearing a blue, long-sleeved shirt," Janzek said, "or a tall, white woman wearing sunglasses and maybe a hat."

Burr nodded. "Yeah, saw the guy in the blue shirt. Remember thinking, dude's gonna get hisself a wicked burn on his scalp."

"Where'd he go?" Rodney asked.

"Out on the *Hooking Up*. Dude didn't look like much of a fisherman, though."

"You know the owner of that boat?" Janzek asked.

303

"Sure, Jiggy Grannis, buddy of mine."

"How long ago did they leave?"

"I'd guess an hour or so."

Janzek gazed past Burr's shoulder and thought for a second. "Could you call him? Find out where he's going?"

"Yeah, no problem," Burr said, pulling out his well-worn Samsung wrapped in duct tape.

"Keep it casual," Janzek said. "Can't let his passenger get suspicious."

"Gotcha," Burr said. "Jiggy's passenger do something wrong?"

Janzek nodded. "A lot of things."

Burr dialed a number and managed to sound relaxed and low-key as he greeted his friend.

"Just wanted to know if you wanna have a beer when you're done," Burr said to Grannis, his phone on speaker.

"Sorry, man, gettin' back pretty late."

"Oh, yeah, why's that?"

"'Cause I'm goin' to Nassau."

"Cool, maybe tomorrow night, then?"

"You're on," Grannis said and clicked off.

"Good job," Janzek said, pulling out his phone. He dialed the number Rhett had given him for Quinn McCartney and put it on speaker.

"McCartney."

"Hey, Quinn, my name's Nick Janzek, Charleston, South Carolina, PD. My part—"

"Yeah, spoke to him earlier."

"Right. So, I located my homicide fugitive. She's somewhere between here and Nassau. Left about an hour ago by boat."

McCartney didn't hesitate. "Tell you what you do. Where are you?"

"Port Lucaya Marina."

"Okay, hop over to Lighthouse Pointe at the Grande Lucayan. I'll pick you up in my police boat in ten minutes."

"Sounds good. I'll be there. Thanks."

Rodney had a wide grin on his face. "You're in luck, mon."

"What do you mean?"

"He's got the fastest boat around. It's called an Apostle Interceptor, goes like a bat out of hell. Thing's got four Yamaha 300s."

"Sounds good," Janzek said, then to Renwick. "How fast can the *Hooking Up* go?"

"Guessing you should catch it an hour, hour-fifteen, max."

Janzek extended a hand to Renwick. "Well, thanks, for all your help."

"Happy to be of service."

Janzek looked over at Rodney and took out his wallet. "Well, my man, I'll take it from here."

Rodney shook his head. "You can't leave me behind for the fun part," he said, just shy of pleading.

"It could be dangerous."

Rodney smiled ear to ear. "Danger's my middle name. Besides, you don't even know where Lighthouse Pointe is."

Janzek nodded and smiled. "Okay, Danger, let's go catch our ride. Give Marquis a call and tell him to head home; he's done for the day."

SEVENTY-FIVE

THE BACKSTORY ON THE 41-FOOT APOSTLE INTERCEPTOR was intriguing. Turned out that in 2013, the U.S. government essentially donated it to the Marine Services Unit of the Royal Bahamas Police Force. According to an article that Janzek read later, the boat was meant to be "deployed in missions including search-and-rescue, maritime security, emergency assistance, and interdiction of illicit drug and human trafficking."

Whatever its purpose, the blue-hulled Interceptor was one of the sleekest boats Janzek had even seen and had a top speed of 54 knots, more than 60 mph, on the open sea.

Which was approximately the speed the police vessel was doing with Quinn McCartney at the wheel, Janzek and Rodney in passenger seats.

"Pretty smooth ride," Janzek said to the blocky, bearded police officer.

"Yeah, not bad," McCartney said. "Calm seas help. So, this woman, disguised as a man, killed three people?"

Janzek nodded. "At least."

He was sitting next to McCartney with Rodney behind

him. Turned out Rodney and McCartney knew each other slightly. They had daughters in the same grade in school.

They had passed a few boats coming toward Freeport and caught up with a few others going in the direction of Nassau, but none was the *Hooking Up*.

McCartney, who seemed like a competent cop and a man who wouldn't mind making the six o'clock news, made a call to the central police station.

"Got an idea," McCartney said to Janzek, putting his hand over his phone, "Hey, Arnie, question for you: When we put those transponders on the charter boats, was one of them the *Hooking Up*?"

McCartney listened, then, "Yeah, check it out, will ya? And get right back to me."

Janzek nodded his thanks. "That would make our job a lot easier."

"See—" McCartney turned and glanced at Rodney, then lowered his voice, apparently not wanting him to hear "—we suspected one of the charter boats was smuggling coke from a drop in Nassau to Miami. Never caught anyone, but we still got transponders on like five or six boats."

"Let's hope the *Hooking Up* was one of 'em," Janzek said.

A few minutes later McCartney got a call on his cell. "Hey, what'd you find out?" He listened, then shot Janzek a smile and a thumbs-up. "Thanks, man."

Janzek was psyched. "So, this transponder... you can pick it up—"

"On my screen. Just like a plane on radar." McCartney gave Janzek a fist-bump.

Janzek turned around to Rodney. "Ready to meet and greet our girl?"

Rodney smiled. "I'm ready, boss."

TWENTY MINUTES later they had tracked down the *Hooking Up* and were within 300 yards of its stern.

Quinn McCartney turned to Rodney for confirmation. "That it?"

"I think so. I've only been on it once."

Janzek was looking through McCartney's binoculars at the stern of the boat. "Can't quite make out the name."

"Gotta be it," McCartney said, sounding sure of himself.

A few moments later, the name of the boat came into focus. "Yup, sure is," Janzek said, lowering the binoculars.

McCartney cut the throttle a notch. "I'm gonna try to come up behind 'em so they don't hear me."

Janzek nodded. He felt naked without his trusty Sig Sauer but knew he wouldn't need it since McCartney was packing a Beretta 92 in his holster. The Interceptor's engines were much quieter at half-speed. A minute or two later, they had pulled to within twenty feet of their quarry. Janzek motioned to McCartney to pull up on the port side, the side where Tipton was sitting.

McCartney nodded and eased closer. Janzek raised the bullhorn McCartney had handed him earlier.

"Tipton Hill," he called out, now no more than ten feet from the port side of the *Hooking Up*. "Put your hands up. The United States and Bahamas governments are charging you with multiple homicides. Hands above your head!"

Janzek saw Hill pull something from a bag, then caught the glint of a knife as his suspect flipped it overboard into the ocean.

Without hesitation, Janzek dived in. He didn't see the knife at first, but then about two feet below him caught its reflection. He reached down, grabbed the handle, then kicked for the surface. He dog-paddled over to the Interceptor and handed it up to Rodney.

Janzek swam over to the *Hooking Up* and hoisted himself over the side and on board. Janzek looked back at Quinn McCartney at the wheel of the Interceptor just a few feet away.

"I'll do the honors," he called out, and McCartney flipped him a pair of handcuffs. He turned to Tipton Hill, who remained seated.

"Stand up, please."

She did.

He walked up to her.

"You're charged with the murder of three men in Charleston, South Carolina and the attempted murder of another man aboard the cruise ship, *Fantasy*... that would be me."

"Sorry, I failed."

He looked her over.

"Nice disguise."

She looked like she wanted to haul off and deck him.

"Looks like you've put on a few pounds, Tipton," he said. "Seconds at the breakfast buffet on the *Fantasy*?"

She spat in his face.

He wiped his face with his wet sleeve. "Sensitive about your weight, huh?"

She was not amused in the slightest.

SEVENTY-SIX

JANZEK WAS AT SHEILA LESSING'S HOUSE ON TRADD Street. He'd flown back from Nassau the day before with his travel companion, Tipton Hill, who had not been in the least bit talkative.

He'd just recounted the high points of his cruise, of which there weren't many, and the capture of Tipton Hill. Which made it worthwhile.

"So, what are you expecting?" she asked. "That you can match the cut marks on your book with the knife you dove into the water for?"

"Yup," Janzek said. "But even better, to the fatal wounds on Jamie Swiggett and Peabo Gardner."

"How can you be so sure it's the same knife?"

"I'm not," Janzek said. "I just know that somehow she smuggled that knife on board the *Fantasy*."

"How do you know that?"

"Because they sure weren't selling knives like that with bikinis and Tommy Bahama duds in the Style Shop. Plus, a

Heckler & Koch Karma is a nasty-looking sucker with a blade you could shave with."

Sheila set her drink down and smiled. "You could shave with," she said and stroked his stubbled chin.

"You think she'll get sympathy at her trial," Janzek asked, "'cause she was so brutally raped when she was a kid?"

Sheila sighed. "Yeah, I do. I definitely do."

"But, I mean, cutting off one guy's hands, another guy's tongue, and a third guy's—"

Sheila put up a hand. "Bastard's deserved it and, yes, she'll get plenty of sympathy," she said. "What is truly amazing to me is that someone could successfully carry off two wildly different identities for ten years."

Janzek nodded. "I know. It's pretty incredible. I never got a chance to check her out when she was drop-dead gorgeous Tipton."

Sheila nodded back at him. "She was that. Nothing like that shaved head albino you described on the *Hooking Up*."

Janzek put his arm around Sheila's shoulder, pulled her close, and kissed her—a kiss that lasted for a while.

Finally, she pulled back and smiled. "Wow. Where did all that passion come from?"

"Well, for one thing I've been out at sea for what feels like months, and for another, you said something about *hooking up*."

Sheila shook her head. "You're incorrigible."

"That's a good thing, right?"

Sheila put her arms around him. "Sure is."

THE END

311

Sign up for Tom's latest newsletter and receive all subsequent ones, which include special deals, promotions, and news on events, podcasts and launches.

tomturnerbooks.com

The second book in Tom Turner's popular Savannah series, *Savannah Road Kill*, will be out in January The beautiful and tenacious Farrell sisters are off on a road trip that takes them from Savannah to Nashville then on to Miami in pursuit of a trio of ruthless killers. Here's a three-chapter preview.

CHAPTER 1

THE SAVANNAH MORNING NEWS CALLED IT, "ONE OF THE most bizarre murders in the long, storied history of our beloved city." Jackie and Ryder Farrell, sisters and private investigators at Savannah Investigations, hadn't been around Savannah long enough to compare the Federico Giraldo murder to other murders there, but they concurred, it was indeed bizarre.

The murder made the national news, too, and CNN, FOX, CBS, ABC and even the Tennis Channel dispatched crews to cover it.

What happened was, Giraldo, a 25-year-old tennis player ranked 227 in the world, was shot dead while playing in a match at the Savannah Challenger, a tennis tournament that featured players a notch—actually, more like two notches—below the Rafael Nadal's and Novak Djokovic's of the world. Most of the players in Challenger events were destined for lives of nagging injuries, gut-wrenching losses, then eventual obscurity, though a small handful would make it to the ATP tour and play for big money and multi- million-dollar endorsement deals.

That would never be the case with Federico Giraldo.

That he died in such a way was considered not only bizarre but totally perplexing to Jackie and Ryder: Bizarre in that, who would ever expect a sniper in a tree to pick off a man running down forehands and backhands on a tennis court? And perplexing because it raised the simple question, why? Sure, tennis star Monica Seles had been knifed by a fan while playing in a tournament in Hamburg almost thirty years before, but the attacker in that case had been a mentally deranged fan obsessed with Seles's rival, Steffi Graf.

Federico Giraldo's murderer... who knew?

The murder had taken place four months before Jackie and Ryder caught the case because two detectives from the Savannah Police Department, Walter Newell and Zed Murphy, had been assigned to it right after it happened. And though they had a number of suspects, they never made an arrest, and it seemed like the killing was headed to the cold-case file. That was when Benedetto Giraldo, Federico's grief-stricken father, walked into the office of Savannah Investigations, said how he'd read about them solving another high-profile murder, and pleaded with them to investigate his son's murder. Benedetto, clearly heart-broken about the tragedy, reminded Jackie and Ryder a little of their father, so, after clearing another case, they agreed to take it on. Solving murders, they also agreed, looked really good on their resumés and allowed them to jack up their prices.

In the beginning, the sisters had four suspects. Well, not exactly suspects, but four people—all men—who could have had a motive to kill Giraldo. The first was the assistant tennis pro at Mercer Island, where Jackie lived. He was a thirty-year-old, former number-two player on the University of Florida and was known to have a fiery temperament on and off the court. It seemed that his wife, also an assistant tennis pro at Mercer

Island, had struck up a friendship with Federico Giraldo the first year he played in the Challenger, and she had rekindled it —reputedly, even more passionately—when Giraldo returned to play a second year in the tourney.

A friend of Jackie's told her about an incident that had taken place in a locker room being used by Challenger players. Apparently, the assistant pro, whose name was Ted Bostwick, had stormed into the locker room after Giraldo won a match on center court. He'd pinned Giraldo up against a bank of lockers, his hands around Giraldo's sweat-drenched neck, and accused him of having sex with his wife in the back seat of Giraldo's car. Two other players had stepped in and broken it up before fists were thrown, but afterward Bostwick had shouted, "If I find out it's true, I'll kill you, you motherfuckin' spic!"

The upshot was that the Mercer Island tennis pro, Bostwick's boss, had gotten wind of the incident and Bostwick's racist threat and threatened to fire him unless he apologized to Giraldo and signed up for an anger-management course at a place called Georgia Outreach Counseling. Most people's reaction had been that the pro should have given Bostwick his walking papers right on the spot.

Jackie had called Bostwick numerous times to interview him but he had not called her back. Frustrated, she'd found out where he lived and parked outside his house with her sister one morning at nine, minutes before his normal work-departure time.

Bostwick lived in a townhouse development that was part of Mercer Island: four pods of attached two-story units that overlooked a golf course. On one side of Bostwick's front porch stood a rusty lawnmower, on the other, several broken flowerpots with a profusion of weeds growing out of them.

"Clearly, the dude's a pretty serious gardener," Ryder said with a smile, a mug of steaming coffee in her right hand.

316

Jackie chuckled. "Yeah, a real green thumb."

The story making the rounds was that Bostwick and his wife were history, or about to be. But, then, wild rumors were always floating around Mercer Island.

The front door opened and a tall, skinny man with a three-day growth and a coffee mug with a Nike swoosh on it, walked out, stuck a key in his front door lock, and turned it.

"Let's go," Jackie said, opening her door. Ryder did the same.

Bostwick hearing the car doors close glanced over at the sisters as they approached him.

"Hey, Ted," Jackie said. "I'm the one who called you. Jackie Farrell. Can we talk?"

Bostwick eyed Jackie, then Ryder, then Jackie again. "I've seen you around. You a tennis player?"

"Marginally," Jackie said, trying to be friendly. "My sister here's the jock in the family."

Bostwick turned to Ryder. "And what's your name, Sunshine?"

"Ryder," she said. "And please... don't call me Sunshine."

Bostwick shrugged. "How 'bout Sweetlips?"

` Before Ryder could do anything rash, Jackie cut in.

"Can we ask you a few questions?" She paused to explain. "We're private investigators on the Federico Giraldo murder."

Bostwick chuckled. "All PI's should look like you two."

"Thank you," Jackie said, biting back a sharp retort. "Can we go inside?"

Bostwick shook his head. "Nah, it's a mess. Plus, you might smell pot. Call the cops on me or something."

Jackie shook her head. "We don't care what you do in your spare time."

"You give tennis lessons stoned?" Ryder asked.

Bostwick nodded and smiled. "Sometimes drunk, too."

They ignored his attempt to shock them.

Jackie plowed in. "Nobody got a close look of the man who shot Federico Giraldo," she said, done with the small talk. "Where were you at the time it happened?"

"Right here. Watching the tube."

"And what about your wife? Name's Gabby, right?"

Bostwick nodded. "Watching lover boy play."

"Giraldo, you mean?"

Bostwick nodded.

"She was there in person?"

Another nod.

"So, nobody was here with you?" Ryder asked.

"Just me and my bong."

Ryder cocked her head to one side and scratched her lower lip. "Are you trying to impress us with how much of a badass you are?"

Bostwick rolled his eyes. "Nah, just making conversation."

"So you have no alibi?" Jackie asked.

"No. Like I told the cops. But I could give you every detail of the movie I was watching when Girardo got popped."

"It's Giraldo."

"Whatever."

"Okay, what was the movie?"

"*Ford vs. Ferrari*," Bostwick said, hoisting his backpack over his shoulder. "What else do you want to know?"

"That incident with Giraldo in the locker room," Jackie said. "Supposedly you threatened to kill him."

Bostwick scratched his bristly chin. "If every guy who ever threatened to kill someone went through with it, half the population would be dead."

Ryder glanced at Jackie, then Bostwick. "Sounds like a line a lawyer would come up with. Did you talk to a lawyer after the murder?"

"A guy here who I give lessons to is a lawyer. We had a few conversations."

"Why?"

"'Cause the cops kept coming back and hassling me."

Jackie nodded. "The question is, why'd they stop?"

Bostwick's eyes narrowed as he glared at Jackie. "Why the hell do you think? 'Cause they had absolutely nothing on me."

Jackie held up a hand. "Okay, okay. We're just trying to do you a favor and rule you out. The way the Savannah detectives apparently did."

"Definitely did," Bostwick said. "So how come both you and the Savannah detectives are working on this."

"We were hired by the Giraldo family. After the Savannah police didn't seem to be getting anywhere."

"I doubt those clowns could solve a candy store hold-up with security cameras on every wall."

Ryder chuckled.

Bostwick cocked his head. "Are you married?"

"Why you asking?"

"Because I'm going to have a lot of free time pretty soon."

Ryder nodded. "I'm guessing that means you and the missus are headed for splitsville."

"Good deductive reasoning," Bostwick said. "So, are you?"

"No," Ryder said. "But you're not my type."

"Well then, the hell with you," Bostwick said, walking between them. "I gotta go hit some tennis balls."

"Thank you for your time," Jackie said, following him. "You don't happen to have a rifle, do you?"

He turned back to her. "Give it up, will you? The detectives already went down that road. Last time I ever shot at anything was a squirrel with a BB gun when I was a kid.... I missed by a mile."

CHAPTER 2

"What a charmer," Ryder said, sliding into the passenger seat.

Jackie nodded as she turned the ignition key. "Just what every parent dreams of: a guy teaching your kid tennis while he's stoned."

"That was just some bullshit to impress us. You know the type."

Jackie nodded. "You weren't impressed?"

Ryder shook her head. "Guy's a douche."

"So, what's your read on him... as a suspect?"

"Not our guy. He'd never shinny up a tree and go to all that trouble. Too damned lazy. Plus, I believe him about the BB gun."

"Yeah, me too," Jackie said. "So, we got the doctor at 2?"

"Which really means 2:30."

"What do you mean?"

"He's a doctor."

"Yeah, guess we better bring reading material."

*****

Dr. Ron Winooski was an eye doctor based out of an office at 4720 Waters Avenue.

He was a suspect—albeit it a long shot— because it was the tradition of second-tier tennis tournaments like the Savannah Challenger for players to stay at houses owned by people who were tennis fans and lived near where the tournament was being played. That was mainly because the aspiring tennis stars couldn't afford hotels. Winooski and his wife, who lived on Mercer Island, had volunteered to have a player or two stay at their house over the years. One of them had been Federico Giraldo.

It seemed that while Dr. Winooski was performing cataract operations, Mrs. Winooski, a pretty, well-toned 38-year-old named Babs, was performing something else. With Giraldo. Or so people had been hearing on the grapevine.

The question that Ryder and Jackie had asked themselves, more than once, was how Federico Giraldo had any time for the sport that allegedly was his livelihood?

Jackie and Ryder arrived at the eye doctor's office a little before two. They checked in and were told the doctor would be right with them.

Forty minutes later, Dr. Winooski finally showed.

"Hello, ladies," Winooski said, then to Jackie. "You look familiar."

"Pickleball, I think," Jackie said.

"So you both live on Mercer Island?"

"Not me," Ryder said, "I live in town."

She meant downtown Savannah. Mercer Island, a large, upscale, gated community was twenty-five minutes from the downtown on an island called Skidaway Island.

Winooski nodded. "Well, come on into my office. Which one of you did I speak to?"

"Me," Jackie said, still bothered by the fact that doctors never felt the need to apologize for being late.

"So, you mentioned that this is about Federico Giraldo's death?" Winooski asked, leading them into his office.

The good doctor reminded Jackie of a dirty-blond Mr. Rogers. He seemed mild-mannered, meek and sincere and had small hands and big ears. But his eyes and facial features were so like Mr. Rogers's that Jackie half-expected him to break out into a sotto voce version of "Won't You Be My Neighbor?" at any moment.

Jackie and Ryder sat in his guest chairs while Winooski stayed on his feet. Jackie noticed a framed photo above Winooski's desk. It was an attractive woman in short blond hair and a dazzling smile. Presumably, Winooski's wife, a/k/a Babs.

"So what can I tell you, ladies? What is it you want to know?"

"You put Federico Giraldo up at your house for the Challenger tennis tournament. What was your impression of him?" Jackie asked.

"A charming young man," Winooski said, putting a hand on his chin, "absolutely charming—" and apparently half the women at Mercer Island thought so too. "I could see him going far with his tennis career...except..."

"He was shot."

"Well yes, but I wasn't even referring to that, though, obviously, it's true. What I meant was that Federico was what used to be called a Good Time Charlie. He enjoyed life to the fullest, but didn't put nearly as much focus on his game as the top players do."

"Good Time Charlie... can you define that, please?" Ryder asked.

"Oh, I think you know," Winooski said. "The man liked the

ladies. I know the reason you wanted to talk to me was because there were rumors about Federico and my wife."

Your wife and a half a dozen others. "Well, was there anything to it?" asked Jackie.

"Not a thing. Federico was a natural flirter. I doubt he ever met a woman, girl, lady, or anyone of the female persuasion he didn't flirt with. But beyond that—with my wife, anyway—there was nothing."

Ryder, far more cynical than her sister, didn't look convinced. "But you can't say that with a hundred percent certainty, can you?"

Winooski gave her a look that was not in Fred Roger's repertoire—pure malevolence. "I know my wife," he said with clenched jaw. "Look, what was your purpose in coming here anyway?"

Jackie cut off her sister. "As I said, we're investigating the murder of Federico Giraldo and speaking to as many people as we can who knew him while he was here at Mercer Island. Obviously, in hopes that we can eventually ascertain who his killer was."

"So, you came here to size me up. *Ascertain* whether I might be his killer."

"You were not high on our list, Dr. Winooski. Not before we came here, and not now."

He laughed and shrugged. "That is such a relief, because I thought you were about to read me my Miranda rights."

"But, just for the record," Ryder said, "do you happen to own a rifle?"

He turned back to her and his eyes got beady. "You have a very irritating manner."

Ryder put up her hands. "I just asked a simple question."

Winooski's gaze darkened. "Get out of here," he said,

pointing at the door. "We're done. Get the hell out of my office, right now."

Jackie and Ryder stood and headed to the door. Jackie turned back to Winooski. "Well, thank you for your time."

"You're not welcome."

Jackie sighed as they left the building. "You gotta work on that personality of yours a little."

Ryder laughed. "Yeah, I know. Not like he's the first guy to say I have an *irritating* manner."

CHAPTER 3

RYDER GOT THINKING ABOUT TED "THE DOUCHE" Bostwick and how she was always getting hit on by guys like him ever since she first arrived in Savannah ten months before. Bars, restaurants, her gym, the place where she played tennis, even church once. Even though, God knows, she wasn't much of a church-goer.

Why was it that Jackie and legendary homicide detective, Harry Bull, from one of Savannah's oldest families, were head-over-heels-in-love and Ryder only had bozos like tennis pro Ted Bostwick working their pathetically lame lines on her? Not only was Harry Bull smart and good-looking but he was nice, too. And funny. Lucky Jackie.

Ryder had met just one guy like that since she had been in Savannah, His only problem, which he conveniently forgot to mention, was that he was married. There was another guy who was a blind date and, reputedly, the finest architect in Savannah and quite possibly the whole state of Georgia. He picked her up in his snazzy Tesla Model S, whisked her off to Chive, one of the finest restaurants in Savannah, ordered up a really nice bottle of wine, looked deep into her eyes and proceeded to spend the next forty-five minutes telling her what an amazing southern belle his mother was. After a while, Ryder wondered why he didn't just bring her along on the date.

So, suffice it to say, Ryder was in the market for the right man. And, truth be told, she was not easy to please. But then, why should she be? She was beautiful, smart, articulate, athletic...okay, maybe a little irritating at times, but Christ, who the hell was perfect?

ALSO BY TOM TURNER

Charlie Crawford Palm Beach Mysteries

Palm Beach Nasty

Palm Beach Poison

Palm Beach Deadly

Palm Beach Bones

Palm Beach Pretenders

Palm Beach Predator

Palm Beach Broke

Palm Beach Bedlam

Palm Beach Blues

Palm Beach Taboo

Nick Janzek Charleston Mysteries

Killing Time in Charleston

Charleston Buzz Kill

Charleston Noir

The Savannah Series

The Savannah Madam

Other Books by Tom Turner

Broken House

Dead in the Water